THE JOURNAL OF EDWIN UNDERHILL

My left hand rested like thistledown on his left shoulder now. I pulled him towards me gently, like a lover. His chest brushed against mine. Our lips could have met. Gently, I took his soft-stubbled chin in my right hand, resting on my curled index finger, thumb closing on the girlish roundness beneath his lower lip, thumbnail brushing his white teeth, inches away. I turned his face into the crook of my arm lifting the lower jaw a little until his head tilted fully backwards and the column of his throat was mine for the taking . . .

The Journal of Edwin Underhill

Peter Tonkin

CORONET BOOKS
Hodder and Stoughton

What profit is there in my blood;
When I must go down to the Pit?

Copyright © 1981 by Peter Tonkin

First published in Great Britain 1981
by Hodder and Stoughton Ltd

Coronet edition 1983

British Library C.I.P.

Tonkin, Peter
  The journal of Edwin Underhill.
  I. Title
  823'.914[F]   PR6070.0498

  ISBN 0–340–32045–1

Printed and bound in Great Britain for
Hodder and Stoughton Paperbacks, a
division of Hodder and Stoughton Ltd.,
Mill Road, Dunton Green, Sevenoaks,
Kent (Editorial Office: 47 Bedford
Square, London, WC1 3DP) by
Cox & Wyman Ltd, Reading

JOURNAL

January to July

THE STAKE

It is midnight and I cannot sleep. Therefore I have taken up this book and started to write in it. First I borrowed the pencil old Mr. Agee in the bed next to mine keeps by him, then I sat on the window-sill here with my legs drawn up as supports and my left arm in its sling against the panes. I am sure there must be a full moon tonight — it has flooded all the ward, and I can see as if it were day. My left hand hurts where it is pierced, but endurably.

I have loved Rebecca for more than a year. This journal is a present from her. She is the daughter of the Reverend Hugh Gore, vicar of my home parish, Dunmow Cross. "Is this the new English teacher, Miss Featherstone? My God, he is a plain little man!" This aside, painfully audible, was said on our first meeting at the school staff Christmas ball a year ago.

But by July she was calling me Underhill, by September sometimes Edwin. Often she spoke to me kindly, and I hoped. Then came the invitation to her New Year's Eve party and, even though everyone who was anyone in the village was going to be there, my hopes grew.

I presented myself at the vicarage door on the dot of nine last night, with a small but expensive box of chocolates in my overcoat pocket. I rang, and after some considerable time Rebecca herself answered, holding a glass of champagne. She was dressed in a gown of green velvet cut tight to the hips and low on the breast. She waved me in and I entered, suddenly terribly aware of the shabbiness of my appearance. I hung my coat in the hall and followed her hesitantly into the loud brightness of the party. I was so overcome by the heat and the din that it was a moment before I realised my mistake: the room I had entered in my blue lounge suit was

7

full of people in formal evening dress. Overcome with embarrassment, I turned to escape when I heard her call me.

She came through the crowd towards me, playing the perfect hostess: but when she saw how I was dressed she stopped abruptly. "Oh, Eddie!"

"I didn't know," I said, far too loudly in the sudden silence.

The moment passed as these moments will. My colleagues from school did their best to hide their smiles while certain other guests didn't even try — the local Rugby Club and Young Farmers' Association sniggered openly.

I took the offered glass and retreated to a corner where I spent a dreary evening watching Rebecca dancing in the distance. Even the champagne tasted strange . . . it was some time before I discovered it was in fact champagne cocktail. I had eaten nothing before coming out and by the time food was announced — some time after half-past ten — I was ravenous and rather drunk. I tried to reach the buffet table but was elbowed aside by Rugby Club members and Young Farmers, all in a hurry to get their escorts fed and watered in preparation for the inevitable subsequent bedding.

All they left me was some badly undercooked beef, some pungent rice salad, and a piece of ham which was mostly fat. I ate little, but continued to drink. One by one the groups I tried to join ostracised me. As in all country villages, our society is strongly stratified, and as a schoolmaster — and with a degree from Exeter rather than one of the senior universities — I did not fit. Thus I was left with no one to talk to. It was not yet midnight. I could not leave. And there was worse to come.

At about eleven thirty I decided to give Rebecca her box of chocolates, and fetched them from my coat in the hall. However, she was nowhere to be found. I wandered through the vicarage until finally there was only the conservatory left where she might be. It was in darkness, but through the icy glass I could just see her seated on an ornamental bench. The skirt of her green dress was high above her knees. The bodice was partly undone. There was a man kissing her. As I blundered in, her eyes flicked up at me over his shoulder.

Completely lost for words, I stood there, dazed, swaying

8

drunkenly as she put one casual hand against her lover's breast and pushed him away. "Yes, Eddie?" she said to me quite calmly.

The man turned. It was Andrew Royle, the heir to Bishops End Farm whose lands march with the A130 most of the way to Chelmsford. She put a restraining hand on his arm so that he could not rise. "Yes, Eddie?" she said again, mocking me.

"I've brought you a present," I blurted. She held out her hand in an imperious gesture, and I placed the chocolates carefully in it. She looked at me but I could not read her eyes. "Your present is under the tree," she said. "It is the one in the blue paper." My heart leaped. A present: a sign that she had thought about me after all.

As I rummaged confusedly throught the pile of presents beneath the bright Christmas tree the room seemed to empty behind me. Although it would soon be midnight, I thought nothing of this: my mind was on the search. The blue package was at the bottom. It was weighty and solid, slightly concave on three narrow sides — a book, obviously: this journal, in fact. I removed the wrapping paper, admired the rich red binding. Of course, I went back to thank her.

This time she was alone. I held up the present. "I found it," I said.

She patted the bench and I went over and sat beside her. Then suddenly my hopes and my passion overflowed and I found myself on my knees before her, the book forgotten, fallen to the floor. I searched desperately in her velvet lap for her hands as I gabbled drunkenly, "Rebecca, I have loved you since I first saw you. Oh Rebecca, I love you so much. Please say you'll be mine . . ."

There would have been more but I paused for breath. And then, deep in the shadows, someone tittered. The titter spread, was joined by giggles. The shadows moved, attained substance, became people. It was then, as their laughter bellowed round me, that I realised where all the dancers had gone, and the cruel trap they had set.

Rebecca suddenly rose to her feet and shouted, "Shut up and get out!"

I thought she was talking to me and I was glad enough to go. I rose to my feet and ran. Behind me she called, "Wait, Edwin, wait!"

Perhaps the joke had gone further than she had intended. Perhaps she wished to apologise. I turned, part-way across the vicarage lawn, and waited. But out of the darkness came no apology — simply my Christmas present to smash into my chest. I caught it and for some reason then I understood: the plain wrapping amongst the bright paper; the lack of a label — it had not been specifically for me at all. It was a general purpose gratuity, kept in reserve to be given in return for an unexpected gift.

I took to my heels once more and pounded across the back garden, through the gate and into the churchyard, weaving drunkenly down the path between the ancient graves.

Beyond the covered lich-gate leading out of the graveyard is a path and beyond that the village green and the crossroads. The green has always been there — perhaps an acre of rough grass, even allowing for the roads and pavements. I ran across it heading for the crossroads themselves and the sanctuary of my one rented room in the ugly Victorian terrace beyond. I was drunk and full of black, bitter self-recrimination. My glasses were misted. My mind, like my vision, was anything but clear. I do not remember crossing the green itself, but suddenly I was at the crossroads. Behind, the church clock began to chime the quarters of the midnight hour. Then the ground seemed to give way under me and I fell.

I landed flat on my face, legs splayed out, my right hand clutching the frosted grass verge. My chin crashed down with stunning force, and my glasses spun away. Beneath my left shoulder the clay at the edge of the tarmac had crumbled. My left hand, fingers forced back by the soil, reached incredibly the full arm's length straight down into the earth and, as the hand went down into the black ground, the palm was pierced by something long and sharp. The pain was more than I can describe. The point entered the middle of my hand and, forced further through by my full weight, ripped out at the other side. I could feel the bones being forced apart and I screamed.

I found my arm was caught fast. I could not move it. In an instant I was covered with the icy, sweat of shock. I vomited, choking on the sweet iron taste of blood in my throat, and began to call out wordlessly for help.

It was thus that they found me, Rebecca and Andrew Royle. Amongst the midnight chimes of the church clock came his bored, supercilious voice. "My God, look at him: too drunk to walk. Heavens, what a noise . . ."

But then Rebecca, approaching, quieter and more gentle: "No, Andrew, look at his arm. I think there's something wrong."

A moment later they were beside me. A small crowd was gathering, but I could see Rebecca's feet before my face. "Miss Gore," I said, "I think my arm is broken."

"Careful now, old chap," said another voice, deep and warmly sympathetic. "The ground seems to have caved in . . . What on earth has happened?"

I felt fingers at my shoulder, pulling. The agony in my hand intensified. Everything was very clear for a couple of seconds. Distantly, in the vicarage, they were singing 'Auld lang Syne'. The stranger released me and said to Rebecca, "His hand seems to be trapped. We may have to dig him out."

"No," I said, feeling strangely calm. "No, hang on, it's all right . . ." I tensed myself, held my shaking body still, breathed deeply once and jerked my left shoulder up. Deep in the earth something tore, and blood suddenly began pumping out of me.

"Mr. Underhill! Edwin! Wait!" cried Rebecca. I paid no attention. I jerked my shoulder up again. Agony. Blood turning the soil around my hand to warm ooze.

And then I seemed to feel something move. Slowly, almost voluptuously, it writhed against my spread palm as though awakening from a long sleep. I made a guttural sound, jerked my shoulder up again, and a few inches of my arm was resurrected. Then my strength failed.

"Help me," I cried. "Miss Gore, please . . . please put your hands under my shoulder." She did so: taking firm hold. A pair of man's patent leather dancing pumps shifted anxiously before my face as the stranger watched over us. My hand felt more movements in the ground below and, "Now!" I yelled, my voice breaking, "pull!" We tore my shoulder upwards in unison, and the arm came free.

I rolled over completely on my back, my arm high in the air. I could see it silhouetted by the beams of a street-lamp and I held it there for a moment, gazing at it. The sleeves of both jacket and shirt were pushed up past the elbow. The light hair on my forearm and wrist was matted with mud and blood. My hand was clawed against the yellow light, the fingers twisted. And through the centre of the palm there was a thin stake of black wood more than a yard long. Almost a foot of the point had been pushed out of the back of my hand. With the black bolt of wood through it, my hand had ceased to look like a human hand at all.

Sunday 7 January:

THE FIRST VISIT

Today she came to see me, her visit sandwiched between tea and early Evensong. I had passed the day, like many of the last seven, in an uneasy doze born of my inability to sleep much at night. I awoke from a cat-nap and she was there, thoughtlessly smoothing a lock of her dark red hair.

"Hello, Edwin," she said quietly. "How's your hand?" I got it out from under the blankets. It is covered by a light bandage now, and is healing fast. I pulled the gauze away from its back to show her the pink mass of the scar where the stake had come through. Long ridged legs reach out to the edges of my hand where the skin tore open, all held together by stitches and smeared with yellow ointment. It looks evil, somehow, like a spider crouching on the back of my hand. Rebecca drew back, pale.

I covered it up. "I'll be out soon," I said. There was an uneasy silence. "Who was the man who helped me?" I asked.

"Oh, haven't you met him?" She welcomed the change of subject. "That's Richard Burke. He's just taken Whitethorn Cottage for a few months. Until the end of the summer, I think. He's a psychiatrist. He moved down here from London to do consulting work at Morden Hall, the asylum."

Morden Hall was the psychiatric hospital where Mrs. Gore, Rebecca's mother, had been receiving treatment for several years. I looked away, embarrassed. "How did the party go?" I asked, more for something to say than out of any real desire to know.

"It broke up almost immediately."

"No one left to laugh at," I said, suddenly bitter.

She looked as though I had slapped her. "I can hardly be responsible, Mr. Underhill, it you become too drunk to control yourself! Still, now that you've brought the subject up, there *are* one or two things I'd like to say . . ."

It was clearly a prepared speech: the reason, in fact, for her visit. I had done enough to merit it, I know, but it hurt nevertheless. I ought to look at myself, she said: what sort of a person was I — how fit was I to offer myself to any woman? Perhaps, before I started making protestations of love, it would be better if I pulled myself together and tried to make something of what few qualities I did possess . . .

She was soon finished. The doors slammed shut-open-shut behind her, leaving me to contemplate wretchedly the sad truth of her words.

What sort of a person am I? Well, to be frank, I am a slob. My hair, what there is of it around a large bald patch, is too long and always looks a mess. My clothes are baggy and usually grubby. I'm five foot six inches tall, my shoulders stoop, and I have no chest to speak of and a pot belly. All this might be acceptable were I an absent-minded professor-type, unworldly but creative. But instead I'm simply a down-at-heel schoolmaster in a fairly down-at-heel private school . . . In short, Rebecca was quite right: I've precious little to offer any woman, let alone one as beautiful and intelligent as she.

It wasn't a happy realisation. But at least, once I had faced the truth about myself, I felt better for it, knowing once and for all where I stood.

And now, tonight, I have been visited by something else: a nightmare at the very least, a horror so terrible that I can hardly write of it. It began as I seemed to waken out of a fitful doze into the quietness of the midnight ward. Outside, a faint wind moaned against the windows, making them rattle. The beds stretched away in ranks, curiously indistinct to me, even in the achingly bright moonlight. I found myself sitting up, looking round anxiously as if I expected something to happen. The air was so cold my breath clouded upon it. An inexplicable shiver of fear shook my whole body.

Old Mr. Agee in the bed next to mine grunted, coughed, and turned over. Then the moment was gone. Silence flowed in. Even the wind died. I lay down again. The whole hospital seemed then to be held in a vibrant stillness, as thought the night's dark cloak had fallen over the sprawling building and deadened every sound. Then out of the silence there grew the tiniest of whispers. I turned my head like a dog towards the door, the better to hear the sound. One faint voice infinitely far away, seeming to sing a song without words. Was it in the hospital? Some child in a distant corridor humming dreamily, perhaps. The whisper in the silence sang a little louder. My skin rose to gooseflesh. My scalp too tight from neck to eyebrows. The strange voice quavered, gaining strength. I thought, *I must move*! but the voice chained me down, nearer now, louder. Surely someone else must hear it?

Was that a movement? the night-light immediately outside the ward flickered, dimmed and died. The glass door-panes seemed black as though painted. The air in the ward freezing, and thick enough to drown you. I shuddered as the absolute knowledge came to me that it was there, whatever it was, just outside the doors in the corridor.

The doors began to rattle. The voice, a woman's now, lingered hauntingly on the air above the abrupt sound of the shaking wood, utterly strange and beautiful, terrifyingly sinister. Then, all at once, silence, more terrible than a scream.

CRASH! The doors slammed open. I jerked back, smashing my head on the iron bedstead. Blackness flowed in through the door, a shadow of impenetrable dark, perhaps five feet high, twisted, almost human in shape, and yet totally unhuman. It soaked up all the light around its twisted, stump-limbed body into two points of eye-brightness. How could a monstrous thing like this, I thought, have a woman's voice?

I leaned across to the vague mound of Mr. Agee in the next

14

bed and shook him wildly. No reaction. The dark was coming towards me, its feeling of absolute evil washing over me. I froze once more, as the thing lurched to the end of my bed and rose erect there, shadowy stumps waving from hunched, uneven shoulders. For a moment of utter terror I felt it watching me, the light soaking up from around it focused in two bright eyes, red, like almonds of blood — eyes without iris or pupil. My left hand came up off the bed, reaching towards it, thrusting it away, still like a claw from the wound.

It seemed to laugh: for a moment the ice-heavy air bore the foulest stench imaginable, and then the presence was gone.

Light flowed back into the ward. Heat. Breathable air. I slumped down on to the pillows and gradually my horror passed and the pounding of my heart slowed. The glass door-panes cast a warm, reassuring glow on to the ceiling of the ward. I looked across at Mr. Agee — he was lying flat on his back, peacefully asleep, quite undisturbed . . . so my dark visitation had been a private fantasy, a nightmare, no more than that. And I'm writing of it now, in the moonlit ward, while its frightfulness is still fresh in my mind, with the simple intention of exorcising its evil memory.

I do not, indeed, ever mean to dwell on it again, and I pray that it may never be repeated for I fear for my sanity should I be forced once more to suffer such mindless, all-encompassing terror.

Sunday 4 February:

CANDLEMAS

My strange experience in the ward was not repeated. I was released from hospital within the week and returned at once to work. The other teachers from my school who had attended Rebecca's party had circulated the story of my embarrassment, so that I found myself even more ostracised than usual. By everyone, that is, except Jane Martin, a colleague of mine in the English department.

A warm-hearted young woman with wide brown eyes and a ready smile; the friendship she offered me was sorely needed. It even included cheerful advice upon the diet which Rebecca's cruel words had prompted me to begin, and the suggestion that my general fitness might be improved if I took up jogging. And two days ago, last Friday, it came to a climax with an invitation to dinner at her house that night, an invitation that I was delighted to accept, little thinking what horrors it would bring.

Jane's family have resided in Dunmow Cross for many generations. It was not surprising, therefore, that, after attending teachers'-training college in Bristol she should have returned here to teach. Her parents, like mine, are both dead, and she now lives in a rambling old house on the southern outskirts of the village, tucked discreetly behind a neat garden and a tiny, but impenetrable, coppice of ancient elm trees.

At half-past six precisely I pushed the white gate open and crunched up the ice-brittle pebble path. A light wind made the branches above me click and whisper together. I pressed the bell and the door opened almost immediately.

Jane smiled at me. "Oh, Edwin," she said, "how cold you look — you should have worn a coat." Hot air washed over me, making me dizzy for a moment. "You'll get pneumonia," she told me.

"No, it's all right," I said. "I don't feel the cold."

"Well, you'd be better in the warm anyway." She stepped aside to let me in, but just for a moment something seemed to hold me back. I stood there on the doorstep, unable to move, until she said, with a hint of impatience, "Come *in*, Edwin, I'm letting all the heat out."

It took me a second to get used to the warm brightness of the hall. It was my first visit and I was very nervous. "What a beautiful old house," I said.

The walls were oak-panelled. A gracious staircase led up to a shadowed gallery landing. "It's Elizabethan," she said as she led the way through to the living room.

The living room was cluttered: too many chairs were

gathered round too large a fireplace with far too hot a fire. Too many tables carried too many photographs. A great black sideboard with an open cupboard above it bustled with decorative plates. Adding to the busy clutter was a stiff-backed old lady. The ramrod in her back extended up through her neck, throwing back her head so that her vivid blue eyes glared disdainfully down a great beak of a nose. Her mouth was a tight line pulled down at the corners towards a white-powdered turkey's neck. She was perched on the edge of a hard chair by the fire. Her twisted, arthritic hands lay crossed on an ebony cane. She offered me the right one as Jane performed the introduction before vanishing towards the kitchen. She was dressed in black bombazine. Her name was Miss Royston, and she was Jane's aunt, there on a winter visit.

"So," she said, "you are Jane's young man, are you? Come over here, young man: let me get a good look at you. Sit here opposite me." She peered at me sharply as I hesitated. "Don't like the heat, eh? Well, you must have thicker blood than I — that's all there is to that."

I sat opposite her beside the roaring fire as ordered, and she surveyed me for a while in silence. "You've quite a strong aura," she said at last, "I have seen many very much stronger of course, but I would say you have *some* force of character."

"Thank you very much," I said.

"I can tell, you know; tell at a glance." She clicked her false teeth knowingly.

"Oh yes?"

"Oh *yes*. It is a great gift. I can see right inside most people. Into their very souls. See that in them which is eternal and will abide."

Such things as abiding eternally anywhere have always been a source of absolute indifference to me. Out of common politeness, however, I held up my end of the occult small-talk until she suddenly said,

"You know the village has something of a history in that line? Oh yes: they say the old crossroads up by the church are haunted. Why, when I was a girl no one in the village would go near them after dark on a night like this. Or to the Broken Woods, of course."

17

She lapsed into silence. Something of what she said had got under my skin, though: after all, the crossroads had featured largely in my own recent experience. My left hand clenched painfully at the thought. "On a night like this?" I queried.

"Oh yes. Didn't you know?" She leaned closer. "Tonight is the second of February: the Feast of the Purification of the Blessed Virgin. Candlemas. For some reason the chains are light on all things evil tonight: It is a Sabbat."

"You mean a Witches' Sabbat?"

"Yes indeed. Not far from here I know of at least one coven which will be at their dark deeds . . ." She paused melodramatically, looked up, suddenly very still, as if listening. A tall old clock in the corner struck the hour of seven. I jumped . . . which was, I suppose, what she wanted. She gave a sort of leer. "In five hours' time . . . preparation will have begun long ago of course, but in five hours' time the witches will be calling on . . . *evil*."

Such mumbo-jumbo didn't interest me, and I came near to saying so. But at that moment the door opened and Jane announced "There, almost ready. Time for a drink, I think."

As soon as we were grouped around the fire again after dinner, Miss Royston made a suggestion which, from another source, might have been surprising. But not from her. "Jane," she said, drawing herself up on her long, straight back and staring down at us, "you may fetch the table. I feel a Presence."

Her eyes closed in apparent ecstasy. Jane glanced at me with apology and embarrassment. "But, Aunt," she whispered, "surely Mr. Underhill . . ."

"Mr. Underhill may not know it, my dear, but he is a part-believer. We must guide his feet, Jane; guide his feet." Her voice sank to a vibrant whisper on the repetition.

Jane returned with a small round table, a wine-glass and, of all things, an old Scrabble set. The old lady rummaged around the plastic chips and with the speed of practice set out a circle of letters spelling out the alphabet, a clock-face broken at nine and three by the words YES and NO. In the centre of this circle she put the glass, base upwards.

"Now," she said, leaning forward, body tense and eyes compelling, "we will communicate with the Other Side by

18

placing our index fingers on the glass. Do not press. Do not try and control the movement of the glass, you will find it moves of its own volition when the Presence wishes to communicate with us."

She placed the top of a bony finger on the glass. Jane followed suit. They both looked at me expectantly so I leaned forward, suddenly reluctant to be dabbling in this, and did as I was told. The base of the glass was icy cold, pleasant to feel in the oven-like room.

"Concentrate," whispered Miss Royston. "Empty your minds of all thought. Leave yourself open to be influenced!" This is childish, I thought, swept back suddenly to a rainy Saturday of childhood when, with some friends, breathless with delicious terror, I had experimented with the letters of the alphabet scrawled on pieces of paper and a plastic mug on the linoleum. Scrabble chips and a cheap wine-glass seemed hardly more conducive to success. "There are negative thoughts!' rapped Miss Royston, her voice suddenly brisk and authoritative. Her eyes on me. "You must empty your mind." Obligingly I tried to do so, bored already with the stupidity of it.

The glass under my finger was giving off a blessed coolness, so I concentrated on that. "Is there anybody there?" said Miss Royston. Again: "Is there anybody there?"

And the glass moved.

My eyes, which had been closed, jumped wide. The hairs on the back of my neck prickled uncomfortably.

YES: said the glass. As simple as that. By moving across the table, making a slight scraping noise, seemingly suddenly imbued with a life of its own, the glass said YES.

I tried to jerk my hand back, but it would not move. "Don't," Miss Royston hissed at me. "You'll disturb it!"

"Who is there?" she continued, full voice. I looked at Jane. She was white as wax, seemingly in a trance. "Who is there?" repeated Miss Royston.

The glass said: US.

"Who are *you*?"

ME AND ANOTHER, laboriously.

"What is your name?"

The glass lurched into motion once more: ANNE.

"Ah!" said Miss Royston, "I thought so. Anne is my spirit

guide . . . Hello Anne. Do not be afraid. There are only friends here."

NO. The glass slid across the table urgently.

Miss Royston frowned. "There are only friends . . ."

NO. NO: said the glass.

"I am a friend," said the old lady.

YES: said the glass.

"Jane is a friend."

YES.

"Mr. Underhill is a friend."

The glass did not move. I could feel my mind shutting again. It was obviously a fake. The old woman was guiding the glass. "Mr. Underhill!" she snapped. "Your negative thoughts are a serious handicap."

Unaccountably, the glass said NO then.

Miss Royston took a deep breath. The clock ticked. A sudden wind made the windows rattle and the room seemed less stifling for a moment, as though there were a cool draught. "Mr. Underhill is a friend," she repeated.

NO. YES: said the glass.

"What do you mean?"

NO. YES.

Suddenly my arm was unbearably heavy. There was sweat on my face. My left hand in my lap twisted and throbbed. "Explain what you mean!" snapped Miss Royston.

ANOTHER: said the glass.

"Please be clear."

BAD.

"Who is bad? Mr. Underhill?"

WICKED.

"Mr. Underhill?"

EVIL.

And everything went out. The lights went dim. Even the fire died. The burningly cold glass screeched across the table with a new and savage force, dragging us after it like puppets.

"Who is evil?" Miss Royston demanded, still undaunted.

I: it said.

"Who are you?"

I.

20

"What is your name?" patiently.

COUNTESS.

I wanted to call out a warning, to cry out, to scream . . . but I was dumb.

"Who are you, Countess?"

I AM I ALWAYS. Terribly fast, almost tearing our fingers free of our hands. I could feel the shadows dancing. The sense of mortal evil around us was utter and complete.

"Will you tell us your name, Countess?"

NO.

And still the old woman persisted. "You will not?"

NO NAME.

How could she be so totally unaware of the danger? I felt I knew the creature the nameless force in the room, and I knew it would feed on fear. Feed and gain strength on Jane's fear and mine. But old Miss Royston was questioning still. "If you have no name, at least tell us how you are known."

KNOWN I AM KNOWN.

"What do you do here?"

I AM FREE.

"What do you do?"

I AM FREE

I AM FREE

I AM FREE

Perhaps Miss Royston at last felt something. Her voice wavered, "What do you want?"

FREE

She straightened, and held up her other hand. "By all the powers of Light . . ."

FREE

Miss Royston broke then. "Tell me what you are," she whispered. And the thing seemed to laugh. D spelt the glass, and E. It scraped more slowly across the table, suddenly webbed by a network of white cracks, as if crushed under some terrible strain and held together only by the will of the malevolent force around us. The glass spelt out A and, moving back, gouged the wood into trenches. Back and back and back it scraped, towards the first letter — D.

D—E—A—D.

Suddenly Jane screamed, a howl of animal terror which splintered the moment and the room slammed back to reality. Light blazed. Heat swirled like boiling water. The glass wrenched itself away across the room and shattered by the far door. The table came up into my face, scattering Scrabble chips. Jane lurched sideways and crashed down on to the floor. I watched, paralysed, as Miss Royston was hurled backwards out of her chair and seemed to fly across the room, heels dragging on the carpet, until she crashed against the wall to hang there as if held by the throat, crushed against the plaster six feet from the floor. Her heels drummed against the black wainscot now, well clear of the carpet, and her hands fought to shake off the invisible thing that seemed to hold her there.

Then the drumming of the heels slowed and her bulging eyes rolled up. The appalling reality of it penetrated my daze: Miss Royston was hanging there. Really. This was not imagination . . . this was not a dream — there was something in the real world which was actually choking the life out of this poor, crazy old woman. I hurled the table aside sprang out of my seat, and ran full-tilt towards the wall. "Let her go!" I screamed. "Let her go!"

My hands waved uselessly through the empty air until with stunning suddenness I was struck in the centre of my forehead. Something was in front of the wall exactly level with the old woman's throat. I could not see it, but I could feel it. Its end was the stub of hardness on which I had hit my head. It was surrounded by a slight, slimy softness, cold as a slug. My shaking hands explored the length of the thing. I found a shape I recognised — an elbow-joint. Then a forearm, a wrist and hand.

Miss Royston was being held against the wall by an invisible, rigid, unbelievably powerful severed arm.

"Let her go!" I screamed again. My open palms slapped against icy, invisible flesh, bunched muscles, steely tendons. "In God's name, let her go!" And abruptly it did so.

She fell in a heap to the ground, slumped on to her side, and moaned faintly. Jane sat up, the terror still in her eyes. "Get your aunt some brandy," I said firmly.

It was something for her to do, something to distract her mind from the full horror of what we had just witnessed. She was gone for several minutes while I crouched beside the motionless old woman, and when she returned with the brandy she was pale but composed.

I moistened Miss Royston's lips with the brandy and she sighed deeply and stirred. "Are you all right?" I asked.

She nodded gingerly. I gave her some more. She coughed and sat up.

"Phone for a doctor," I said to Jane, but Miss Royston whispered, "No. Help me to my bedroom. I shall be quite all right in a minute."

I protested that she really ought to see a doctor, but Jane's aunt was not someone with whom one argued for long. And besides, she was clearly making an amazingly quick recovery. So I helped her up to her room, and then waited uneasily downstairs. To pass the time I tidied away the Scrabble tiles and swept up the broken glass. The room, in fact, was distressingly normal — it was almost impossible to believe in what I had seen in it with my own eyes, and felt with my own hands, only such a short time before.

When Jane had put her aunt to bed, the old lady sent word for me to stick my head round the door. I did as she asked.

"I have to go home to Scotland in a day or two," Miss Royston told me, "so I won't be able to do much more. It'll be up to you, now."

"What will be?" I asked, surprised.

"Why, to find out what that thing was, Mr. Underhill, and how it got loose. *Free*, it said it was . . ." She smiled at me wanly. "Well, you're just going to have to chain it down again, you know . . ."

Her voice wandered away and her head dropped sideways on her pillow. On her throat, already darkening into bruises, I saw the unmistakable marks of four fingers and a thumb. At the tip of each mark was a curved wound, as though fingernails lengthened into claws had cut into her flesh. The wounds were not deep but blood welled in them softly, bright and strangely beautiful against her wrinkled, powdered skin.

THE CROSSROADS

Miss Royston returned to her home in the north on the fourth, two days after the seance, and last week Jane was called away to nurse her. We both hope her illness will prove to be nothing serious. In Jane's absence my life has seemed to centre around my increasing interest in jogging. I have also pursued a rather dilatory search for information about the ghostly Countess. This has proved difficult. Dunmow Cross, it seems, has seen nearly two millenia of countesses, and following up every single one of them has been a task quite beyond my limited enthusiasm. Until this very evening, in fact, when a chance encounter — for I would not believe it otherwise — has at the same time sharpened my interest and eased my difficulty.

I have made a habit of jogging most evenings and today, after church, lunch and a long boring afternoon, I suddenly felt wildly restless. I changed into my new tracksuit and set out into the gloom. As usual I felt full of running almost instantly. The east wind caressed me, tugging my hair, making my flesh rise in goosebumps. Even the pavement seemed to spring up beneath my feet, thrusting me forward in the darkness. I decided to run out of the village into the surrounding fields.

I do not know how far I ran or for how long, my course dictated only by the windings of the paths I followed: past Jane's house, out of the village, across the A120 main road and up the western edge of the Great South Field to the Broken Woods. The naked branches of the high hedgerows glistened against the black sky. Even in this dead season I seemed to be sailing through a sea of life. Birds soared above me, calling as they settled for the night. The hedgerows and frost-white grasses were alive with scratchings and scurryings. I closed my eyes and ran.

On the coppiced hillock of the Broken Woods I overlooked the distant diamond lights of Great Dunmow. The evening seemed so full of life that I actually sang out loud. Utterly at one with nature I ran from tree to tree, exploring their rough bark with newly sensitive fingers. I felt their quiet life pulsing beneath my hands.

Then I turned and sped down the hill until I came to the great straight Roman road, where I turned for home. In the distance, a mile or two before me, the church bells began to ring: Evensong, I supposed. I ran on, then slowed to a walk as the bells quietened. What I was thinking about I cannot clearly remember. The bells had punctured my euphoria but I was not tired. If anything in particular, I was thinking of food.

I have been very pleased with the way my diet has been going: I have lost more than a stone now and need to wear belts with all my old trousers. It is a simple diet, consisting mainly of meat, fresh fruit and green vegetables. Recently, however, I find I have grown sick of plant pap. And the only drawback to eating meat on its own is its effect on my digestion. I seem to awake occasionally in the night with a terrible burning thirst.

Such mundane thoughts, I believe, occupied my mind as I jogged down towards the village. The church tower reared dizzily on my left, the vacant threatening stare of old empty houses on my right. I speeded up a little. Henry Francis Lyte's immortal 'Abide with Me' lingered like incense on the air behind me and it was that, if anything, which raised the short hairs on the back of my neck. A few hundred yards ahead of me lay the crossroads themselves. The street-lamp which normally illuminates them was not working, but the road seemed to contain its own dim brightness amid the heavy shadows, and the grass positively shone. The signpost stood like a complicated gallows, its four wooden arms pointing urgently away from the place. In the far distance, thunder rumbled again. New clouds moved across the dark heavens, lean and grey, slightly luminous, like a pack of ghostly wolves hunting. The east wind pulled my hair gently, an invisible lover, and I thought suddenly of those other fingers that I had not seen, clamped around Miss Royston's throat. I shivered. For a moment everything was absolutely still. Even time itself seemed to pause.

And at the birth of that moment there was suddenly a figure beside the signpost. It was crouching or kneeling by

25

the thin wooden post. Naturally I went towards it. As I came nearer it began to pull itself up, almost as if out of the ground. "Is everything all right?" I called.

By the time I was within five yards of it I could see that it was a woman, even though her back was towards me. She was fully erect now, leaning against the signpost, looking up at the church. Her head was held at a strange angle, almost resting on her left shoulder. I knew now that here was something wrong. Her hair fell in rats' tails of colourless darkness down her back. Her left hand came away from the post and fell to her side. It was the absolute silence of her movement which triggered the most vivid alarm in my mind. She had on a full skirt which reached the ground and bulked out strangely on either side of her slim waist. Her arm should have made some sound as it fell against the shadowed cloth, but it did not. I froze, every nerve in my body suddenly aflame with an agony of cold. She began to turn. A high lace ruff flashed a pinpoint or two of light. I noticed then that there was no cloud of breath above her on the icy air. Something inside me recognised what this was, and who.

I turned and ran. Ran from the Countess; ran from her who was dead. And free . . . Head down and elbows pumping, bruising the balls of my feet on the black, icy road, I sped out of the haunted shadows down into the bright heart of the village. As I ran I thought of Miss Royston's words: there is something evil loose — and you must chain it.

And soon now, I will have her, my Countess. Already I have begun to tie her down. For I have seen the style of dress she wore in countless illustrations: she was an Elizabethan, my Countess. And it should be easy now to learn her history, to discover why she walks, and armed with that knowledge — to chain her as the old woman said.

THE RECORDS

Every evening after school for the last ten days or so I have gone straight into the Central Library in Great Dunmow to consult all the histories of Essex I could find, but there was no reference to any Elizabethan countess.

By last Wednesday I had looked in all the books immediately available to me and had found nothing. My next step was obvious: the parish records. It was time to go and visit the Reverend Gore. And, of course, I thought that if I was lucky I would see Rebecca also, and could show her how fully I have followed the advice so mercilessly given at our last meeting in the hospital. My jogging continues, I am running faster and longer, and I swear I stand taller these days. And it is all, at least to some degree, thanks to her.

This evening, accordingly, after a high tea of rare steak, I went up the hill to the vicarage. It was a misty spring evening and the declining sun seemed unbearably bright. Dunmow Cross was quite busy and yet I found myself walking alone. Only slowly did I realise that whereas everyone else was crowded on the sunny side of the street in the brightness and warmth, I had elected without conscious thought to walk amongst the shadows.

The vicarage is a huge house for one old man and his daughter to live in. There must be eight or ten bedrooms. It is, as Rebecca had told me, early Elizabethan, built in the distant days when Dunmow Cross was a thriving community and its vicarage one short step only below the bishop's palace. Nowadays, of course, the income from this wasted parish cannot begin to support it, and it is terribly seedy and dilapidated.

I walked up the drive and knocked on the door. Rebecca opened it almost at once. Not long ago my heart would have been in my throat at the prospect of seeing her, but today I was expectant rather than nervous. She was wearing a big, red, floppy, woollen, polo-necked pullover and faded blue jeans. She squinted at me for a moment, slightly puzzled, until I said, "Hello, Rebecca."

"Oh. It's you, Edwin. I didn't recognise you." Her face was pinched. Her eyes were dull and dark-ringed. She did not look well. "What is it you want?"

"Can I see your father for a moment?" I asked.

"My father? Yes, of course. Come in." She held the door open wide. I stepped into the cool, dark hall. It was neat, tidy and sparkingly clean. Even the wainscot glowed dully. They had a woman in, of course — old Mrs. Hope. She had been coming ever since Mrs. Gore had gone into hospital. When was that? Five years ago now?

"He's in his study. This way . . ." She shut the door behind me and led me into the big airy sitting room.

"How are you?" I asked.

"Fine. You?"

"O.K." I held up my left hand, the scar white now, as though I had drawn a starfish with chalk on the palm and the back of the hand alike. On the far side of the sitting room, down two steps, was a dark little corridor. We went along it.

"What do you want to see father about?" she asked.

"Ghosts, actually," I answered.

She stopped and I collided with her.

"Please, Mr. Underhill — under no circumstances mention ghosts to him!"

The tone of her voice was strange, almost frightening. Then she swung away and rapped smartly on a big dark door. A distant voice called, "Come!" She pushed it open, ushered me in, and left me.

It was a tall room, packed with books of all kinds and ages. Mr. Gore sat at a huge desk littered with paper. There were crumpled balls of it on the floor round the desk and in the wastepaper-basket. His white mane of hair was dishevelled as though he has been running his fingers through it. "Ah, Mr. Underhill!" he said, swinging his chair towards me and half rising. "How are you? I haven't seen you much in church lately. What can I do for you? Sit down, do."

I sank into an overstuffed armchair and put on my lap the pile of file paper purloined from school. I cleared my throat a little nervously. The Reverend Hugh Gore is a large, powerful man. They say he was a rugby blue at Oxford. Physically, emotionally and spiritually he is overpowering. Rebecca's warning lingered in my mind: there would be no mention of ghosts. But I had come well prepared.

"I would like to consult some parish records," I said. "I shall need a little guidance as to which ones would be best. I've never done anything quite like this before. It's for a project with one of my classes about the history of Dunmow Cross in Elizabethan times."

"Why the Elizabethan period particularly?"

"Well, I teach English rather than history, and the Elizabethan was the Golden Age of English Literature, after all."

"I see." His tone made it clear that he wished he didn't. "Well, the best place I can recommend to you is the *Victoria County History of Essex* . . ."

"Yes. I've looked there. I was hoping for something of more local note. I thought, perhaps, if there are any parish records . . ."

"Oh, I think you'll find very little of use in there. Baptisms, marriages, funerals . . . Dry old stuff . . ."

"An exploration of local history. Old family names, forgotten relationships. The very fabric of our past," I insisted.

"But I'm sure you will be disappointed. Really. There's nothing of note at all!"

"Does it mention where people were buried?"

"Some family plots, yes. But you can see more by looking at the gravestones in the churchyard . . ."

I was not to be put off. "Some of them are defaced . . ."

"Oh, very few . . ."

"And I have heard that some graves actually lie outside the churchyard wall."

Silence. An icy silence. "Well, Mr. Underhill, I see you have a scholar's tenacity and that weakness of youth which refuses to learn by any experience other than its own. I suppose you wish to see the marriage register."

"No. The records of burials, please."

"Really, Mr. Underhill, you must let me guide you some of the way. There are hardly likely to be any family relationships recorded in a register of interments." His voice had taken on the strange iron edge which had made Rebecca's tone so sinister when she talked of ghosts. He was clearly not going to give an inch.

"Of course, you're quite right. I didn't think of that. The marriage register is exactly what I want." It was on a shelf far back in the room. I paid careful attention as he got it.

For the next hour I ploughed through the several hundred pages of a fat dusty tome dated in faded but beautiful writing: MARRIAGES IN THE PARISH OF DUNMOW CROSS 1560–1575. I sat bemused as the youngsters of a large and bustling provincial town married and inter-married. Dunmow Cross must have been by far the largest town in Essex when Elizabeth was still a young woman. What had happened to it? I was tempted away from my search for any reference to a Countess by that question. "Could I see the next one?" I asked.

"What? " Mr. Gore glanced up from his work.

"The next volume. What is it, 1575-1590?"

"No, no. The next one is locked up. Not available. It would really be most inconvenient."

"Oh, I'm sorry," I said. "I'll just put this one back."

"No. Leave it there. I'll put it back."

"Please don't bother," I said, rising and walking across towards the shelf. "I really don't want to disturb you."

He was on his feet immediately, thrusting his great square body between the shelves and myself. "It's no trouble at all," he said, holding his hand out for the book. But my eyes were busy over his shoulder. Beside the space left by the removal of this fat volume of marriages 1560–1575 was a curiously thin companion labelled MARRIAGES IN THE PARISH OF DUNMOW CROSS 1575–1620. Apparently it had needed several hundred pages to record fifteen years of weddings in the earlier volume and less than half that number in the next to record the following forty-five. Stunned, I pushed the fat volume into his outstretched hand. It was extremely heavy. One hand was really not enough to hold it in. He dropped it, half caught it, fumbled with it, stepped back to give himself more room, and collided with the shelves. As I helped him regain his balance my gaze wandered once more along the dusty rows of books. Three shelves up the words REGISTER OF BURIALS caught my attention, and I ran my eye along the line. 1540–1550 . . . 1550–1560 . . . 1560–1570 . . . 1570 — and then suddenly, on its own, an entire weighty volume, labelled 1579. In that one year, then, there must have been a thousand burials — no, many, many more! A plague, perhaps? The Black Death? or . . .

One of the vicar's great hands closed on my shoulder. I turned to him. He had followed the direction of my gaze, and now in his smile there was a terrible, menacing coldness.

"Is there anything else you'll be wanting, Mr. Underhill?" he asked, challenging me.

"N . . . no, thank you." I'd had enough already. More than enough.

"In that case, Mr. Underhill, I suggest that you leave me to get on with my work. I have a sermon to prepare." He gestured indifferently at the crumpled balls of paper that littered the floor. "And if you *really* wish to interest your pupils in literary history, might I suggest another period? Milton's perhaps? I'm sure they'd find it far more rewarding."

He pointed to the door. "You can find your own way out, I imagine."

I could. And I did. Rebecca was nowhere to be seen, but that did not particularly concern me. What *did* concern me were the reasons of the vicar of this ancient parish for wishing to keep its doings in the 1570s so deeply shrouded in mystery. They would hardly, I thought, have been on account simply of the plague. If there had been a visitation, then there would be more than just the Black Death involved.

Friday 16 March:

THE CHASE

Last Monday brought a letter from Jane. Miss Royston was fading fast, poor old soul, and had been asking to see me. She said she had something of enormous importance to tell me, and I was preparing to travel up to her sick-bed this weeekend when a telegram this morning forestalled me. Miss Royston died last night. And her secret, whatever it may have been, died with her. I do not know what Jane will do, but there is sadly no help I can offer her.

This week, since my confrontation with the Reverend Gore, has been very strange. I have been searching down all the old records once again, my mind full, not only of the Countess, but also of the visitation that Death itself seems to have made to the village four hundred years ago. But all available documents seem to be wilfully silent on the matter.

My concentration on these questions is such that they seem on occasion actually to intrude upon reality. Even at school, once or twice this air of unreality has proved unsettlingly powerful: shadows glimpsed out of the corners of my eye, movements where nothing moved. I am sleeping badly again also, and such rest as I do get is disturbed by visions and dreams. One especially has been repeated: I seem to awaken in my room in utter silence, a silence which is broken, as it was in the ward, by the approach of some terrifyingly evil entity. I can feel it, hear it, on the landing outside my bedroom door. The handle turns. The door is locked. The handle turns further and rattles impatiently. And then the door itself begins to shake as though something enormously powerful and dangerous is about to burst into my bedroom.

In spite of the strong temptation, I have not seen the vicar again until this evening — and even then it was not a social call, but simply an accident. I had gone jogging over my familiar route down through the village, up to the Broken Woods through the fields, and down again towards the crossroads. As I came past the vicarage in the dark, I was startled to see the Reverend Gore astride an ancient bicycle. On the back of the old machine there was a square parcel bound with string. I was about to turn away when in my mind's eye I suddenly saw that bundle once more. It was made up of books . . . All at once I knew they were the parish records! I almost panicked. Where was he going with them? What was he going to do? By the time I had brought my thoughts under control, my legs had taken over and thrust me forward in pursuit.

And so the chase began. The vicar turned off the main road

into one of the little hedge-bound lanes and veered south, squeaking away in the dark. I bounded after him along the silent byways, mouth agape and gums stinging. My glasses — a positive hindrance nowadays — kept slipping down my nose. I took them off and thrust them into my tracksuit pocket.

Low clouds filled the sky. City dwellers are not acquainted with the dark as we are out here. Beyond the realm of street lamps the darkness can be absolute. The dark wraps itself around your head like a black sack, even seeming to impede your breathing.

But this evening there was light from a rising moon, filtering through the clouds and I could see the hedgerows glinting with dampness. I ran in the middle of the road between the busy rustlings of the night creatures in the hedges and the fields, and always, ahead of me, drawing me on, the squeaking of the bicycle.

Abruptly there was mist. It lay in flat sheets on the dead air. Mr. Gore pedalled through it unconcernedly but as I met the first pale swathe I brought my hands up to my head as though there were cobwebs entangled in my hair. I began to shiver. Where was he going? Each step forward made me colder and more tired. The squeaking of the bicycle began to draw away. I gritted my teeth — how my gums throbbed — and ran on at full-tilt. Then, over the sound of the bicycle I heard the first sinister whisper. The hissing, gurgling, bubbling song of running water. The vicar was heading for the River Chelmer and I knew what he was going to do. He was going to throw the books into the water.

I put all my power into the running now, leaping forward in great bounds, grasping the ground with spread toes as though I were barefoot, thrusting onward with every sinew. Suddenly the squeaking stopped. The sibilance of the water filled my ears as though I were surrounded by snakes. By the time the stream came in sight I was drenched in an icy sweat of terror. Why was I so afraid?

The road went down to a tiny ford. The banks gathered up, mist-shrouded, and meandered into the dark on either side. The water was inky. It seemed to give off an aura of night. And the nearer I came, the more strongly it reached for me. I faltered, my fear of it incomprehensible yet sickeningly powerful.

Mr. Gore stood with the square parcel in his hands and his chin sunk on his chest, at prayer no doubt. For all his unhelpfulness I wished him no ill — it was the books I wanted. So I gathered my courage and worked my way left, nearer to the water.

Finally the vicar stopped praying and raised the bundle high above his head. He hesitated. I crouched. Then he turned towards me and the heavy package crashed into the reeds a little to my left. Silent as a cat I dived after it, but the rushes rustled and cracked around me.

"Who's there?" cried the vicar. I scrabbled in the icy ooze at the edge of the water. "Come out, whoever you are," he shouted, his voice ringing on the watery air.

The stream closed on my left hand like jaws. My bones ached. I moaned in terror, wriggling forward, my ears closed to what Mr. Gore was yelling. Elbow-deep, shoulder-deep I pushed my arm, seeking the bundle. Agony. I could scarcely breathe. Past the shoulder. Half of the chest, my hand among the riverbed weeds and slime, numb yet afire. I gulped one agonised breath, mouth stretched, nostrils flaring, and plunged into the water. My finger brushed the package, nails scraping recklessly over the sodden paper, cutting through the wet cord as if they were steel claws, so that the bundle, destroyed by my clumsiness, burst apart.

A book brushed my face. I opened my eyes beneath the water, saw its pages wafting in slow motion on the stream, saw the lines on them blur, run, and fade away as the book itself disintergrated. Then my feet touched bottom and I thrust up.

I exploded out of the river with manic force. Mr. Gore had taken several steps forward and was staring into the dark, obviously perplexed by the noises I was making, and blinded by the darkness. Now his pale face twisted into a mask of horror. He cried out, and something silver sailed lazily over my head to sink into the black water safely behind me — a crucifix and chain. Then there were only his hurried footsteps and the dying squeal of his bicycle.

It was not until then that I realised I was screaming. Screaming with terror and rage and frustration. Screaming like an animal. Screaming so that all the farm dogs for miles around were answering my cries.

ALL FOOLS

After the episode in the river things have quietened. My sleep is uninterrupted, the corners of my eyes are untenanted. All avenues towards a discovery of the Countess's identity seem closed off to me. And I have been glad enough to let it lie, to concentrate instead on the inevitable mountain of school-work which seems to collect at the end of term — added to this term by the portion of Jane Martin's work that I also have to do in her absence. As the holidays were approaching she has decided to stay up in Scotland and try to come to terms with the shock of Miss Royston's death.

Yesterday night, however, by the merest coincidence, interest in my ghostly lady stirred again. It was a gusty, uneasy night. The windows rattled, and strange little draughts disturbed curtains and papers like unseen fingers. The whole of my tiny rented room seemed suddenly packed with ghosts. My unease was so drawn out that when a strange, slithering scratching sound began against my window I jumped from my chair and cowered back against the room's far wall.

The sound persisted, like the whisper of long nails against the curtained glass. It took all of my strength and courage to drive me across the room to it. My hand trembled on the curtain. And when I jerked it back I cried out as if in a nightmare, for a wizened yellow claw was pressed against the dark glass, tapping and tapping, its skin lemon-coloured and scaled . . . It took me anguished moments to recognise it as simply a chicken's foot on a pole. When I pressed my face to the glass it vanished, and I saw half a dozen dark shapes scrambling away across the garden. They were children, and they were playing the ancient Fools' Game.

In Little Dunmow they have their famous Flitch Trial in which, for a side of bacon, husbands and wives are tested. All over Britain we have the bonfires of November 5th. In America, trick or treat on October 31st. Here in Dunmow Cross we have the Fools' Game.

The idea is simple: on this night each year one child — a girl always — begins to creep through the village at sunset. She taps on the windows, summoning the other children out to her. They in turn tap on other windows for other children, until all the children in the village and the neighbouring farms have been called out into the night. Then they all flit from shadow to shadow up to the Broken Woods, where they dance around a bonfire.

The game has not been played for years however, and as I put on my coat to go downstairs I wondered who had started it up again. Of course it had to be the newcomer, the new tenant of Whitethorn Cottage, Dr. Richard Burke the psychiatrist, working extra hard to become an accepted member of the village community. I found him alone in the now-silent street, and joined him.

"Hello, Mr. Underhill," he said affably. "How's the hand? No ill-effects, I hope?"

I showed him the scar, which was fading now, and we chatted amiably about village life while the children flitted between the dark buildings, individuals becoming couples, groups and gangs. Their giggling increased, only just short of hysteria.

"It's one of the most fascinating historic games I've ever seen," said Burke. "What do you think it means?"

"I don't know. It's extremely sinister, though."

"I quite agree. Does it ever start spontaneously?" He tugged at his beard. "I mean, I set this game up myself, arranging permission with parents and suchlike, but does it ever just *happen*?"

I told him it hadn't, not that I'd heard of since coming to the village. We began to walk up towards the Broken Woods where the Fools' Game would end. We talked about children's games and how they made play out of fear.

Here comes the candle to light you to bed,
Here comes the chopper to chop off your head . . .

And the horrific 'Ring-a-ring-a-roses', which is a catalogue of the symptons of bubonic plague, a memory of the Black Death. Like these, the Fools' Game, we decided. seemed to tap some forgotten terror.

Dr. Burke went on up the hill to watch the bonfire. I left him on the edge of the woods and returned to my room. There was something about the prospect of seeing the children dance around that fire that made my hackles rise. The children and my ghostly Countess seemed suddenly to be inextricably connected . . .

I met Dr. Burke this afternoon as well, when I called round to Jane's house after school to see if everything was all right there.

He was in the garden. "Look at this," he cried as I went in through the gate. "It's those damn children!"

A small rose garden at the corner of her lawn had been trampled underfoot so that the bushes lay about with their roots starting out of the soil like black bones. "I was keeping an eye on this one in particular," he said, pointing to a tall standard lying on its side. "It's Miss Martin's favourite — it needs tying up, and I've nothing . . ."

"I have," I said, and went quickly back to my room. A few minutes later I returned with the stake which had stabbed my hand four months ago. We thumped it into the ground and tied the rose to it. "There," I said when we had finished. "That should hold it."

This evening, after correcting a set of exam papers, I changed into my tracksuit and padded out into the night. I had been running for perhaps twenty minutes when in the darkness something squealed. I knew the sound. Looking neither right nor left, the Reverend Hugh Gore cycled determinedly past me.

Without pausing to think I followed him. Down the road we went, through the village heading south. After half an hour or so, Mr. Gore turned into the driveway through a great pair of gates. Interest quickening, I moved forward. By the time I reached the gates he was gone and the gates locked again behind him, but I could hear his bicycle squeaking away up the drive.

There was a notice on a dark brick column: MID ESSEX HOSPITAL PSYCHIATRIC UNIT: MORDEN HALL.

I loped into the darkness. There had been an urgency in Mr. Gore's manner that told me something was afoot. The wall of the asylum grounds was perhaps ten feet high, but a few yards back from the road a small coppice reached up to the cloudy sky. It was the work of only a moment to shin up the tree nearest to the wall, swing out on a limb and drop down on to the other side.

Some two hundred yards away stood the irredeemably ugly building, squat, and square, five storeys high, like a huge Victorian workhouse. It had an air of brooding hope-lessness. Windows blazed, yet there was absolute silence. I moved forward. The grass was shaggy — it would soon need its first summer cutting and it pulled my feet. Along this wing of the asylum there was a stair-well with steps leading down to basement doors, and around it a wrought-iron railing painted black: uprights about nine inches apart, rising to ornate points above a single, flat, horizontal bar at shoulder height. I followed the railings along to the end of the building but there was nothing of interest.

I turned and began to walk back across the lawn. The silence of the place depressed me, I found it dangerously at odds with the tension that seemed to crackle everywhere in the night air around me. I had taken perhaps a dozen steps when the sound of breaking glass made me stop and turn.

High on the wall a window burst outwards, the glass falling in bright arcs like crystal snowflakes. A figure dressed in black dived through the broken frame to pause on all fours like a huge cat balanced impossibly on the sill. It was shriek-ing the high-pitched cry of a woman. Outlined against the brightness I saw long wild hair, great breadth of shoulders, legs as thin as bones.

Its shrieking ceased as the moon broke through fat clouds, and the creature raised its arms in a frantic gesture of one-ness. Then it hunched forward. Its hands sought purchase on the rough brickwork, the hips and buttocks were outlined for a moment and then it began incredibly to crawl head-first down the wall like a gigantic black spider.

Another figure appeared in the vacant square of the window-frame. "Rowena!" cried the Reverend Gore.

He hurled himself out over the sill, reaching down to grasp the foot hooked on to a drain-pipe. "Hang on, Rowena!" he cried, inching forward.

Other figures joined him, held his legs as he pushed clear of the sill, leaning down to grasp the hooked foot with both hands. As he did so a great silver crucifix swung free of his

38

breast and dangled glinting in the moonlight. The creature on the wall saw it and one hand lifted free of a projecting overflow pipe to make a wild gesture. "Hang on, Rowena!" he cried again "Don't let go!"

But the creature howled and kicked against him. A heel slammed into his face. His grip on the other foot slipped. Suddenly the creature looked down and its eyes met mine. It gave a low, thrilling howl, and lifted its hands once more, as it had to the moon.

Lazily, turning in the air like a coin flipped for a bet, it fell clear of the wall. Over and over it went, its scream growing like the whistle of a train approaching out of a long tunnel. It seemed to fall forever.

She was on her back, face up, legs in towards the wall, when she hit the railings. Warm, heavy drops rained on me. One moment she was falling, the next: still. No transition. Suddenly, absolutely, as though she had always been there, she was hanging on the rails. Heels against the iron uprights, hands at the end of arms swinging behind her back to clap quietly in the silence. Upside down and silent — though still wide-eyed — dangled the white face of Rowena, mother to Rebecca and wife to Hugh Gore.

Five years insane, and at peace at last.

Friday 13 April:

THE INQUEST

The Coroner's Court was a small, dusty room, rather like a lecture theatre in a university. There were public seats at the back, seats for a jury at the front, a couple of tables, a witness box and an august bench for the coroner. The coroner today was Miss Hortense Simcox J.P., a formidable lady with hair like steel-wool and the face of a pink frog. But she had sharp, intelligent eyes. I sat at the back, enjoying one of the first days of my Easter holiday. The court was crowded.

The preliminaries were surprisingly swift. A jury was sworn in. The coroner gave a brief talk about the circumstances of Mrs. Gore's illness, about the Gore family and its feelings.

The pathologist was a fat, bald man with a black moustache and artist's hands. He spoke briefly, and forcefully. There was no doubt of his meaning, although many of his technicalities were foreign to me.

The psychiatric expert was Richard Burke. Mrs. Gore, he said, had been under his care for the last few months of his consultancy at Morden Hall. She suffered basically from paranoia, a specialised persecution complex. She slipped into and out of reality quite unpredictably, and was capable of the greatest extremes of violence, both to herself and to others.

Put at its most simple, he said, trying to sound matter-of-fact, Rowena Gore believed that she was a vampire. She feared sunlight and water. She fed only on raw meat, and on her own blood licked out of bites on her forearms. The clearest pattern of her behaviour — if the court would indulge an unmedical reference — would be that of the lunatic Renfield in Bram Stoker's novel, *Dracula*.

My God! I thought, no wonder the Reverend Gore and his daughter sometimes seemed to be carrying a heavy burden! And, even as I thought this, the vicar himself got up to give evidence.

His face was haggard, and he seemed to have aged a dozen years since I'd seen him last. But he spoke out strongly, and with impressive dignity.

"For many years," he began, "my wife believed that there was a curse on the female members of my family and blood. There is a legend in our village about a beautiful foreign lady of noble birth who brought a terrible plague to what had been, up to then, a prosperous town. An ancestor of mine was apparently instrumental in whatever revenge the townspeople took on this noblewoman, and she is said to have cursed his line through its female descendants.

"There is a doggerel which run thus:

40

Women of blood, look to blood,
Make of blood your bread.
Feed on blood until your blood
Feeds the Dead.

"I myself have never placed any credence in this tale, although it is a matter of record that the women of my family have not led long or happy lives."

Mr. Gore paused, took a drink of water, then calmly continued.

"When she consented to become my wife, Rowena knew nothing of this, but Dunmow Cross has been the cradle of my family through many generations, and soon after the birth of our daughter Rebecca I decided to live there. Somehow, not long after we moved in, Rowena discovered a reference to this curse. She brought it to my notice of course, but I explained that is was nothing but a folk tale. My wife and I met at Oxford University where we were both involved in academic study — myself in theology and Rowena in history — and she used her training in methods of research to the very worst ends. In such places as the Bodleian Library and the library of the British Museum she began to check back on the history of the folk tale. In doing so, she became insanely convinced that some powerful supernatural agency was involved, and that the curse would in fact work out its full power upon her, and eventually upon our daughter Rebecca."

Here he paused again. The feeling of concentration in the room was absolute. Every eye was directed towards his tragic, black-clad figure. This was not a ghost story. This was real. He was talking about a woman who had actually lived and believed in such things, and who had died in that belief, because of that belief.

Mr. Gore sighed deeply. "The ideas took root. I offered to give up living in Dunmow Cross and move away, but her fixation was absolute and she refused. She believed that the curse would find her out no matter where she was, and that research in and around the village presented her best chance of fighting back.

"Ten years ago I first took her to see a psychiatrist. Five years ago I was forced to have her committed." He stopped,

41

his head drooping at last.

The coroner cleared her throat, "Can we turn now to the night in question?"

"Certainly, madam." He drew himself up again. "Since the beginning of this year, my wife's illness had become even more pronounced. She seemed convinced that the curse was coming to some sort of climax. That its author, the Countess, was in fact returning to complete her revenge."

"Let me get this quite clear, please," said the coroner. "Your wife believed that someone was returning — returning from where?"

I sat forward, waiting for his answer, fascinated.

"From beyond the grave. From the dead," said Mr. Gore and a stir went through the silent room like a night wind through trees.

"I see," said the coroner. She made a note. "Please continue, Mr. Gore."

"I went to see her as often as possible, of course, to try and bring her some spiritual comfort. But it was no use. She was convinced that she was beyond divine aid. That it was only a matter of time, of very little time, before this creature returned to claim her for ever."

"And in the meantime, she was sure she was a vampire?" You could hear the conflict between sympathy and utter incredulity in the coroner's voice.

"That was just it, you see," cried Gore, his voice growing hoarse now with the strain. "That was the cure: that she should become like that. She believed the curse was that she should become a vampire, completely and absolutely, one of the un-dead, feeding on blood alone."

Miss Simcox waited for the commotion to subside in the courtroom. When she spoke again her voice trembled, but she kept her tone brisk. "I see. Thank you, Mr. Gore. Now to the night in question, if you please."

With a visible effort Mr. Gore took up his story again. "I went to see her as usual, around eight o'clock. It was after dark. She was seated in her room surrounded by her books. At first, she seemed very glad to see me and asked how I was. We talked of the family and the village, just chit-chat really. Then she began to grow restless. She said she could feel something evil coming close. I tried to change the subject by

42

referring to some parish records which she had spent many years studying. I told her, quite abruptly, hoping to shock her back to her senses, that I had thrown them away."

"Just a moment, please," said the coroner, "you mean to say that you have thrown parish records away?"

"Yes," Mr. Gore admitted. "But only records of the late 1570s, now unfortunately so badly aged and damaged as to be utterly indecipherable."

"I see. So you told your wife you had disposed of these. What was her reaction?"

"She asked me why I had done this. She seemed shocked, as I had hoped — and suddenly quite rational."

"So your shock tactic worked."

"So I believed."

"And then?"

"I explained to her that someone else had been going through the records in her absence."

"Who had?"

"A local schoolteacher. He was checking for a lesson. He mentioned something to my daughter about tracking down a ghost also."

"I see. Is this relevant?"

"Not at all except that Rowena also asked who had been looking at the books and why. And when I told her she became most agitated again. She asked me, what ghost? I realised I had committed a serious error in mentioning it and immediately rang for aid. My wife started to scream. 'It is she. It is she!' I tried to calm her but she suddenly went completely berserk and threw herself at me screaming that I had summoned back the Dead."

"What did you do?"

"I have for some time been using the delustions of her illness to control the malady itself — under the advice of course of Dr. Burke. I showed her my crucifix."

"Did it work?"

"She drew back from me, yes. But at that moment two attendants came in and she threw herself between them, and out through the door. I ran after her but I was too slow. She hurled herself through a window at the end of the corridor and tried to climb down the wall. I leaned out of the window and reached her. I caught her foot but she kicked free —"

Mr. Gore choked, and turned his head away. The coroner waited until he was in control of himself again, and then she said, very gently, "Your wife fell?"

"Yes. No. Yes."

"You're not sure?"

Mr. Gore hunched his shoulders. "Not entirely. You see, it was more complex than that. I . . . I think she saw the Countess down there waiting for her."

"*What*?"

"There was something, someone, down there." He stretched out one hand as if pointing. "Rowena saw it. I too — I am certain there was a figure on the lawn. It was tall and gaunt. It gave the impression of being terribly crippled in some way . . . I am sure Rowena saw it and tried to fly down and join it."

Far too quickly the coroner said: "It was obviously some-one from the hospital."

"No," Mr. Gore whispered. He was almost sobbing now. "They were all accounted for. It was no one from the hospi-tal. And there were footprints of a sort across the long grass of the lawn. It was gone, of course, before anyone else saw it. And yet *I saw* it. I know Rowena saw it . . . Why was it there? Where did it go? And so quickly?"

He collapsed then. His testimony was at an end. So was the inquest to all intents and purposes. He was led sym-pathetically away, and the coroner summed up as best she could. A verdict of Accidental Death was returned almost immediately.

On the way out the Reverend Gore was cornered by well-wishers and newspapermen. I caught up with Rebecca who had gone on alone. My part in her mother's death was troubling me. "Hello," I said, as lightly as I could.

"Edwin," She jumped. "I thought you'd be back in the village. Where did you spring from?"

"I just happened to be in town," I gestured apologetically. "I do hope you don't mind, but I was in there for the whole thing. Is there anything I can do?"

She just looked at me.

"I feel so responsible." I wondered how much I dared admit to. "It was I, after all, who started it all, digging around in those old books."

"Oh, Edwin, don't be so silly! Poor mother was quite mad — we've known it for ages. Come on. Let's have a cup of coffee."

Over coffee — which I did not drink because my lips and gums have grown very sensitive to heat these days — I suggested that her mother might not have been as mad as everyone thought. There might in fact have been a curse after all, I said. And my own researches, taken up since I had seen an (I glanced uneasily over my shoulder, certain that someone was standing there) ... an apparently genuine apparition, had more or less proved the existence of the Countess.

She went marble-white. "What?"

"Wouldn't it be of help to you and your father's peace of mind if I could prove that there was a solid historical foundation to this? That your mother's fixation was not *all* madness?"

"That there really was a curse?" she cried. "On all the Gore women? Are you saying that I will become like that, too?"

"No! No, of course not. I'm just suggesting that if we can discover the historical basis of the story, then perhaps you will understand your poor mother a bit better. I really don't think she was half as mad as people like Dr. Burke care to make out."

Rebecca drifted off into thought, as though she were simply too bone weary to bother with the strain of reality any more. As I watched her I wondered what it must be like to suspect that, like your mother, grandmother, like ten generations, all you have to look forward to is madness and violent death.

Finally she sighed. She picked up her spoon and slowly stirred the coffee in her cup. She had come to a decision. "Yes, it's a good idea," she said. "We'll try it. Come to the house sometime next week. We'll go up to Mother's old library in the attic and look through what's left of her papers."

Sunday 29 April:

THE PAPERS

It was a long, low room with dormer-windows and sloping ceiling, immediately under the vicarage eaves. It was lit by three naked light-bulbs. The wind whispered all around it. Things scurried behind its rough plaster walls. Somewhere nearby a tree-branch tapped on the tiles with mindless insistence, as though something were out there, like Catherine's ghost in *Wuthering Heights*, begging to come in.

"I hate this place," said Rebecca with unaccustomed violence. "It's full of death and ghosts."

Now I rather liked it. For all the strange business associated with it, it had an atmosphere I personally found restful, but I agreed with her out of politeness and pretended to shiver. The constraint between us following her New Year's Eve party has mostly been forgotten these days. We meet seldom, but never unfriendlily.

On the right of the attic the ceiling sloped down to the floor, but on the left the room was ten or so feet high. All along that wall were book-shelves loaded with books. In front of the shelves was a desk. I went over and opened it. It was full of stationery.

Behind me Rebecca shifted her feet. "Well," she said, "I'll leave you to it."

"Thanks," I said, hardly bothering to look at her. On the desk was a plastic box full of file-cards. An index. I pulled up the chair which stood by the desk and sat.

"You know your way down," she said. "I'll be somewhere around."

But I was already leafing through the index at random. POLIDORI John: *The Vampire*; POE Edgar A: *Berenice*; STOKER Bram: *Dracula's Guest*; STOKER Bram: *Dracula*. In fiction and in fact, in old editions and in new, in English and a whole spectrum of other languages she had amassed a library on the occult which centred, as her obsession had dictated, on vampires.

Piled on the floor beneath the lowest shelf were older,

darker tomes whose names were not on the cards. *The Clavicle of Solomon; The Grimoire of Pope Honorius, The Arbatel of Magic.* Lists of devils and demons of all sorts — box upon box of them — but always the same basic theme: vampires. Their formation, their habits, defences against their strength, methods of exploiting their weaknesses, their place in the patterns of Earth, their position in the hierarchies of Hell.

All of it interesting enough to anyone obsessed by vampires, I suppose, but all of it useless to me. I was very near to despair when I found, right at the back of the room, a plain brown cardboard box. The top was folded shut and sealed with tape. I peeled this off and tore the flaps back.

I cannot fully describe what happened then. It was as though I had opened a jack-in-the-box, some sort of booby-trap. Something formless seemed to leap out of the box and hit me with considerable force full in the face. A stench as though of putrefying flesh, a white light hurled me back in a strange explosion of power right across the width of the room. Inevitably my head hit the slope of the ceiling and I rolled, helpless, into the narrow dark corner where the roof met the floor.

I was knocked partly insensible, I think, because it seemed only seconds before Rebecca was at my side. She later said that it was some minutes for she was downstairs when she heard the distant crash of my fall. She helped me up and supported me over the chair. "What happened?" she asked.

"I don't know. I was opening that box when . . ."

"This box?"

"Yes."

She leaned over it. "There seems to be something —" She broke off "What a terrible smell! There's something here. *How disgusting!*" She dipped cautiously into the box and brought something out. "No wonder you were startled," She said. "Look at this."

She held up the decomposing corpse of a bat. On its breast there was a tiny silver crucifix tied in place with white strings of garlic. Nausea burned agonisingly in the back of my throat. "Take it away," I croaked. "Please!"

She took it away. My head began to clear. After a few moments she returned. "Are you all right?"

"Yes," I said "I'm fine now."

She stood above me, lingered for a few moments, and then left me again. I waited till she was gone, then turned to look in the box. Inside there were three green files. Rebecca's mother had placed them there, and then the corpse of the bat on top of them. I wondered why. Was the bat intended to discourage innocent intruders? Or had not the crucifix perhaps been placed there to protect the files from evil? I lifted them carefully out and carried them over to the desk.

In many ways those three files have absolutely dominated my days and nights ever since. From mid-morning to mid-afternoon I pore over them in that strange long room which whispers and rustles all around me with such quiet mystery that at times I imagine, if I were only to turn quickly enough, that I would see the spirit of old Mrs. Gore scribbling away in the corner. And even when I walk or jog abroad on the busy streets or in the open fields in the evenings, that whispering still seems to teem about my ears.

The first file looked initially to be innocent enough. It was a history of our village of Dunmow Cross from its beginnings right back in the Bronze Age. A stone circle was built on the hill, its ruins cloaked today by the Broken Woods. In later years the circle was fortified to stand with Boadicea and the Icenii. When Governor Suetonius Paulinus brought his legions over in A.D. 61, the Romans moved the fortress down the hill, and settled the site of the present village where two of their roads crossed: the rule-straight *via* up the Roddings and Stane Street which ran at that time due west from Camulodunum.

The Romans fell in their turn, to be followed by the East Saxons, who gave the whole region their name — Essex — and the town the name it holds to this day: Dun Mow — the Field on the Hill. Then, after them came the Danes, up the River Chelmer one night in the mid-ninth century to slaughter the townsfolk and put everything to the torch.

And yet by the time the Domesday Book was compiled two hundred years later, here was a thriving town again. It grew during the Wars of the Roses to be the premier wool-market of East Anglia. By the reign of Elizabeth I it was set fair to become a force to be reckoned with in the South of England: at least five thousand people dwelt there in the 1570s.

But then it all ended. Not temporarily, as the slaughter by

the Danes had ended it, but permanently. Inexorably the records in the file revealed that something had happened there so evil, so powerful, that the whole town had died. It had ceased, never to live again.

Rowena Gore had photocopied the pages from the Register of Burials which I had not been allowed to see. There were thirty-seven pages for January 1579 alone. Fifteen entries per page. More than five hundred deaths in that one month. As many as 150 dead in a week, for week after week.

'Ann Spooner 18 yrs Spinster this P'sh. Dead of the White Plague. St'd.'

Page after page like this. All dead of the White Plague, all young, each with that cryptic 'st'd.' at the end of the entry. January, February and March of 1579 went past. The graveyard became too full. They put the bodies in the crypt of the church. When that too became full, they found somewhere else.

By All Fools' Day 1579, the busy town of Dunmow Cross was dead. It fell out of history. Even the roads moved. Stane Street, nowadays the A120, bent north, while the B184 up the Roddings bent east. They circled away from the accursed, derelict spot where the Roman roads had originally crossed. A new crossroads was made, and a new town: Great Dunmow. So it remains on the maps today — two perfectly straight roads, which look as though they will cross at right angles, turn aside instead and cross at Great Dunmow, only to turn back afterwards to their original straight ways ... Dunmow Cross is the place they avoid, a tiny shabby village now, unremarked upon even by the makers of maps ...

After this brooding, sinister history, the second green file came initially as something of a surprise, for it began with methodical examination of the probable locations for an old house, now long vanished. The place had been called Coul Hall. When Dunmow Cross had been an important town, Coul Hall had apparently been one of its most famous buildings — amongst the greatest architectural wonders of East Anglia. And the conclusion of the first part of the folder surveyed the geographical evidence and suggested that the hall had stood close by the Broken Woods, on the top of the hill.

Turning to the second part, however, I saw at once why Coul Hall had clearly been so important to Rowena Gore.

In 1578 the hall had suddenly acquired a new tenant. A beautiful lady, a member of some foreign aristocracy, took up residence there. As the year aged, she became the hub of Dunmow Cross society; as it died she threw party after party in the bright rooms. In the icy mid-winter her guests thronged the place. They danced, they ate, they drank . . . Then they began to die. According to the records, almost every person in the town aged between ten and twenty-five sickened, infected others, died. Their disease came to be known as 'The White Death'. They were buried in the graveyard, in the crypt, finally even in the cellars of Coul Hall itself. And in the spring the few remaining townspeople took the house, stone by stone, and tore it down with their bare hands, so that only the faintest memory of the place remained.

And what of the curse that so weighed on Rebecca's mind? And what of the beautiful tenant of Coul Hall herself? The third folder told of both, the curse and its originator: Stana Etain, Countess Issyk-Koul, bringer of the White Plague, witch, monster, the Dead.

Certainly that was what the townspeople had believed her to be. Rebecca's mother had documented their sufferings with obsessive thoroughness. And if she herself shared in their belief, did that make her crazy? When I finally went downstairs carrying the folders, late on that first afternoon, I had little enough to tell Rebecca, and nothing for her comfort. The curse was historical fact. She could believe in its effectiveness or not, I had to say, as her own convictions persuaded her . . .

And now dear Jane Martin has returned, seeming to bring the spring with her. All through her long absense we have corresponded, letters full of increasing affection. She had told me more or less how long she would be staying in Scotland, of course, but not the exact date of her return, Indeed, I did not even know she was back in Dunmow Cross until yesterday afternoon, when a note from her was pushed through my landlord's door.

She's looking well. As soon as I received her note yesterday I put aside the folders and went to take tea with her. The sky was cloudless, radiant, and there was a south wind full of the scent of young blossoms. The elm trees round her house were delicately green as their new leaves unfurled in the balmy air. So warm was it, in fact, that we took tea on the lawn.

She seems slimmer, a little quieter than I remember, but full of a new strength that I find both appealing and impressive. She embraced me in the doorway and kissed me warmly on my check. "Oh, Edwin!" she said, "it's so lovely to see you again."

"Welcome home!" I said, returning her hug enthusiastically. "You've been away too long. I've missed you."

With our arms still around each others' waists we walked through the house. "You *do* look well," she told me. "You've lost so much weight! It makes you look much taller, you know."

In the garden, Richard Burke was sitting with a bone-china teacup expertly balanced on his knee. He rose as we came out.

"Edwin! How are you?" he asked.

We shook hands. "Very well, thank you. And yourself?"

"Fine . I was just telling Jane how we've been keeping the garden in line."

"Oh, come now! You've been much busier than I have. I haven't been round in a week or more. I've been . . ."

"Well, it was you who saved the standard rose . . ." he gestured across towards the rose tree we had bound to my stake.

There was indeed a tall bush, rich in branches and buds. We went across and examined it with increasing interest. The rose, in fact, was stunted and dying. It was my stake which was branching into life. "That's amazing!" said Jane. "What sort of bush is that?"

We didn't know, but such was our fascination that we decided to check there and then. Jane kept much of her gardening equipment and several books in the cellar. This was a large dark room at the foot of a flight of stairs, tucked behind a narrow door beside the entrance to the kitchen, in the hall. As Richard and Jane pored over assorted gardening books, I explored the cluttered dusty room and discovered, beyond it, a tiny room behind another door. Here Jane's grandfather had kept his woodworking tools on an old trestle-table. The windowless little room was very snug — there was even an old gas fire there. I would have lingered for some time, had not Jane called, "Well, that's it: it's not here. We'd better give up. Come on, Edwin, The tea will be getting cold. And I want to hear what else has been happening while I've been away . . ."

The most lurid news current, of course, was that of Rowena Gore's death. "Yes," said Richard, nodding sadly over a new cup of scalding tea, "I was involved. Mrs. Gore was the main reason I came down, you know. I'm spending the second half of this year doing a series of lectures both here and on the continent about certain types of criminal lunacy. Several of the lectures will centre on so-called 'Vampirism', and Rowena's case was the most vivid example of it in years. Well, since Haigh, actually . . ."

Richard Burke is a charming, friendly person and he was so naively excited by the prospect of the lecture tour, it was a delight to listen to him. The tour was the goal he had striven for during many heart-breaking years of obscure work. He was determined to take the establishment by storm. Overnight — well, within six months — he was going to become famous. Rich.

But Jane, my quiet, fair-minded Jane, did not let him have all the limelight. "And what have you been up to, Edwin?" she asked at last.

"Well, it brushes against Richard's concerns really . . ."

"Is that so?" Richard leaned forward eagerly, interested at once.

"Yes. It arose out of Mrs. Gore's inquest. I was there, you see, and heard your evidence, and it occurred to me that there might be some basis in fact for her obsession."

"That's fascinating!" Richard tugged excitedly at his beard. "And is there?"

"Well, I've been going through her folders —"

"Folders? I never knew . . ."

" — and it seems that there *is* a certain basis. You see, in 1579 there was a woman living in a place called Coul Hall just outside the village, up in the Broken Woods somewhere. This woman, whose name was Stana Etain, Countess

Issyk-Koul, brought some sort of a plague to the village, and —"

"What sort of plague?" Richard demanded. "Black Death? Bubonic?"

"I don't think so." I shrugged. "They called it the White Death, whatever that might have been. Anyway, so many people died of this plague that the villagers who were left took revenge upon the Countess. They accused her of witchcraft. They said she was a creature they spoke of as the Dead. They tried her, hanged her, and buried her at the crossroads."

"That's fascinating. *Stana Etain* . . ." He thought for a moment. "That wouldn't have been her real name, of course. It's obviously a cypher for Satan Innate . . . so it's no wonder that they buried her at the crossroads. And I tell you what — it must have been *her* grave you pushed your arm into on the night of the party!"

"Obviously." I had already worked that much out for myself. "Perhaps that's also why . . ." I went on to tell him something of my experiences with the ghost, the apparition at the roadside.

"And you think your disturbing her grave has been enough to bring her back?" he asked when I had finished.

"Well, I can't think of anything else I've done," I said.

Richard swung round dramatically, and pointed at the black bush growing strongly beside the dying rose. "You've done that!" he cried.

At first I did not understand his meaning.

"The stake," he explained. "The stake through her heart — you've removed it. If — just for argument's sake — you admit that vampire lore has any basis in fact, then the removal of the stake is bound to bring her back. Isn't it?"

I hesitated, sensing from his manner that he was trying to trick me "I'm not sure," I muttered.

"Wise man." He smiled at me approvingly. "You see, the snag is that if she were truly a vampire then her *body* would have risen. She wouldn't appear to you as a ghost — she'd seem to be an apparently normal person."

I was about to agree with him when suddenly Jane spoke up "Unless," she said, looking from me to Richard and back again, "unless the people who buried her found some other way of destroying her — something more than just the stake through her heart."

Richard frowned, momentarily nonplussed. For me, however, her words came as a blinding revelation, for I remembered all too vividly my terrible experience at her aunt's seance — the powerful presence of evil, and the severed arm that had tried to choke the poor old woman. There had also, before that, been the shapeless, semi-dismembered apparition in the hospital ward.

"Of course!" I cried. "The townspeople must have cut her up. Chopped her limbs from her body . . . perhaps her head also . . . That's why, even though the removal of the stake has released her from her grave, she *still* cannot take on human flesh again. She needs another body. *And I think she's looking for one.*"

Silence fell across the garden like a sudden shadow. Richard shifted uneasily in his seat. "It's an interesting theory," he said.

His words were calm enough, scientific, carefully objective. But behind them lurked a fear, a primeval dread, that would not be hidden. Even a man of science such as he would not be arrogant enough to deny the existence of the Unknown. Nor, deep in his bones, would he be too arrogant to fear it.

Monday 7 May:

THE HALL

Now a new urgency has entered my researches into the life and times of Stana, Countess Issyk-Koul. Jane helps me with them, and together we have come to the conclusion that there is little more to be wrung from the general history of the village, while Mrs. Gore's maunderings about the Dead itself bear far too much the stamp of lunacy to be worth our serious attention.

Not so her work on the location of Coul Hall, however, and here we have concentrated our main endeavours. Although all reference to the place has been expunged from records after 1579, Mrs. Gore discovered some hints in earlier documents, and, so finally with the aid of her notes, a large-scale map and a good deal of guess-work, we set out this afternoon to find the site.

We started near the road and, with the hulk of the Broken Woods towering on our right, began our slow exploration of the ground, pausing every now and then to consult our maps and diagrams. The day wore on: we found nothing. At sunset, with the road far behind and out of sight, we sat down side by side like lovers to watch the red disc of the sun settle behind the smoke-grey horizon. Jane rested her head on my shoulder, rubbed her cheek there thoughtlessly like a child, and fell asleep.

The view was beautiful. The slight roll of the countryside, the chequered fields, the hedgerows already plump and green. The first twinkling lights in the vales on the shady sides of hillocks. A distant spire stark against the sky.

As the last of the sun vanished, threads of mist appeared among the hedgerows. Even as I watched, the threads became webs and the webs tiny white clouds. A coldness crept out of the woods behind us. I shivered and glanced back, careful not to move my shoulders for fear I should awaken Jane. The woods seemed more threatening now, the black tree trunks breeding shadows. Everything was expectant, silent and still.

"What's that?" cried Jane suddenly.

I jumped, looked where she was pointing. There was a glimmer of movement. We froze. It was repeated. Someone was wandering silently in the twilight at the farthest edge of the coppice, a mile from the quiet road, five hundred yards from us.

"Hello?" I called, and the faintest of echoes came: "Hello?"

The figure did not pause or turn. I did not call again. My skin prickling, I caught Jane by the hand, rose and plunged forward up the slope. It was the Countess Stana, I was sure, pacing the vanished ruins of her home. The figure became clearer as we ran, and yet somehow it remained indistinct. I could make out only paleness, silently moving among the great black columns unhindered by undergrowth, unencumbered by brambles.

We drew level with the edge of the trees and, turning right without letting go of each other, entered the wood. Our progress slowed and when we reached the place where she had walked there was nothing. She had vanished. We began to cast about for some sign of her, but it was useless. Darkness began to gather. I had matches in my pocket and lit one. Even with the maps shading it, the match blew out immediately.

And then the ground opened beneath me.

One moment I was standing on firm ground, the next, incredibly, there was a sharp crack as the earth tilted and tore itself into ragged jaws. I fell between them precipitated down into a musty, echoing dark. My ghostly Countess had led me well.

Immediately I was knee deep in soft soil. I panicked and floundered about, fearing I would sink as though into quicksand, until Jane's head thrust into the rough square of light above my head. "Are you all right?" she asked anxiously.

The need to reassure her calmed me. "I'm fine," I said. And I was. My feet had found firm ground now, paving stones or levelled rock.

"It looks as though you trod on some kind of trapdoor. Are those steps under that earth?"

I felt about. "I think so.'

"Good, I'm coming down."

In a moment we were both standing in what seemed to be a shadowy little room, perhaps one-quarter filled with earth. Straight ahead of us a doorway gaped absolutely black, the soil flowing through it like a stream in suspended animation.

"Someone went to a lot of trouble to fill this room with earth," Jane whispered, "but then the door there must have given way."

I did not answer. She clutched my arm and we both moved forward, blundering through the strange clinging soil. At the doorway we were stopped by the stench. We stood there for a moment. There was just light enough to see that the floor fell away again into another set of steps.

Beyond that there was only darkness.

But the atmosphere of the room told me what we would see if there were more light. It was the distillation of all the terrors felt at midnight in a thousand graveyards. Some timeless memory in me knew well enough the peculiar odour of ancient putrefaction.

And yet I was utterly unprepared for what I saw when I lit a match and held it high in the still air. It was a sight I carried with me as I fled with Jane up the soil-slick stairs and out of the gathering shadows of the woods. It was a sight that burned a vision of horror indelibly upon my mind.

They had not rotted to skeletons. The atmosphere must have been kept dry by the thick, stone, cellar walls and the location high on the hill. Nor had it mummified them — not properly. And of course worms and insects had been busy for four hundred years.

Like grey-green leather the skin clung to their bones, holding thigh to hip and arm to shoulder, holding wild-haired skull to neck. Nearly a thousand children, the records had said. They were piled like wood — one row atop another. Once, no doubt, neatly and reverently. Now the weight of those on the top had crushed those beneath. The highest rows were toppled outwards as though, even in death, trying to escape. They had fallen in attitudes of crawling, and the match flame's guttering flicker made them seem to move. But it was not the corpses which so deeply shocked me — not their number nor their condition. It was the final understanding they gave me of the White Death, the cryptic 'st'd.' after each name in the register of burials: for through the breast of each tiny corpse there was a sharpened piece of wood.

In that nightmare winter four centuries ago the towns-people had staked their dead children for fear they would rise again, with stakes like the one I had removed from the breast of the Dead itself.

Tomorrow, I think, we must go and see Mr. Gore. At last we have something to tell him.

THE GRAVE

That Saturday, the twelfth, we went to see Rebecca's father. She was out, and the old man answered the door himself. He was not pleased to see us, and let us through into the library only after I insisted that we had discovered something of great importance.

"Look, sir," I said as soon as we had sat down, "I know you don't believe any of this, but let me put it to you the way I think I see it. Your late wife's records show that four hundred years ago a witch lived at Coul Hall. She called herself Stana, Countess Issyk-Koul. The villagers called her the Dead, believe her to be a vampire. Early in 1579 they summoned a 'Cunning Man', as they were called, a sort of folk-wizard, from the village of Theydon Mount to help them destroy her. This man, Gore, was the progenitor of your family, and he advised the people of Dunmow Cross how best to lay the witch to rest. Eventually this was done, but as she died she cursed Gore and his family. You repeated the doggerel yourself in court:

> Women of blood, look to blood,
> Make of blood your bread.
> Feed on blood until your blood
> Feeds the Dead."

He nodded, an expression of extreme distaste on his rugged face. I continued, undeterred. "By that time, however, nearly a thousand young people in the town had died and the townspeople, believing this to be the work of the vampire, drove a wooden stake through the hearts of each person before they buried them."

"But this is preposterous!" he exploded, "a childish legend."

"They did the same to the Countess."

"Nonsense! She was hanged for witchcraft. There were records. I have seen them. *Hanged!* This vampire stuff, the curse, the Dead, it is all make-believe, childishness and lunacy."

"No," said Jane quietly, "it is not!"

"Hah! I'm sorry, Miss Martin, but if you believe that then you are as mad as my wife, poor soul!"

"No," I said. There was madness, but not ours. Nor, at the beginning certainly, your wife's." I leaned forward, intensity burning in me. "And not your daughter's either . . . yet!"

"What do you mean?"

"The stories, they are true," whispered Jane. "What those people did is true. As for what they believed . . . well, of course, that is another matter, but they did stake the children. We've seen it. We can prove it."

He sat back in his chair, stunned, as though she had hit him *"Prove it?* How can you prove it?"

"We found where they buried the children."

"In the crypt . . ."

"No," I said, "in Coul Hall."

Again he lurched. "The Hall? But it is gone. People have spent years searching . . ."

"We found it. There are cellars. We have been down. The children are there."

"Sacrilege! *Blasphemy!*" He rose, arms raised, white hair wild and floating.

"Neither!" I snapped. "Accident. Good luck. Perhaps I was guided. Have you thought of that? Guided? What does it say? 'To give light to those that sit in darkness and in the shadow of the Dead, and to guide our feet into the paths of peace . . .' "

He swung towards me. For some reason my throat burned as though I had drunk acid. "I have not heard that translation before," he said, more calmly.

I said nothing. Jane reached across and touched my hand.

Mr. Gore considered the two of us. "You must show me what you have found," he said.

He brought a briefcase, I took a torch. Jane begged to be excused: she said that once was enough for her, and went home.

The sun was bright as Mr. Gore and I set off at a brisk pace. He began to perspire almost immediately, mopping his face with a great white handkerchief. We talked hardly at all until the Broken Woods closed over us like a black wave breaking.

My companion shivered as soon as the shadows of the trees clutched at him. We walked more slowly, both of us suddenly reluctant to reach our destination. It must have been after six when I found the hole. It gaped silent and sinister like a dark wound in the earth. I lit the torch. The blackness gulped at the puny beam.

"The steps are covered with earth," I said "You'd better watch it."

I put one wary foot in, and explored until I found the faintest edge of stone. Then I went down, backwards, until I was in the antechamber, up to my knees in soft black earth once more. I shone my torch around, briefly illuminating walls, floors, the squat lintel on the inner door.

Mr. Gore came down as I had done. "It smells horrible," he said. The darkness seemed to consume his words, as it did the light. We paused for a moment.

"There's nothing here," I said. "We have to go through there." I pointed with my torch beam into the shadows of the second room.

He took another torch from his briefcase. We waded over to the doorway and stumbled down the slope into the vaulted chamber beyond. It was not until we stood together on a sure footing that either of us looked up. Mr. Gore retched drily. His torch beam wavered up the walls of the dead to those few still packed up high against the ceiling, and fell again to the floor. "I would not have believed it!" he cried. "It's incredible. They must have been mad. Oh, the stupid, criminal, *blasphemy* of it all!"

His voice rang out and dust filtered down among dead bones, disturbed by his echoing words. He fell to his knees, opened his case, and began to set up a little altar.

"There is no need for that, surely," I said harshly, turning away, "I'm sure they were all blessed and shriven by good Christian men just after the stakes were driven home."

"Don't, don't," he whispered. "A sacrilege. A perversion. How terrible."

He began to mumble prayers. The stench upon the air grew richer. It was then that I noticed that all the bodies seemed to be directing the gaze of their cavernous eye sockets

60

at one spot in the centre of the room. The impression was so strong that I stepped forward, past the man and his prayers, to the long tongue of earth which thrust down from the antechamber above. At the place at which the skulls were staring so fixedly, I kicked desultorily at the earth and my foot struck hollow wood. "There's something here," I said, and knelt.

Mr. Gore did not hear me. I began to scrape away at the earth with my hands. Several prayers later I had uncovered the head of a stone tomb. There was a thick lid of rotting boards. I scrabbled the earth away down its length and hooked my fingers under the edge. "Help me!" I cried to Gore. "Help me here."

The prayers faltered into silence. I tugged again. There came a quiet grating. *"Help me!"* I tugged once more as I spoke, and the lid burst free, tumbling earth into my lap. The torch cartwheeled away, slicing the darkness with its beam.

As I picked myself up the old man came over, his torch aimed strangely high, like a knife in my eyes. He hesitated, staring oddly at me. "What is it?" I asked. He mumbled something about shadows. I laid my hand over his, guiding the torch beam down into the stone box. He resisted momentarily, shuddering, then acquiesced.

There was no body in the coffin — only a piece of parchment marked with dark writing. I picked it up and looked closely in the torch-light. The writing glistened slightly as though there were scales on it. I rubbed a dot with a thumbnail. It flaked away. I wet my finger and it stained my flesh dull red. It was blood.

In blood upon the parchment someone had written: THE DEAD WHERE SHE RESTED.

And through the parchment they had driven a sharpened wooden cross. Disgusted, I tore it out and threw it away. As I did so, the shadows seemed to leap around us. I looked over my shoulder and thought I saw a crippled shape lurch away into invisibility. I swung back towards Gore. He was dead white. Had he seen it too? His eyes went down to the parchment. "Blasphemy," he whispered. Then he turned back to his makeshift altar.

"There's nothing more we can do here," I said. "I've shown you as I said I would. Now we must look to Rebecca.

Here is the origin of the curse — we must find a way to lift it."

Then he did a strange thing. He turned towards me, still on his knees, the light of his torch lending fire to a silver crucifix. I stepped back easily and turned away to recover my torch. "What's the matter, Vicar?" I asked as I straightened again.

Leaning forward, as though against a strong wind, I walked towards him. Something — proximity to so much putrefaction, perhaps, brought bitter vomit to the back of my throat. I lifted my right hand as if to protect myself, although against what I did not know. "Mr. Gore?" I queried.

He seemed confused for a moment, then he lowered the cross, took my hand and allowed me to help him up. "You're right," he said. "We should seal this place and bless it. Perhaps erect a cross, an epitaph."

"Your wife has an epitaph in a book in her library," I said. I was not serious but he did not realise it. "The vampire's epitaph: 'What profit is there in my blood: when I must go down to the Pit?' "

"Yes," he said, his eyes strangely bright. "Yes. Let us do that immediately."

"Not yet," I answered. There was an idea suddenly forming in my mind. On the way up out of there, and on the way home, I explained it to him — how we should take the Countess from her grave at the crossroads and return her to this place where she had rested, so that she perhaps might find eternal rest again.

He heard me out. "Well, I don't know," he said uncertainly, "I suspect we would need a special dispensation from the bishop, not to mention the civil authorities . . ."

"For Rebecca," I said. "If she believes in the curse then this will surely lift it."

I needed to say no more.

The arrangements took him a fortnight. While we waited, Jane and I left off our ghost-hunting. It was a quiet, gentle time. We saw each other every evening for tea or dinner and I could feel a mutual regard blossoming almost minute by minute. Once I had loved Rebecca and perhaps I loved her still. Is it possible for a man to love two different women in two different ways? Jane and Rebecca. Calm and passion.

And now, this evening, the exhumation has taken place.

Jane and I reached the crossroads at seven. Five minutes later a police car drew up quietly, and then a blue van. Three constables in shirts-sleeves began to unload a set of green canvas screens which they erected in a rough square on the grassy corner of the green where I had fallen on the night of the party. Then they produced a small generator, a battery of lights, spades and a pickaxe and some black plastic bags, all of which were taken behind the screens.

At a quarter-past seven more people arrived in official cars. There was quite a crowd of villagers now outside the first terraced houses of the Cross on the far side of the road to the village green. A representative of the Department of Health and Social Security talked briefly with a uniformed police inspector. The coroner, Miss Simcox, arrived. At half-past seven precisely Mr. Gore came down through the churchyard with the sexton, Rebecca, and a tall stranger dressed in black clerical robes. Jane and I moved forward at last.

I had not seen Rebecca for some time, and her simple proximity set my heart racing. Jane fell into conversation with the stranger while I drifted across to Rebecca. "How do you feel?" I asked her solicitously as we moved into the floodlit square.

She was pale and her face was marked with strain. She smiled wryly.

"Frightened," she said.

I had no time to react to this, for Jane was at my side again: "Edwin, this is Brother John Warlock. Brother Warlock, Edwin Underhill."

He was tall, his hair thick and wavy. His eyes were bright blue and piercing, and his hand was almost as cold as mine. I grunted some reply and turned away.

The grass was floodlit, flat and green. The sexton and two constables had spades. We witnesses gathered round. The place where my arm had gone through the earth by the road was still visible. The coroner nodded and the men began to dig there. It was as simple as that.

They cut the turf into rough squares and laid them to one side. Then the medical officer turned to Mr. Gore and said, "Are you sure this is what you want?"

The vicar's arm tightened round his daughter's shoulders

63

and, loudly and clearly, he said, "Yes. I am."

The spades bit into the earth, wrenched it free, dumped it with a dead sound on a mound by the graveside. They were no more than two feet down when the first spade struck something solid. They dug the hole wide enough to leave a walkway of a couple of feet on one side of the coffin, and stood on this as they carefully uncovered its plain wooden boards.

These were completely featureless except that in the centre, above the heart, there was a ragged hole, presumably caused by my hand. The sexton reached for the pickaxe. One blow wedged it under the boards. He tugged, but they would not yield. The nearest constable joined him and they leaned on the haft together, rocking with all their strength, trying to prise the stubborn lid up. The rest of us gathered round the head end, the floodlights blazing above us. Every crack in the board stood out clearly.

There was a groan, as of someone in great pain. The constable and sexton strained at the lever and abruptly there was a sharp crack as the ancient wood split apart. About four square feet of the head sprang free and fell back thunderously against the hollow length of the coffin.

On the other side of the lid, uppermost now, there was a severed head, fixed to it by an iron staple driven into the gaping eye sockets. Incredibly, greenish skin still stretched to obscene fullness over rotten flesh. Long hair, matted, writhed with worms and insects. The flaccid mouth fell open as the lower jaw swung down. Teeth projected over swollen black lips, the canines two shining scimitars of white bone.

Rebecca fainted, was caught by the medical officer as she teetered on the edge of the hole. Jane staggered back, dragging me with her, and Mr. Gore fell scrabbling to his kness. The three men in the hole leaped out, vomiting as the first putrid stench on the thing tainted the still air. Brother Warlock, however, moved forward unafraid. He prayed in silence, tranquilly, over the shattered coffin until order was restored around him.

Eventually the head was placed in a plastic bag and the exhumation continued. There was little more of note: the rest of the skeleton, mere dry bones, was put into further plastic bags for later examination. Then the hole was filled in. I left then, taking Jane home and then returning to my rented room. I dined here alone, on rare steak and warm milk.

Afterwards, for some reason, I found myself terribly restless. I crept downstairs in my tracksuit and ran out into the dark. I was running with no object other than for the exercise, and along my usual course, out of the village and on to the pathways between the fields, then across the main road towards Great Dunmow. As I neared the westernmost corner of the Broken Woods I saw a flicker of light in the blackness.

I froze. Then I realised that it was not the ghostly glow of some spectre but the flashing of an ordinary electric torch: nothing supernatural about it at all. I crept forward, both curious and silent. As I drew near I heard voices.

"*I must!*" Rebecca's voice.

"But you don't know what is down there, Rebecca." They were by the entrance to the vault. "Brother Warlock and I will do it."

"I don't care. I'm not frightened of dead children. I must come down. I want to be there when you read the service over her remains."

A pause. Then the deep, infinitely calm voice of Warlock himself. "Let Rebecca come, Hugh. If we do ill, we will protect her. If we do good, she must share in it."

The light went out. I reached the trap-door and paused. After a few moments I followed them down.

They knelt by the side of the stone tomb and their heads were bowed in prayer. In the coffin lay the bones and, still stapled to its piece of wood, the head of Stana, Countess Issyk-Koul, mistress of Coul Hall. In the coffin lay what was left of the Dead, and all around her lay her children.

They had placed a candle on each corner of the great stone box and these illuminated the cellar with a clean holy light which seemed obscenely out of place. It drove the shadows back, revealing each separate horror of the thousand tiny mouldering corpses. And yet even as I looked, a shadow seemed to creep in front of my eyes. I took a step forward; the shadow lingered; I took another step. Then my foot slipped and I crashed sideways against the door opening. All three of them leaped to their feet. Rebecca's arm hit a candle and it tumbled, miraculously still alight, to roll away across the floor. Before any of us had time to react the bodies burst into flame, first their brittle hair and then their paper skin. In an instant the whole wall was a sheet of crackling spitting fire.

"Run!" I yelled and grabbed the vicar by the shoulders, hurling him towards the steps. Warlock needed no second bidding. Rebecca stood still, riveted by the speed and ferocity of the inferno. I swept her bodily into my arms and ran with her up the stairs, behind Brother Warlock and her father.

Outside, we paused for a moment, and only for a moment. There was a roar from within the earth's heart. The ground quaked. A column of fire swirled out of the vault's dark entrance as if from a gigantic flame-thrower, shrivelling the grass and blackening the rich summer green of the trees overhead. Then we staggered gasping away, Rebecca still close against my breast, and seeming to me so hot there that she might have been a live coal herself.

The service of commital, I gathered, had not been completed. I saw this as in some measure my fault, and I apologised. But my words were waved away, for none of us then — not even the wary Brother Warlock — doubted that the destruction of those foul remains would have led inevitably to the laying of Stana's evil ghost and the lifting of her four-hundred-year curse.

Now, however, as I write this in the quiet of my room, I begin to have my suspicions. The dark calls to me, and somewhere, somehow, the Countess is waiting.

THE STAKING

In the week since we opened her grave I have slept only fleetingly. Listless and sick by day, I am restless and burning with energy at night. This is not sudden, I know: looking back I see the process starting at the beginning of the year — sleeping through the alarm in the morning: too overtired to do more than catnap at night. And of course there have been the dreams. Even now as I write this in the empty hours before dawn, I could swear that I hear my bedroom door begin to shake as though there were something terrible out there battering the flimsy wood to come in to me.

And this is what happened last night. I seemed to awake from a fitful doze at the first whisper of sound — like the lightest brushing of long talons against the wood. I sat up, mesmerised, as the round porcelain handle began to move. Three-quarters of a turn one way it went, screaming softly, then three-quarters of a turn the other way. The door stayed closed. I could see the key that I had turned before getting into bed, locking it. The talons scratched the paint again. Then the door began to rattle back and forth as whatever stood outside it tried to break it down.

And at last, goaded beyond endurance, I cried, "If you must come, come then. Come in! *Come in!*" And the rattling stopped abruptly. Silence clotted my ears. The door did not open but shadows obscured it for a moment. I lay back, half propped up by my pillows, and suddenly she stood there, inside the room. How can a sane man describe a nightmare? She was tall, her body clothed in a plain white robe which fell from shoulder to ankle. Her hair was a dark mass tumbling. Her face was pale, on her full lips glinted the points of sharp white teeth, and her eyes were blood-red almonds. I have never experienced such absolute terror in all my life. My breath clouded on the icy air. She walked towards me, and as she did so her left hand reached out. I shrank back into the corner between bedhead and wall.

When the white cloth of her gown touched my counterpane she stopped. Very faintly through the fullness of her body I could see the door. She was not a thing of muscle and bone, then, I thought. Those sharp white teeth would break no skin.

Her hand reached out to touch my forehead in its centre. She did no more than stand there for a moment, then turn and vanish into shadow. But it was as though a splinter of ice had been driven into my brain which lingered even when she had gone. Exhausted by the excess of my terror, finally in my dream I slept.

But in my sleep of dreams I had a dream. And in this dream I stood at the foot of a gallows high on a hill. From one arm of this gallows hung a body bound by strange ropes woven with dead white flowers. There was an odour of garlic on the air. The body was that of a woman, dressed in a long white nightgown. Its hair was long and Titian red. A great blade of tongue lolled out of the side of the mouth. Its neck was broken and yet, beneath the ropes, the body writhed, fighting against the knots and the garlic which bound it. If she could release herself, the neck would heal in time. And she had time, Stana Etain, Countess Issyk-Koul, she had all eternity. Unless . . . .

Unless down in the town of Dunmow Cross hard at the bottom of the hill, Master Rawley looked to his daughters. Or Napier, or Potter, or any of the rest to their children. Unless Cunning Man Gore returned, for he had dangerous knowledge.

In the distance, suddenly, a great scream mixed of heartbreak, revulsion and terror. The scream was echoed throughout the Cross. They cried as they must have cried in Egypt when Moses also had loosed the Angel of Death to the firstborn of the land. Time would be short now. Swaying even in the calm, the Countess writhed against the ropes — but long before an inch of freedom could be gained they came. Lights like a river of fire surged through the town.

They were led by the Cunning Man of Theydon Mount and their cry was all *revenge*! Great carrot-topped Rawley and his friend Tom Piper followed, then Napier the blacksmith and the rest. Napier cut the rope which had hanged her and she fell, broken-boned, in a heap to the ground. The Cunning Man made a sign. They moved forward, silently and with terrible purpose. They lifted her and threw her on to the bare boards of an open cart as though she were a sack of offal, the depth of their hatred far beyond words or tears. The cart creaked into motion, down towards the crossroads at the heart of the town.

The long watches of the winter's night were drawing to a close when they came to rest on the green outside their tall old church. Some had already started digging the grave at the foot of the four-armed signpost. A coffin of plain, white wood stood ready, its lid leaning erect against the upright of the post. Cunning Man Gore pointed to this. The only sounds still were the roaring of the wind in torch flames, and the crunch of frozen earth yielding to their spades. They dragged the white body off the cart and held the lolling, inert length upright against the coffin lid while the Cunning Man lashed her with more garlic ropes to the rough wood, then stood back silently.

Then Piper, overcome with a lust for personal revenge, reached forward. "This strumpet," he roared grasping the bodice of her shift, "this Countess whore shall not go to her grave in virgin white while I yet live!" He tore downwards with all his force. The white material yielded, revealing white flesh. The shreds of fine silk writhed about her as the man, his eyes fixed upon her cold nakedness, pulled them free. The last jerk dislodged the rope from her arms.

With the speed of a striking serpent her left hand reached for his throat, the strength of the dead sinews choking his scream before it was born. Like a puppet he was jerked towards her. Her head, lolling on the ruined column of her neck, was suddenly alive. Eyes like pools of blood sprang wide. There was a grating of broken bones loud on the air as her head moved, then the great blades of her teeth were like daggers in his breast. Blood gushed steaming down her naked body.

Her gruntings, like those of a feeding hog, seemed to fill the air and the spell was broken. "Her eyes! Look away from her eyes!" cried the Cunning Man, and they were all quick to obey.

Already she had cast Piper aside, dead and drained, and was plucking at the ropes which bound her — she could not break them, but if she could unloose the knots she would be free. But once again they outwitted her. With loops of their

69

garlic rope they caught her wrists and lashed them once more safely to her sides.

She tried all her tricks upon them then, writhing and howling in such a manner that every movement drew their eyes and every sound was a promise. But there were a thousand dying children in a wall between these men and her wiles. They did not look at the flawless beauty of her body. They did not look at the limitless power of her eyes. They finished the grave yawning silently at her feet, put the open coffin in it and stood back.

Then Cunning Man Gore threw a sack on the ground and drew from it a jumble of iron and wood. There were staples, a mallet, an axe, a stake. They pushed the points of the first staple into her left leg, just above the knee. There was no blood. Her screams held no pain, for she felt none: they were those of a beast defeated. "Look to your daughters, Gore," she screamed. "Look to your daughters to the end of time. I am the Dead and I will abide."

Gore pushed the staple home until the points grated the bone and then, with a stroke of his heavy mallet, drove them through and into the wood. He did the same with her right leg. The metal was like two grey scars over her dimpled knees. The flesh seemed to smoke. In a few moments more, he had done the same over her elbows.

And she cried out again in a high sing-song — "Women of blood," she cried, "look to blood. Make of blood your bread. Feed on blood till your blood feeds the Dead."

The last staple was more than a hand's length long, but half a finger's length wide. A length of rope hauled tight in her grasping mouth stopped its motion and its screams. Gore rested the points of the staple on the blood-balls of her eyes and pushed home. For the first time blood flowed as they burst, and cascaded down her face. The man from Theydon held the cold, slippery metal with a shaking hand and then drove it home, home, home. Even then she screamed. But there was one more wound: one more lesson that Cunning Man Gore had learned.

He rested the point of the plain wooden stake on her breast above her heart. Napier took up the great mallet and swung with all the might of his great blacksmith's shoulders. The point went through her torso, through ribs and heart,

70

through the thin wing of her shoulderblade, through the white cold flesh of her back, through the soft wood to stand there, more than a foot of its bloody point clear of the back of the coffin lid.

A great torrent burst from her. It did not pulse as though driven by a heart, it simply roared out of her, pushing the flesh back from shattered stubs of bone, to thunder into the coffin at her feet. Gallon after gallon, as though her sagging body were just a shell filled to bursting with it. As the coffin filled, so she seemed to shrink. On to the skin sprang a web of wrinkles, the flesh beneath it wasting away, until finally the flow faltered, slowed and died.

But the man were otherwise occupied, making assurance doubly sure. Cunning Man Gore caught up the axe at his feet, then, reaching forward with careful aim he struck with all his strength at the top of her thigh. The flesh parted at the first stroke, the white stick of bone at the second, and at the third the leg fell free. When each limb was held only by a staple, and the head by its staple, and the torso, anchored only by the stake through the breast, was beginning to slide to the right, Gore gave the back of the lid a mighty kick and it fell into the grave with a great dead crash.

Rawley said, "Now it is over."

But the voice of the Cunning Man echoed in my ears as I awoke, saying, "No. It has just begun."

Sunday 17 June:

THE CHANGES

For some reason, when I woke on that morning after my dream, I was struck at once by the paltriness of the room in which I had lived for so long. It measured a mere twelve feet by ten. One mean window, for ever rattling in its warped and twisted frame, overlooked the back yard of the

George public house next door, and to it the stench of putrid rubbish rose with clouds of fat iridescent flies whenever the sun came out.

One thin-mattressed bed pushed its foot at the crooked door. One narrow wardrobe stood in a corner where two outside walls converged, its interior always cold and damp, breeding pinmould on my clothes. A low cupboard was topped with a single electric ring, upon which I did what little cooking I now care for. There was a bookcase beside this, infested with some nameless life form which ticked in the night like a hesitant clock.

On one wall there hung a cracked washbasin whose ancient taps gushed rust-red water, and above it a mirror so marked and flyblown as to be utterly useless . . .

It was, I think, the sudden recognition of all this tawdriness that Sunday morning that told me how far I had outgrown the place. For months past I had been striving to bring myself up to the standards of fitness and self-assurance demanded of me so long ago by Rebecca. I believed I had been successful. And could the new man, the new Edwin Underhill, remain in the den of the old?

In less than an hour I had packed my bags, run down the rickety stairs, slammed the front door, and posted through it a letter of explanation enclosed with my last week's rent and the keys. It was almost noon, so I went into the George, dumping my cases beside the bar. There was a sign of the wall which said ACCOMMODATION: BED AND BREAKFAST, £10 A NIGHT. A week's rent every night! But I was feeling reckless enough not to care — especially when the landlord's daughter came bustling in.

Theresa Potter had just turned eighteen and was in the sixth form of my school. She gave me a beer, chattering gaily with that self-conscious mixture of familiarity and formality that pupils use to teachers out of school. A pity I didn't teach her any longer, she said, making eyes at me across the bar. I was taken aback. She had always seemed to dislike me. Yet here I was, unshaven and undeniably scruffy, and she was quite blatantly propositioning me. I asked her about the room to rent and, with more teenage ogling, she said she must talk to her father.

At last she drifted away to serve another customer and I

was left staring, still somewhat amazed, into my beer. Then the bar door opened behind me and Jane came in. "Hello, Edwin," she exclaimed. "I've never though of you as much of a pub-goer — what are you, doing here?"

I told her my story, and when I had finished there was a little silence. Then she smiled as if she had thought of the most wonderful thing. "You must come to me," she said. "I have spare rooms, spare bathrooms, spare everything. It's such a big house really — you can have the whole east wing for twelve pounds a week."

I stared at her. "The east wing?"

"Well, it's not a wing really, of course — I just call the two halves of the house 'wings' to sound grand."

"But — "

"But what? The gossip?" She tossed her head. "Who cares?"

I thought again of the dingy little chamber of horrors upstairs next door and smiled gratefully. I said I didn't want to be any trouble and she replied eagerly that she would be glad of the company.

The east wing of Jane's house is fairly well self-contained. When you come in through the front door you find stairs leading straight up opposite you out of the spacious hall to a gallery landing. This leads off right and left — each side to a small bedroom, bathroom, large bedroom with smaller withdrawing room *en suite*. We share the kitchen, dining room and lounge downstairs.

That first afternoon I unpacked, while Jane fussed happily about with towels and suchlike. She was obviously delighted to have me there. Later on, while she made tea, I lay full-length on the bed and felt my being fill the room. It took only a few moments, but in that time the whole east wing seemed to become mine more comfortably, inevitably and absolutely, than the vision-haunted kennel above the George's dustbins had ever been.

During the following week Jane and I settled down well together. We were fond, loving even, but we did not become lovers. Something held us back — I thought at the time it was propriety.

At the end of the week, when I went shopping in Great Dunmow, a couple of strange things happened. I had decided to buy a new suit, and therefore went into one of the larger gentlemen's oufitters. But the size I asked for, the size I had worn for fifteen years and more, came nowhere near to fitting me. Clearly the constant exercise over the last six months had shrunk my waist and deepened my chest more than I would have believed possible.

I was undeniably taller also, and I ended up buying a black three-piece suit that fitted me excellently but that only a few short months ago I would have said was made for another man altogether.

The second episode was even more bizarre. I went to get my hair cut. Jane had recommended Richard Burke's hair-dresser so I chose this establishment, thinking more about my elegant new image than about my growing aversion to water. As soon as I was seated in the chair, however, things started to go wrong. The huge mirror in front of me was so disgust-ingly marked that I could not bring myself to look in it. The barber gently pushed my shoulders forward, over the white porcelain bowl immediately below the spotted glass. I leaned forward but when he turned on a hand-shower attachment and water was suddenly swirling within inches of my face I could not stop myself from jerking back. The terrible hissing filled my head. Clouds of steam threatened to choke me. The very droplets seemed to scald my skin. "Is anything the matter, sir?" asked the hairdresser, surprised.

I controlled myself as best I could. "No. It's just a bit hot."

"Sorry." He adjusted the heat and leaned me forward again. I managed to stay calm until the stuff actually touched my head then I jerked away once more. "Still too hot?" He adjusted it further. "There you are: dead cold."

For ten minutes I had to control every jumping muscle in my body as the stuff ran like scalding slime over my skin. Lather. Rinse. Lather. Rinse. I watched it pour away as one watches something utterly disgusting, nauseated but unable to close my eyes.

Finally, to my profound relief, it was over and he began to cut. We fell into a strange conversation: was I an actor? he wanted to know. No, I was not, I was a school teacher. Ah. Had I just been in the school play, then? No, I had not. Had I just been to a fancy-dress party? Dressed as a monk, perhaps?

At that I lost my temper. "No!" I snapped. "Why do you ask?"

"Well," he said huffily, "I could have sworn you've recently had your head shaved in some sort of tonsure, and now it's growing back." His fingers were on my bald patch. "You feel it?" he asked. "Stubble. Hair growing here."

All I could feel were his fingers, hot and distasteful. I brought my own hand up — it was true, there was stubble there. My hair was returning, and thicker than it had ever been!

I had used my left hand, and now I heard his quick indrawn breath as he saw the scar on it. His reaction gave me just the clue I needed to come up with a reasonable explanation.

Of course!" I exclaimed. "The doctor *told* me there might be side-effects. I used to be going bald, you see, but when I injured my hand I was given a massive blood transfusion and the doctor said it might effect my metabolism . . ."

Now, at last, over the last few days, I have been forced to admit and to come to terms with my steadily changing appearance. I do not consult a mirror — I do not need to for I can sense the changes within me, coursing powerfully through my blood. Inevitably Jane has noticed them also, and earlier tonight she came to me.

I had awoken from yet another strange but unremembered vision with a burning thirst, my teeth and gums aflame. I found myself half in and half out of bed, and at first I did not recognise the figure that stood over me.

"Edwin?" she whispered. "Edwin — what's the matter?"

Relief flowed through my body. I eased myself back into the bed and sat up. "What do you mean?"

"Edwin — oh, I've been so frightened. What's happening?"

When I didn't answer, she collapsed on to the edge of my bed and reached out her hand like a child seeking reasssurance. "But you must have felt it! There's something *evil* here in the house. It must be the Countess. Oh Edwin, I'm so frightened . . ."

Spontaneously I threw one arm round her quaking shoulders and hugged her to my breast. She came willingly enough, pressing her fiery cheek to my cool flesh.

"But now that I'm with you, it will be all right," she murmured. "Six months ago I wouldn't have dreamed this could ever be possible. But you've changed so much."

"Me? Changed? How?" I was wary.

"Oh Edwin — you know very well you have."

I snapped on the light by the bed. "I haven't changed *that* much," I protested, still unsure of her reaction.

She sat up, and cradled my face in her long hot hands. She looked at me, frowning with concentration. "Yes," she said, "even your face. It's different somehow."

"It can't be."

"It is," she insisted. "I suppose it's partly what you said Richard's barber has done to bring your hair back, but your forehead looks definitely broader. Your eyebrows are shaggier, too. And now you don't wear you glasses any more, your eyes look bigger . . ."

Her hands moved down from my face, down my neck to caress my shoulders and the new, hard muscles of my chest. Her cheeks were flushed and she was smiling. There could be no doubt now that, whatever the changes in me might be, she found them to her liking.

She leaned forward, looked up into my eyes. "And you're different in *yourself*, Edwin. One's body is so important, my dear . . . yours is so strong now, so powerful — it's made *you* strong and powerful too. You're . . . you're the most exciting man I've ever known, Edwin —"

She pressed herself against me, passionately, tenderly. The need for words between us ceased . . .

I write this now in the grey light of dawn. Jane has left me. I have slept fitfully, and now I am awake again. And in my sleeping I have dreamed, for once a dream of exaltation, and it is with me still:

It seems in my dream that even as I close my eyes I open them again and find myself in the charred undergrowth of the Broken Woods. The smells of ripeness and ash are bitter on the air and burn at my tongue and throat. I lift my nose, sniffing shallow breaths, trying to sort out the different scents around me. The high moon makes my blood reel. I move, and so discover that I am on all fours, although there is none of the uneasiness of movement associated with crawling. I slip through the shadows gracefully and without sound until the trees part before me and I am on the edge of the meadow watching its rolling bosom in the moonlight.

I run forward, my presence upsetting the calm of the summer's night. Panic movement spreads out in ripples from my dive into this pool of life. An owl drops noiselessly on to the back of some creature I have disturbed. Silently I trot onward, breaking into a gentle lope, bouncing off my broad grey pads as though I had springs in wrist and ankle. The rich air smells good. The waxing moon calls with her timeless call, and I begin to run in earnest, bursting with the eternal joy of it, forelegs close together grasping the ground, shoulders hunching, back arching. The wind tears at my face and body and howls in my ears . . .

The Great South Field speeds past beneath me. A hedge with a gate which I clear in one bound. Sheep scatter in panic. Another hedge. Along deserted roads and pathways. Then into a farmyard, setting all the dogs tugging at their chains to join me — to join the spirit of the wild and free.

Saturday 23 June:

THE PSYCHIATRIST

When we arrived home from work on Wednesday evening there was a letter awaiting us. Would we like to go to the vicarage on Friday evening? Miss Rebecca Gore would be celebrating her birthday.

When Friday came — yesterday, in fact — Jane was dressed in a brown evening gown which left bare her arms, shoulders, and the upper slopes of her breasts. I had shaved carefully with a new electric razor and I wore my new black suit. We wandered arm in arm up to the vicarage, past the crossroads with its sinister square of dead grass where Stana's grave had been. We talked quietly of intimate things, already like lovers of long-standing. The night wrapped itself around us gently and delicately, free for once of the shades which frighten us. I felt buoyant, excited. I was with a woman I possessed, going to see a woman I desired. I was massively self-confident — the feeling dizzily stealing over me that I, and I alone, was ordering events.

Rebecca answered the door, immediately, as though she had been waiting for my knock. "Edwin, you look magnificent! Positively Byronic. Come in. You will break a few hearts tonight."

We went in and handed over cards and presents. I had brought her also one of the blood-red blossoms which have sprouted on the strange tree in Jane's garden that grows out of Stana's stake. She fixed it to her fine silk corsage. Against its fullness her flesh looked utterly white so that it revealed the fine blue traceries of the veins just beneath her skin. Then we went through to the room of my humiliation of six months ago.

It was full of the same people: the headmistress, her deputy, half the staff from school. Andrew Royle, of course. The Rugby Club, the Cricket Club, the Young Farmers.

As with my last entrance, many eyes turned towards me, but this time it was very different. I had Jane on one arm and Rebecca on the other: the two most attractive women there. I was dressed with a great deal of elegance, newly shaved and with my hair (so much more of it) well cut. I felt as though I were master of all I surveyed.

Jane and I danced every now and then but both of us were content to circulate. Most often I saw her beside the bearded Richard Burke. Once or twice they appeared to be deep in heated conversation, but I saw no cause to interfere. Theresa Potter openly offered me drinks and, almost as openly, herself.

A little later Rebecca appeared at my side. She pressed my hand fondly, and kissed my cheek. Then she moved reluctantly away. "Father would like to speak to you," she said. "He's in the study."

I went through and knocked quietly. A voice called, "Come in." I went on through. He was sitting in the great wing-backed chair. John Warlock perched on the edge of the desk, his keen blue eyes hooded but watchful. "Edwin," cried the old man, half rising. "We were just talking about you."

"That's very flattering, sir. Good evening, Brother Warlock."

He half smiled and nodded at my greeting. There was a feeling of power about him which made me feel uneasy. "You seem to have become something of an expert in occult matters," he said.

I pretended modesty. "Not really," I said. "I just found a few old books in Mrs. Gore's library and hoped to help Rebecca by using them."

"Yes. Your strategy seems to have been quite faultless."

"I'm glad to hear it. She certainly looks much happier tonight."

"Yes." The Reverend Gore laughed — it was the first time I had ever heard him laugh. "She's calling tonight her first birthday. She says it's a completely new start."

"Oh, that *is* good news."

"It was very selfless of you to risk both your sanity and your salvation in the way, just to help another," Brother Warlock persisted, probing like a dentist at a suspect tooth.

"Not really." I dared play with him. "I don't actually believe in it."

"In what?"

"In any of it — black magic, ghosts, vampires."

"I see. And you found this a source of strength when dealing with the Dark Powers?"

"There are no Dark Powers," I explained patiently. "It's all in the mind."

"There are few people who really believe that," observed Mr. Gore.

"Oh, I don't know. There's a great deal of the Doubting Thomas in us all, I think. We have a scale of incredulity, our own thresholds of belief. For myself, I simply do not believe in ghosts. Nor in exorcism."

Brother Warlock smiled tolerantly. "Exorcism is only as powerful as a man's belief in it. It isn't all like that sensation-mongering film. Most of it is quiet and mundane. People get worried — they think they see things. So a place gets a reputation and the local priest or someone like myself requests permission to hold a special service there. The

79

bishop or Synod eventually agree. Then the service is read and . . . well, things quieten."

I folded my arms, "It *is* all in the mind, then?"

"No, no, — by no means. But actual physical manifestations are rare. It makes good sense if you look at it logically from the Devil's point of view. If he manifests his powers too clearly — as in the case of demonic possession, overt diabolic influence and so forth — then he will only prove his own existence and therefore, in so doing, prove equally the existence of his eternal antagonist, God."

"And you believe in all of this, do you? That in and around us there are hierarchies of Good and Evil involved in our every action?"

"Except that I include the element of free will, yes. The Powers of Light and those of Darkness."

"And life after death?"

"Certainly."

"If you can really believe in that, then why don't you believe in all the rest of it?"

"All the rest of what?"

"All the other occult mumbo-jumbo. The un-dead. Werewolves. Vampires. All that sort of thing."

He paused for moment. "There is no need," he said, "to step outside the formal structure of my religion to explain these things. Ghost, vampires, even Satan himself — if these are not all a part of my spiritual framework, why do they fear my holy symbols?"

"But they fear other symbols too. How does your theory fit with their aversion to garlic, mirrors, silver, iron, running water?"

"You have answered your own question of course. These are all chosen as symbols of goodness, concentrating their power more fully against things of evil."

I shrugged easily. "It's all magic really," I said. "And who believes in that these days?"

"So in your world," Brother Warlock observed, "the exorcists you need are psychiatrists, not priests."

It was a good point — and the psychiatrist was what I got later on. Warlock, Gore and I chatted amiably through one or two of the more ridiculous conundrums of occult theology, and then I excused myself. Almost immediately Jane came

80

up to me with Richard Burke in tow.

"Richard wants you to fill him in on the final chapter of the Stana saga," she said, but her troubled eyes suggested there might be more.

I was reluctant to say much, but under her gentle prompting I lowered my guard and told him the tale. Jane, who knew most of it, drifted away.

"I see," Burke said when I had finished. "And how has this affected you in yourself?"

"Me?" I laughed. "Hardly at all."

"You find your sleep undisturbed by nightmares? It's given poor Jane a few. It would give me nightmares too, I can tell you."

"No." I met his gaze squarely. "I don't dream much. Quite honestly, I don't sleep much anyway. I'm a bit of an insomniac."

"Have you always been like that?"

"Not really." Burke too, like Brother Warlock, could be played with. "Only this year or so."

"That's very interesting. And the ghost — why did you see her, I wonder. You had experiences like this in your childhood?"

"Not that I remember. No."

He paused, looked down at his drink, spinning it in his glass. I thought back to our last meeting over tea at Jane's. How could I have actually *liked* this man? He glanced up, as though divining my hostility. "One or two people say you've changed a good bit, you know. I was just thinking as you came in tonight that if I hadn't seen you on and off since the New Year I would hardly have recognised you at all."

"Is that so?"

"Yes." He watched me keenly. "Strange, isn't it? You even seem to be taller."

He was boring me now. "Look," I demanded, "where is all this leading? What is it you want to know?"

"Do you ever dream of being an animal, Edwin?"

"Certainly not. No."

"Do you dream about death? Blood?"

"I told you — I don't dream."

"Do you still see the Countess Stana? The Dead?"

"What are you talking about? Look, what *is* this all

81

about?"

"Listen to me, Edwin. Here's my card — feel free to call me, any time, day or night. I'll still be at Whitethorn Cottage for the next few weeks. It's just across the road from Jane's."

"How dare you! What exactly are you getting at?"

"It's Jane. She's worried about you and I think she may have good grounds. I know what I'm talking about, Edwin. Remember Mrs. Gore."

"Don't be ridiculous . . ."

"When did you last look at yourself in a mirror?"

Months ago. "That's none of your —"

"You eat your meat raw and bleeding, Jane tells me. And you only drink milk."

"I'm on a diet."

"Come and see me when you need to, Edwin. I can help."

"This conversation is serving no purpose. Good evening, Mr. Burke!" I turned and stalked away across the floor.

After the party, when we got home last night, Jane and I quarrelled bitterly. I did not think she should have told Burke so much about me, and I said so. Inevitably she defended herself. We fought again this morning and she took a train to London in a huff. I went out for a walk instead, up past the vicarage, my mind a strange mixture of regret, of exultation and terror. In every distant propect I saw the promise of Rebecca, while in every nearby shadow I saw the terrible spectre of Stana Etain, Countess Issyk-Koul, mocking my paltry assumptions of power.

I needed Jane, but my pride and my harsh words had sent her away.

THE LORD OF FLIES

I am worried about Jane. Our quarrel that Saturday two weeks ago was soon made up. But she is looking most unwell. Her colour has gone and her hair is dull and lank. Although we are still lovers we sleep apart for I cannot stand the burning heat of her body in the night. I keep telling her to go and see a doctor but she won't. I think she sometimes visits Richard Burke instead.

For myself, after a restless week, dream-infested, I went for a walk this afternoon. I wanted to think things through. The ghost-woman Stana keeps me company continually, filling every shadow with her obscene presence. It is only a madness in me, of course, I have no doubt of that. Only I am not sure what to do about it. Perhaps I should go and see Richard, like Jane. Or Brother Warlock. There is a rumour in the village that he wants to exorcise the Dunmow Round, the small circle of Bronze Age stones up in the woods close by where Coul Hall once stood. Perhaps he should exorcise me while he is at it. It would be as much use as anything else, as far as I can see. But something must be done.

On my walk the weather was overcast and threatening. Great fat clouds rolled in, their black bellies slick as though drawn tight with the strain of containing the deluge. The wind was hot, clammy on the skin, and the whole afternoon slowly took on the aspect of a huge dank cave full of hot fetid air.

I walked through Dunmow Cross in my shirt sleeves. The suffocating weight of a jacket was too much even to consider. I was lost in thought, and shouldered my brooding way through the mass of early weekend shoppers. A woman half turned towards me: she had Stana's face.

I walked up past the crossroads and towards the Broken Woods. There was no beauty in the wretched fields. No growth, no movement, no life. Only columns of flies and mosquitoes humming and dancing in the sullen grey air. And she was there again, filling the shadows with her pale form. I found a stick but my wild slashes and thrusts passed through her as if through a mist. At last, striking at her dull red eyes, I broke my stick on a tree and hurled the stump away.

The afternoon gathered stiflingly around me as I stumped on. A headache throbbed behind my eyes. The phantom woman, the exorcist, the psychiatrist, Jane, my life, the weather — all sickened me. I carried a weight of agonised frustration which eventually bore me down. With the hog's back of the hill humped up on my left, the woods like a strange, spiny cloud at its top and a quiet little valley cloaked with clover at my feet, finally I flung myself on my back to look at the low grey sky.

In a moment I was asleep.

And awake, in a dream, once again in the great wolf's body. I raised my long head. Odours rose to my nostrils in stunning array, but in the breathless heat of the afternoon they brought no pleasure to my keen animal senses. Silently I padded forward into the rough undergrowth. Each touch from a fetid leaf brought a rumble of anger to my throat. Every whiff of the damp fullness of life just on the edge of rottenness caused my black lips to rise in a snarl.

Only slowly as I crept forward, moving my body with relentless deliberation, did I realise that I was hunting. Abruptly, the lust to destroy suffused me with an excitement that was almost sexual. My heart thundered in my throat. My grey flanks rose and fell . . . Then, suddenly, a scent of the hated prey swirled along the delicately nerved corridors of my muzzle. Cleanness, soap, a hint of perfume, they were all on the air and I was tracking them.

The sound of voices came. Whispers at first, then words half heard. I crept forward, my belly sweeping the lank grasses. The smell of flesh; young and sweet. Saliva pumped so fast I drooled great threads of it. A growl rumbled in my throat. Careless in my ravening, I put one pad on a dead twig and it broke like my thunder.

"What was that?" She.

"Nothing, darling. It's all right. No one comes here." He.

They were lying on a rug in the middle of the circle of the Dunmow Round. On the ground beside them articles of clothing — a green blazer, a pullover, his shirt, her blouse.

He lay half on top of her, his gray-flannelled thigh cunningly pushing up her skirt. Their hands, mouths and minds were busy. I crept forward, three long steps, and my grey tail was free of the bushes. Pause. Crouch. And then the charge.

I leapt on to his back. His head turned, looking up over his shoulder, too stunned even to react. My jaws closed on his fat, freckled face and I dragged him back, worrying at him, ripping his flesh away from forehead to chin. He struggled, his hands beating at me, trying to fight back, choking on screams. I jerked my head from side to side until his writhings weakened.

But a distraction disturbed my feeding. The girl. Coming out of her shock, she leaped to her feet and ran. Instantly I bounded across the body of her lover, and was after her. Wild with panic, screaming uselessly in the empty woods, she tore through the undergrowth between the sullen trees. Bushes laid traps for her. Branches clubbed her. Crab-grass tripped her and I caught her.

She was pulling herself to her feet as my forelegs landed on her. And then there was only the blood.

I awoke screaming. My body arched, writhed with the dream sensation of blood on my skin. I lay for a moment, waiting for my head to clear. Then I looked down. My shirt ballooned out from my chest. The wind might have moved it but there was no wind. I brought up my shaking hand to open the buttons. My shirt sagged apart and beneath it my breast was black and shiny.

At first I thought it was blood from the dream, but then my vision cleared. The blackness was flies. Like a shirt of mail they clothed me, several layers deep. Those on top were crawling down, trying to reach my skin. Even as I watched, the ghastly sensation, as though I were being touched by millions of cold pins, spread to my arms. The back of my hand was abruptly thick with them.

I lurched to a sitting position. My face was immediately in a hovering screaming cloud of them. They settled like cobwebs closing on my skin, and clung buzzing. My nose clogged. My ears. I could feel on my lips each individual foot with its scratching hairs and sucker, each individual tongue kissing. I squeezed my eyes shut and felt them clotting on my eyelids. They infested my hair. All over me, on every inch of my skin, they crawled.

My mind said: This is not happening; you are imagining this. Do not believe what your senses are telling you. Be calm and it will end. Be calm.

I was calm. I did not open my mouth or my eyes. Blind, I rose and took a step. Blind and dumb, I began to run. If I beat my arms across my chest, I thought, I will kill some and the rest will fly away: but I did not beat my arms. If I find a stream or lake, I thought, I can jump in and they will drown: but I found no stream or lake. If I fall down and roll on the ground I will crush many and the rest will fly away: I did not fall. If I open my eyes I will at least see where I am going: I did not open my eyes. If I open my mouth I can call out and someone will come to my aid: I did not open my mouth.

Running full-tilt, I tripped. Blind and deaf and dumb I fell, rolling over and over, until mercifully I lost consciousness . . .

When I recovered I looked frantically in all my clothes and ran my fingers through my hair: there will be many dead flies, I thought. But there was none.

Wednesday 25 July:

THE LAST DAY

It was the last day of summer term today. Jane went to work alone this morning. Her sickness is worsening: she has about her now a constantly haunted look, as though she sees in every shadow something too horrible to express. I wonder whether I too look like that. Even as I write this, waiting for the end, if I glance up I can see the phantom Countess where the shades are thickest, her eyes like blood, the red rose of her mouth beckoning.

This morning I stayed at home, nursing my madness. But she drove me out relentlessly into the streets, and wherever I went she was before me still. Finally, desperate just to talk to someone, I knocked on Richard Burke's front door. Once — how long ago now was it? — he had offered me his help.

He welcomed me in, strangely unsurprised to see me, and we sat in his chintzy front room. I came to the point at once, asked him if he believed in malignant spirits.

He shook his head gently. "They're all in the mind, Edwin."

"They have no will, intelligence, or power of their own?" I insisted.

"How could they have, when they don't exist? They're pure imagination."

His words gave me little comfort. "And vampires?" I asked. "Does the same apply to them?"

"Of course." He smiled. "I could hardly write off ghosts and then grant genuine powers to other occult creatures. No — vampires, werewolves, they're both simply the products of our own fears: hysterical attempts on our part to explain phenomena that are really not at all supernatural."

"I can't believe that."

"You *must*, Edwin. Look at vampires, for instance. All the great centres of vampire folklore are in mountainous areas — the Carpathians, the Hartz Mountains, the middle of Greece. Now, in areas like those the soil is thin and graves are therefore shallow."

"Obviously. But—"

"Listen to me, Edwin. Vampires are linked with bubonic plague in the Germanic tradition, right?" I nodded eagerly, thinking of Stana and the White Plague. He went on: "The scenario is easy to imagine. Great numbers of plague deaths, bad medical facilities growing worse under the strain, increasing numbers of cataleptic trances being mistaken for death . . . and therefore premature burials, victims awakening out of their catalepsy, being able to dig their way easily out through a couple of feet of light soil and returning to their families for help." He spread his hands. "Hey presto, the myth of the un-dead — vampires!"

He became suddenly serious. "And so, Edwin, from vampires to wolves. In those same mountainous areas the woods must have been full of wolves. As one lay in bed at night listening to them howling, how easy it must have been to imagine them possessed by evil spirits."

"But all that was hundreds of years ago — if there's really nothing in such ideas, why should they have lasted so long?"

"Because they answer some of our darkest fears, Edwin." He looked at me narrowly. "Tell me, what are *you* most frightened of?"

I thought of the Countess. "The dark," I said. Then, "And dying."

"Exactly — darkness and death, the two things most men fear worst of all. And the vampire, in its own mad way, is lord over both. Hence the lunatic-based fixations; lycanthropy and vampirism. There are well-authenticated cases of both, you know."

I looked up at him, surprised.

He nodded. "Oh yes — there was a Countess Elizabeth Barthory in the Middle Ages, and a Marshal of France called Gilles de Rais a little later — both drank blood and bathed in it. They really did. Haigh, of course, is the classic case in this century, but there are many others. In one particular strain of chronic anaemia the sufferer will actually try to suck blood in a vain attempt to replace his own missing red corpuscles . . ."

"But such people are quite mad," I cried.

He frowned. "I prefer to think they're sick. And I find it perfectly understandable that a certain sort of mind — one with a morbid fear of death and darkness, for example — once presented with the complex of legends surrounding vampires and werewolves, should become interested . . . and then pathologically fixated. After all, a vampire is a creature of geat sexual power also, and how many of us have not wished at one time or another that we had only to say a girl's name and look into her eyes for her to be ours?"

I left him soon afterwards. His calm rationality irritated me — *he* might find such things understandable, but I did not. And sick or mad, the difference seemed to me to be one of words, nothing more. And how understandable would he have thought it if I had told him of the Countess, standing all the time in the shadows by his fireplace while we talked, standing and silently laughing?

Jane returned in the afternoon. School had closed early.

"They've found them," she said, as if I would know what she meant, And when I asked for an explanation she gave it coldly, almost dispassionately.

Children playing in their lunch hour at the edge of the Broken Woods had discovered two corpses, inexpertly covered with broken branches. The face and throat of the male corpse had been torn away, and the female's head had been crushed. The sixth-former, Theresa Potter, had been missing from her home the previous night, and evidence pointed to the female corpse being hers. The dead man had not yet been identified.

When Jane had finished she just sat and looked at me. It seemed that she could not know the terrible visions she had conjured up in my memory.

"It . . . it must have been a dog," I said at last.

She nodded. "Something like a dog."

"What do you mean by that?"

She hesitated. "Sometimes when I wake up in the middle of the night, you are not there," she said slowly. "But if I listen carefully, I can often hear a wolf, howling in the woods."

"NO!" I cried, lurching to my feet.

She shrank back. I cannot describe what went through my mind then, as all the careful layers of self-deception which had bolstered up my sanity crumbled away. For weeks I had supposed poor Jane to be frightened of the horrors I thought I saw in shadows: now I looked into her eyes and realised that all that time she has been terrified of *me*.

She ran from me, out of the house and I followed her. Bright burning sunlight splattered like acid on my skin. Defeated, I covered my face with my hands and felt the flesh blister as the sunlight touched them. Blinded and agonised I staggered back into her house. She had fled, to fetch the police no doubt.

I slammed the door. Locked and bolted it. "I am not mad!" I cried.

In the bathroom was a mirror. I put my hands on either side of it and stared full into the glass. At first I could not hold my head still. It would jerk away to either side like the pole of a magnet approaching the like pole of another. But eventually I held it unmoving and looked into it. There was no reflection. Nothing. Like a square black pit it reached back into infinity beckoning so strongly that I almost tumbled down it to who knows what damnation.

But I did not: somehow I forced my gaze away — and I sit there now writing these words so that everyone may know. Richard Burke was right, it is a sickness after all. The figure in the shadows leers and shows me the face of poor Mrs. Gore. Looking into her mind I have caught her madness.

I am in the little room in the cellar. There are no windows at all. I have blocked the flue and the bottom of the door. Jane had an old gas fire in here and I have turned it on full. It is not lit.

Had it not been for Theresa and her dead, nameless lover, I might have tried to face my madness and even seek a cure. But the thought of myself, wolflike, creeping through the woods to leap upon them and kill them in such a way is more than I am willing to accept. To be such a thing is more than I can bear.

This not a large room. The gas from the fire roars like a storm of wind. It should not take long. It is very cold.

NOCTURNAL

August to December

AWAKE

My first thought was: I am not dead. But there crept through me, with that realisation the first stirring of unease. I felt the weight of my face. I catalogued its vague outline traced by tension in the muscles of the brow, a movement of eyes behind closed lids, the flaring of nostrils, the turning down of the lips. The mass of the flesh pressed upon the bones at the front of my skull and cheekbones jutted prominently. My tongue lay along the roof of my dry mouth, its tip caged by teeth. My chin pressed a shirt-collar and the knot of a tie into the hollow of my throat.

These things on the one hand: my mind was alive, sensation existed. But on the other hand, I felt no pressure of the weight of my body on shoulders, back and buttocks, nor from the weight of my head on the back of my skull. I felt no weight of arms on my breast although my fingers felt, as though through thin gloves, the material of a jacket. There was no all-pervading throb of heartbeat sensible to innumerable delicate nerve-ends. There was no rustle in nostrils and throat from the tidal surge of breath. There was no automatic pumping of ribs and diaphragm. And there had been, before awareness came, no dreams.

Now I lay in silence, feeling nothing in my body, two trains of thought in my mind debating one simple question: am I alive or dead? How long I would have lain thus I do not know had it not come: terror, unreasoned but overwhelming. My eyes jerked open, dry lids sliding back, and saw nothing. My ribs rose fractionally. So the first sounds I heard were the hiss of breath in my throat, the catch of it jerking across the back of my tongue. I screamed, and my body exploded into action. But each part of me that moved came into contact almost immediately with an unyielding surface. Head, foot, sides, floor, lid, all inches away.

Thus I discovered the coffin.

No other explanation for the presence of these strange restrictive walls even occurred to me. What else could they have been? The terror stilled in me. I lay quiet. My movement had brought about several results.

Wads of cotton wool and gauze had been knocked loose in my mouth. I turned my head to one side and spat it all out. Bemused, I ran my tongue around the inside of my mouth, finding rudimentary molars at the back, and at each side a complex of canines building up to the thrust of fangs. They crowded my gums so that the whole shape of my mouth was different. It was squarer and a good deal longer. The whole shape of my face was different: I jerked my right hand up to feel the shape of the new face. My knuckles crashed against the coffin lid.

It was then that the unreasoned feeling of restriction began to squeeze in on me again. Breath hissed through my throat again as I prepared to make animal sounds of distress. My hands slammed palm-up against the quilted lid of my coffin and pushed up until the wood screamed in protest. It was in my mind to break open the fragile wooden roof and dig my way up through the thick earth to the surface. But there was something in me which knew better than that. *Do not destroy your home.* It was as though there was a voice which whispered in my ear. *Do not tear down the wall when all you need do is open the door.*

Slowly my arms relaxed. The lid settled back above me. I lay absolutely still. At the very centre of my mind a lake of utter blackness beckoned. I relaxed my grip on the reality which surrounded me and slipped into the dark. There was a moment of absolute terror as the totality of it swept over me, then the earth around me trembled and heaved, thrusting me upwards and out into the light. The rich stench of the living world washed into my nose and I knew, at last, that I was no longer of its number.

I stood at the head of a new grave in the silent graveyard amid the crystal purity of a summer's night. It was precisely that time of evening when the trees lose colour and form to become intricate silhouettes against the stained-glass sky. The west was pale gold, edged with rose and crimson, the east smoke blue and shadowed. The first star gleamed like diamond. My joints creaked as I turned. Like a cat I stretched, clawing my hands and pushing them up towards the sky. I rocked my head back, mouth agape, experiencing an overwhelming desire to howl. It would be a first-quarter moon tonight.

There was no surprise in me. A moment before this body had been entombed. It had just passed through six feet of earth. And yet it was real enough. I struck my chest with my hand. My chest was hard. I looked down. My hand stood out against the shadowed soil. I moved my fingers, watching the play of the muscles as they stretched and tensed. And it seemed to be wearing a white glove. Above the glove, the arm of my black suit. I lifted my hand closer to my face. There was something strange about the glove: it had features — wrinkles, finger-prints. It looked like white wax. Like an animal I brought it to my mouth. I tasted it: sniffed it. It had no particular taste. It smelt of me. I fastened my new needle-sharp teeth in it and tugged. It would not come free. It seemed to be attached to my wrist. I tugged again. It remained stubborn. I released it and folded my cuffs back expecting to find the top of the glove neatly tucked away. There was nothing. The white of the glove ran into the pale skin without a flaw. It was then that I realised. As in the coffin, the dark animal in me took over, knowing what to do. The new razor fangs traced lower wrists with gentleness and care until I felt the skin part beneath my lips. I did the same with my left hand, and peeled off my old hands like gloves. My new hands were long and thin. Thick, horn-yellow nails curved wickedly at my finger-ends. When I closed my fists the points of the nails lay on my wrists and in the centre of the palms there was a pattern of dark silky fur.

I wadded up the waxy skin from my hands and eased the cold ball past the incredible array of my new teeth. I could not chew. My lower jaw, used to moving from side to side as the molars worked, could only move up and down now. As the tasteless thickness of skin was slowly shredded in the dry cavity I studied my wrists and forearms more closely. The edge of skin cut away by my fangs was like an obscene lace cuff below my shirt cuff. The skin of my forearm seemed to be covered in tiny white blisters. There was no pulse in my wrist.

I stood in the middle of the graveyard as the night gathered about me. I could not at first get used to the absolute stillness of my chest. No breathing. No heartbeat. A part of me wailed with utter horror. I choked down the lumps of half-chewed skin and went questing into the night.

It was the beauty which held me first and holds me still. I found on every side *light* — as though a rainbow had been shattered at my feet and lay now glittering on the earth. Everything living seemed to have an aura of energy flowing about it: from the tall majestic shimmering of a tree to the bright bolt of the sparrow nesting in its bosom. I walked upon a lambent carpet of grass broken only by pools and rivers of non-life: gravestones, slabs, paths, eventually the roadway. But even here there was magic: the faintest glow of a lichen, the sudden irridescent scurry of a beetle. On the pavements, bright filaments of grass and moss at the square edges of the flags. The lingering glow of a leaf dying in the gutter. I began to run silently north towards the Broken Woods.

A little bolt of lightning hurled above my head: a house martin hunting. A ball of fire before me on the ground: a cat, turning and gone even as I reached out towards it.

Then the meadow gathered itself before me in a great lucent wave, breaking at its crest into the brightness of the Broken Woods. The splendour of it made me reel as I went in among the trees: would have robbed me of breath had I been breathing, would have made my pulses race had my heart been beating.

I paused and brushed a bright leaf with my finger. There was a thrill like a tiny electric shock. The skeleton of life upon it flickered and died. Something massive in me stirred at the sensation. By tomorrow, it told me, the little spade of green would be sere and crisp. I had killed it with a touch. The dark thing in me stirred again, rejoicing in the destruction, leaving the slightest memory of laughter on the air. I examined its power. The thing was evil. Unhuman. It is the thing which keeps me un-dead, of course: it is the Dead. I half expected it to have character and personality — to be Stana herself; but it had neither and was far more elemental even than she.

They say that vampires go home first. Richard Burke had

told me this was natural — the victim, confused, starving, terrified, would go home, looking for aid. I was not looking for aid. I was not even fully in control. It was the Dead itself which directed my feet home to Jane's house.

I approached it from the back, scaling the garden fence with supple ease and dropping silently on the phosporescent lawn beside the strange tree which had grown out of my cursed stake. Only that plant, alone among all the others, had no glow of life-force. It has a shadowed aura like that which surrounds me, and its crimson blossoms are like black holes in the very fabric of my new reality.

The house was in silence and shadow. It was midway through the night. I thought she would be asleep. I pushed the French windows and they opened to me. As I crossed the threshold I felt a tug as though there was some force warning me that I should not enter lightly, but it had been my home in life, therefore I went in.

The house itself glowed with electricities, life-forces, the dying memory of life. The doorway had a faint sheen: it was wood. I could distinguish the wooden parquet flooring in the hall, the wooden banisters, and the wooden stairway, which I now ascended. Anticipating her body asleep between the sheets, I felt the stir of animal excitement, but by the strange alchemy of the Dead, it set my sharp new fangs to throbbing — and not my loins. My long claws clicked against the faint ghost of her door and it opened. The Dead led me in, prowling across the carpet to her bed, filling me within, massively burning. How can I describe what I, Edwin Underhill, felt at the presence of this commanding cancer of the spirit within? At the casual ease with which it had started my body awake and sent it hunting through the night.

But she was not in her room. She was nowhere in the house. I searched it from attic to cellar, and laughed to see the brute within me frustrated. My clothes were all there untouched, but many of her clothes and two of her suitcases were gone. She had clearly gone away, presumably on holiday. So that the beast, which had waited so long, must wait a little longer.

For the rest of the night I have been busy. Close by the graveyard, in the sexton's garden, I found a spade and rope. By the light of the fattening moon I parted the earth above my coffin. The rope slid around it and tore it effortlessly out of the grave. By moon-set the hole was filled again. I cleared the coffin's silken interior of the wads of gauze packed into my cadaver by the undertaker, and half filled it with soft earth from the grave. There was nothing on which to transport it, so finally it was rested on my shoulders and my new-clawed hands grasped the handles.

I have put it in Jane's cellar, in the small windowless room where Underhill succumbed to the gas. Among the books in my old bedroom I discovered this journal, and the thought has come that I may continue to record my experiences. While just beyond the curve of the earth the gaudy sun approaches, and the Dead within me awaits Jane's return.

Friday Night 17/18 August:

COMPANY

She returned on Wednesday afternoon. My eyes sprang open. I knew it was not yet sunset, and I lay still for a moment, every nerve at full stretch. I heard footsteps on the path and the grinding of a key in the lock. Against my will my face twisted in anticipation and a growl rumbled in my throat. My long hands were suddenly pressed on the white silk above my face, but I saw in my mind's eye the great gold disc of the sun and I could not lift the lid. The front door swung open. She put heavy things on to the hall floor. Iron rivets on wood: suitcases. I hissed, helpless. Leather on wood, click-click as she walked. The door swung closed: she was alone. The footsteps moved from thick parquet on to planks masked with rugs. A stair creaked. Then she was on the gallery landing, and then in the west wing. I had ears in the floors but my body was bound down here.

I listened to her unpacking. I needed no chronometer to tell me the length of the chain which held me.

Wood on wood, screaming: drawers. Wood on wood, with a faint whisper of hinges: doors. Light doors brushing wood, heavy doors sweeeping over carpeting. Feet on the carpets

Feet on the stairs. Feet in the hall. She would make supper now. And the sun yet twice its diameter above the black blade of the horizon.

As I listened to her, my lips stretched back on the bone-blade teeth. The weight of the lid above my hands became intolerable. Blackness seemed to exude from every dry pore of my body and fill the coffin like smoke. Her mind opened to the questing of the Dead. A vision — Burke the bearded psychiatrist; then an emotion — tenderness. Then fear: *What was that noise?*

I realised I was screaming. I closed my mouth, the points of my fangs meeting and sliding down upon each other. I fell silent. Too late. Her footsteps approached on the parquet of the hall, on the cellar stairs, hesitantly on concrete floor. Click of light switch in the next room. My hands slammed down flat on either side of me, grasped the black earth filling the black box beneath me. The sun was still high in the sky. If she came in here she would see the coffin on the trestle-table among her grandfather's tools. There was nothing I could do.

I saw through her eyes the outer cellar room. The cob-webbed and shadowed walls. Red-brick and cankered whitewash. The canes, spades, forks, rakes, the gardening books. Emotion came to her — again a poignant stirring of fear. She looked round the room until her gaze fell on the closed door leading in here. A sudden vividness of memory: the trestle-table, the swinging light, the choking stench of gas, the hunched body, my own, the hands which clasped the open journal . . .

Terror flooded her body and she turned and fled. Doors slammed. Cellar door. Front door. Two things lingering: her scream and the face of the psychiatrist in her mind. She would go and seek his help.

Like the first kiss of the returned beloved, the rim of the sun touched the horizon. Moments now, mere moments. I writhed slowly, arching, falling, my fists like thunder on the cushioned wood, as the Dead sifted information, trying to find her and predict the moment of her return.

The sun vanished. The night lay upon me. The coffin lid slammed open of its own accord and I was out, a vortex of sensation still swirling in my head. The woman was returning, and now he was with her. Feet running on wet gravel. Front door . . . "I don't know, Richard — somehow there was a feeling of such *evil* . . ."

Two pairs of shoes descended the cellar steps. Outside the cellar door they faltered. I crossed my dark sanctuary and positioned myself, towering beside the doorway. They stumbled into the main cellar. In her mind there was still terror. His mind assessed: admittedly the air was icy cold, but that was not uncommon in cellars; and the sensation of evil could well be more than an association of ideas.

His voice came then, professional, soothing. "It was only to be expected. I should never have let you come home alone. Look. There's nothing here . . ." He looked at the shut door to my sanctuary. Our minds met. *You will not come in here,* I thought.

Time stopped. Then: "Let's just go upstairs for a cup of tea and a chat . . ." They turned and walked away. The light snapped off. I swirled through the door, silently into the cellar where their scent, their very heat, still lingered on the chill air.

I stood in the shadowed hall outside the kitchen door and heard the man say, "Look, Jane, perhaps it would be better if you came and stayed with me for a while."

"No," she said, with iron in her voice. "This is my house. I will stay here."

"Then let me move in for a couple of nights, until you've settled down again." Silence, then, "Shall I get my overnight things? I've put off my lecture tour for a month so I can look after you for a while — I might as well do the thing properly." He was Daniel, and he did not know it, coming to the lion's den.

"Yes," she said at last. "That would be very kind."

I would have to find some way of keeping them out of my cellar, I thought. But no: "What about the cellar?" she asked.

"Take out the gardening stuff, then lock it up and throw away the key," he answered.

I turned away across the hall, out through the front door and into the night.

When I returned in the grey time before dawn, I stole like a shadow into her room to stand at the foot of her bed. Such was the beauty of her simple humanity that I felt tainted. She writhed and moaned in her sleep, and a vision came to me of her dreams: a hideous terror, bestial, without mercy. The psychiatrist rose in the next room, coming to her. I fled carrying with me that loathsome vision of myself.

It has not occurred to me before to see myself like that. But I realise now that the beast that keeps me company within knows well enough what sort of thing it is. And rejoices.

The cellar door is locked now, bolted and barred against all save myself, a safe stronghold, yet despair has opened like a pit. And at its bottom lurks the black strength of the Dead — the desire for destruction, for revenge against the beauty of the world.

Dawn is like the breath of dragons on the roof-top: the upper windows catching fire, the dawn chorus and a cock-crow. I must lie down upon my stinking earth. Gently I must close the lid.

Saturday Night 25/26 August:

JANE

The shadow-stalker, the skulker in shade, the thing inside me grew impatient as night after night Burke lingered. Each sunset it took me far away creeping from darkness to darkness, haunting the fields, learning the fleetness to feed on animals. First it caught a stupid rabbit in a field. How horribly it lingered on its feast, feeling the little body convulsed in terror between long hands, rubbing it over my face and mouth before forcing its head between the bone blades of my fangs. As the Dead was at its feast I thought, *This then is what I have become: a creature without glory, a horror*. And hatred burned in me for everything that was greater than the thing I have become. For everything that has life, that has hope, that has the slightest tincture of divinity about it. For everything which *is*, and which is not the Dead. That hatred burns

101

in me still.

Sometime yesterday the psychiatrist left, with protestations of affection and mutual promises to write: he has gone at last on his lecture tour and will not return until Christmas. The house once more belongs only to Jane and myself, and the tension of awaiting the dark racked me more than I can tell.

As soon as it was evening I arose and prowled the house. It was empty, but I knew she would return. I went out into the fields to feed but my mind remained clear. I wandered amongst the Broken Woods lost in thought. I had no mirrors: I did not know what I looked like any more, and I feared the knowledge, yet burned for it. Reflectively I ran my fingertips over my face. They discovered smooth cheeks, thick hair. My body was almost invisible to my eyes for it gave off only a tiny part of the energy I saw in other creatures and, like the strange stake-tree in Jane's garden, it has no life-flame. Were there bloodstains on the dark suit? Was there mud caked all about me? Was there a stench of death like a miasma on the air I inhabited?

With these thoughts darkly in my mind I sat beneath the moon. The reason for them all was the same: Jane. I thought — feared — that the Dead would take this opportunity to kill her. But if my hatred of it were strong enough, then there was hope. In the small hours of the morning, therefore, I rose, my senses tingling and began to walk towards the village and the little white gate to Jane's house. As I reached it the trees broke in a wave of brightness up and over its roof. Ivy clung to its walls like a seaweed made of fire. There was a rush and roar of air: leaves flew in a blazing spray. I glanced up. Thunderheads closed across the face of the moon and a wind whipped through the village, armed with lashes of dust. The trees roared again. Thunder snarled. Shutters rattled. The houses trembled.

I pushed the gate open. A sharp twinge of pain in my arm warned me that I had touched something toxic to me. I glanced down: the iron latch. I walked up the gravel path, the wind wild about me. The door opened itself to me, then closed against the storm. I paused. The hall glowed dully. A bolt of lightning flashed like the flicker of an enormous arc lamp and thunder boomed. The stairs were drenched in a waterfall of light. I crossed towards them and stood at their foot. Rain and hail combined like pebbles on the window-panes above. Step after step, I slowly mounted to the gallery junction. The easternmost window went livid blue. A fiery wave of static electricity rolled down the hall. Dazzled, I was forced to turn my back on it. Thunder crashed like the feet of giants running over the sky.

I stood before her tall bright door for some time, my mind seized in a paralysis of conflicting fear and expectation. Then I reached out towards it and it swung open.

Instantaneouly the cavern of the room was lit, surfaces blue, angles black. Each vertical tuft of carpet stood out. The chairs were littered with clothes, nylon glowing with electricity, silk and wool with filaments of life-brightness. Swiftly then I moved until my back was to the windows and I looked down upon her from the foot of the bed. Lightning visited the black sky behind me. The bed lit up stark with the dazzling blue. She lay revealed by the light, restless on her back, caught in mid-movement, tossing her head. Then the light was gone and I saw her with my vampire's eyes. The first woman the Dead within me had looked upon.

The clothes had fallen back a little from her breast. Filaments of electricity flickered on her nightdress as it rose and fell. She herself was a creature of flame and darkness, of light contained in layers and planes as in the heart of an opal. The dark ruby thrust of her life constricted in the channels of her throat. The electric impulses of motor-nerves relaying bright messages to restless muscles. The golden filigree of sensation all about her. The plain, untarnished depth of the silver life-flame which clothed her, shining even through the heavy blankets. I could do nothing but stand there and look at her, robed as she was in beauty. I could not move or utter sound. Until another lightning flash lit the bed with absolute clarity and I realised with aching bitterness that, in the face of so much radiance, so much vitality, I the vampire lacked even a shadow.

I do not know what prompted me to wake her in the way that I did. I might have aroused her in many ways, but I chose to wait for a silence in the storm and, with tongue and strange jaws unused to words after more than a month of rest, the consonants fitting ill against my teeth, I quietly called her name. "Jane," I whispered to her. "Jane."

She stirred. My face slipped into her dreams. My old face. Emotion: love. Emotion: horror. The dream released her then and her eyes flickered. "Edwin?" she murmured.

And I again, her name like bones in my long mouth: "Jane!"

Her forearm moved across her bright brow. Her mind filled with things of the Dead, a grave, wreaths . . . Terror. She sat bolt upright, the flame of her bright against the wall behind her. A creature reared vividly in her mind, a thing of immense horror. Tall, wild, utterly evil. Blood-red eyes ablaze. Hands armed with yellow talons, great fangs in a cavernous mouth. A sense of evil beyond the bearing of sanity.

"Jane," I cried. "That is not I. That is the Dead. *It is the Dead.*"

But there was madness in her face, madness in her head. I stepped forward, seeking to help. The vision in her mind loomed. Her last faint hold on reality began to weaken. And it was I, I the Dead, I the vampire, who was doing this. Another moment of horror and she would be insane.

It was then I found within me a new sort of strength, a power of command. It closed on her mind and all thought stilled there. And even as I concentrated so completely on the matter in hand, I remembered Richard Burke's words and reeled with exultation at my power. *You have only to say a girl's name and look into her eyes for her to be yours . . .*

Eventually it was done and to the utmost limit of her mind she belonged to me. "What is it that you want?" She whispered. "This?"

She threw herself back upon the pillows arms wide. Her movement jerked me forward, my attention focused to the curve of her jaw, and the soft round flow of her neck down to the hollow of her throat. She turned her head to the right a little, the long muscle pulling from the inner point of her collar-bone up and back beneath the tumble of her hair. In the shadow of the ridge it made, the powerful thrust of life flowed on her skin like a river of ruby. I felt the tug of her invitation in my fangs and on my lips.

But she leapt up then and stood beside me, shrugging off the shoulders of her nightdress to let it tumble crackling down her life-bright length. "Is this what you returned for?"

she cried.

I reeled with Burke's sense of power. The woman was mine to command. Her mind was in my control. I caught her by her blue-veined shoulders, and felt my finger sink into the pliant flesh. "Tell me," I whispered. "Tell me what you *see!*"

I felt the wildness and some of the strength draining out of her body. I could have torn into her at that moment, fastened wolf-like on to her throat, drinking her essence. Temptation answered only with hunger. And my hunger the hunger of the Dead. Unchecked, it would bring destruction.

I released her and she swayed. Only the iron rivets of my gaze held her erect, like the staples hammered home in Stana's eyes. Her will rose like a candle in a storm, only to gutter out. Her terror crumbled. "Tell me what you see," I said again.

She described me to myself then. She was my mirror of words. We perched, knees almost touching, at the edge of the bed and she told me of myself.

A tall man, she described, long of arm and leg, whose hands, though claw-nailed, could fly into sudden courtly gestures. The fur on their palms somehow divided the broad spades of flesh into the plump bulges of a dog's foot. "Or a wolf's," I said.

"Yes," she answered her voice blank, "yes, I suppose so."

There is about his long body a feeling of suppressed power and savagery — revealed in its stillness and rapid, precise movements. The clothes are marked with mud and spotted, especially on the lapels, with points of green mildew. A white shirt, unstained. A dark tie. Shoes crusted and scuffed.

My head, she said, is long and lean. My hair thick, my ears high-tipped without lobes. The long brindled hair all but covers them. My forehead has become broad. It slopes back sharply above the shaggy thrust of brows. Beneath these brows, in deep caves, dwell huge almond-shaped eyes. These would be of surpassing beauty were it not for the fact that the eyeballs themselves are a blazing blood-red. My cheekbones are high, my cheeks hollow. My nose, although long, is flattened and spread at the nostrils by the forward thrust of my upper lip and strong, square chin. Although my full, red lips almost conceal my teeth, when I move my mouth to talk, an array of bone-white, finely honed points comes instantly on view.

Then I stood as she undressed me. Suit to one side, shirt to another, underwear. And all at once, her stomach was heaving and my mind was forced to close around her once more, and bend her will to mine again. I saw in a flash what she saw — the tall, lean, well-muscled body marred by strange blotches: from shoulder to thigh, front and back, my torso was covered by huge blisters of dead skin, beneath which matted tufts of black hair curled like sleeping worms.

I stood for an hour or so while I made her remove the dead skin from me as though I were somehow terribly sunburned and peeling. And I made her find pleasure in this simple service.

At last the cold tide of dawn washed inexorably across the roof-tops. My hands reached out towards her. "Come," I said, "it is time I was at rest." Her hands came up, fluttered and settled in mine. She looked entirely lovely. "What can I give you?" I asked.

"Please," she said — filigree golden sparks among her hair as she began to think a little — "please, I would like to sleep . . ." Her head raised, her eyes sought mine. They were dark-ringed, red-rimmed. Her face was lined with fatigue. "I would like to sleep without *dreaming*."

I threw back my head like a wolf and laughed — my first laughter in many months. My right arm slid across her back and beneath her arms. I scooped my left arm across the backs of her thighs, sweeping her up against my chest. I felt the vital heat of her in my hands and on my face. "Come down with me and you will sleep without dreams," I promised.

And so I lay down in the coffin and she lay by my side, thigh curled over my loins, left arm on my breast, face burning in the crook of my neck. We slept thus, I at first aware of her few movements as she pressed more of her body on to my chest. But her weight on my ribs, and her heat, no longer disturbed me as it had done once. Why should it, when my ribs no longer rose and fell, when my coldness was impregnable, that of the Dead, and when the sleep I granted my Jane for that first day was that of the Dead also — the dreamless sleep that only the Dead know?

ENEMY ACTION

I am still in two minds as to what to do about what has happened this evening. An incursion of the enemy into my lair, you might say, though probably no more than the result of simple curiosity. Alternatively, of course, the visit might have been an excuse for poking around. They might, after all, suspect something.

I heard men's footsteps on the doorstep just before sunset. My eyes opened wide. The bands of day still tight about me, I writhed in the coffin but could not open its lid. Deep in the house the doorbell jangled. Jane's soft footsteps came downstairs and across the hall. She sleeps up in her own room again now but still, whenever her routine allows it, in the daytime.

The door opened. "Good evening, Miss Martin." It was the voice of Mr Gore.

'Good evening." Jane's quiet voice in return. "What can I do for you, Vicar?"

"May we come in?" Warlock's voice now. What was he doing, still here? Had he not exorcised the Broken Woods and gone about his business? I writhed the more on hearing him, for I feel he is deadly dangerous to me. "May we?" he repeated.

"Well. . . " she hesitated. With Burke away, I had not expected many visitors, and so I had not told her how she should react to them.

"Please?" Warlock, pressing.

"Of course." Inevitably she yielded. Footsteps moved above my head, turning away into the lounge. I tried to reach her with my mind. I caught glimpses of the room, cavernously dark behind curtains kept constantly closed. The two men stood courteously till she had seated herself. Then they too sat down. She did not open the curtains or switch on the light. I have trained her to love darkness like myself. Neither did she offer them food or drink: to offer sustenance is to give of your strength — that too I have taught her. "What can I do for you?" she asked.

"We were asked to call by a mutual friend," said Gore.

"Oh, who?" Interested, but distant.

"Richard Burke," said Warlock. "He hasn't heard from you for some time. Your telephone seems to be out of order. He's on his lecture tour now, but he's asked us to call and see how you are."

"I am fine, thank you."

"We haven't seen you in church lately, Jane," Hugh Gore probed gently. At that moment, as the last curve of the sun slipped out of the sky, my coffin lid slammed open. I sat up slowly, still listening to the conversation above.

"No," said Jane.

"Is there any reason for that?" Dear, gentle old Gore. Look to your own child, man, I thought, and to Stana's curse . . . Immediately I noticed that the thought of Rebecca stirred within me something I had thought to be dead—lust. With Jane I have so succeeded in subduing the emotions of the Dead within me that only domination remains.

But Gore had asked Jane if she had a reason for avoiding church. "Not really," she answered calmy.

"Richard is really most concerned. Will you write to him?" Warlock, his voice now impatient.

"Perhaps." Still that quiet, dead intonation.

"Is someting troubling you, my child?" Even the vicar had noticed that something was not quite right.

"Nothing," she said as indifferently as ever. I frowned: she should be getting angry. If the two men were to be convinced by her behaviour then there should be hostility in her at their inquisitiveness — but of course there was not: there was nothing I had not formed and put there. I could feel Warlock's mind seething with uneasy questions. I stepped out of my narrow bed, crossed the cellar and caused the door to open to me. Silently I mounted the cellar stairs and crept into the hall.

"Excuse me," said Warlock quickly, "but might I use your bathroom, please?"

"If you wish."

I faded back into the shadows as the door swung open and he came out across the hall. He did not see me. At the foot of the stairs he stopped and looked around. Supposing the coast to be clear, he passed the cloakroom door, climbed the steps two at a time, and vanished on to the landing. I had to follow him, or course, even though I was acutely aware of how much I was risking, for I still do not know the full extent of his power. Or of my own, for that matter.

Had he the knowledge to unmask me and the power and means to destroy me? Quite possibly. But I had to know what he was doing.

I took the stairs as he had — two at a time, and in silence. A movement in Jane's bedroom. I crept to the door. He had left it slightly ajar; the pressure of my will swung it silently wider. He was searching the place quickly but thoroughly, and what he was finding elicited the occasional click of his tongue against his teeth. One muddy footprint: a man's. A man's shoes, with a little earth on one. Supposition in his mind: a lover.

I realised for the first time how noticeable the change must be that had come over Jane's behaviour. From a cheerful extrovert she had become a virtual recluse. Clearly Warlock and Gore had supposed — prompted no doubt by Burke — that it was the shock of Underhill's death; now Warlock thought again. He swiftly searched the other rooms, found nothing more and returned to the head of the stairs. I withdrew into the shadows at the far end of the landing. He glanced my way, paused, frowned as though he thought he could see something, and then went down.

I watched him as he crossed the hall. At first I thought he would return to the lounge, but he did not. He went instead towards the doors which lead to the kitchen and to the cellar steps. I took the stairs in a rush. He was just turning to go down into the cellars as I arrived outside the lounge. Desperately I sought Jane's consciousness. Savagely, more savagely than I needed to have done, I sent pain into her. The response was a keening scream of agony and the slump of a falling body. Warlock left the cellar steps and rushed back into the darkly-curtained room. As he did so, he came very close to me.

He paused, feeling something of my presence in the thick shadows. I stepped back and back, burning under the hostile awareness of his mind, then Gore called his name and he went in throught the door. Jane lay curled on the ground. They picked her up and sat her in a chair. She quickly regained consciousness. '

"I'm all right," she said. "Please go." I was totally in control of her every word now. She became righteously angry. "Really, there is nothing the matter with me. If I was upset then it is you who are upsetting me. Just go away and leave me alone!"

Suspicion sparked between them then. But they left the house as she had demanded and quiet returned.

By now Jane remembers nothing about their visit. I wish I could clean Warlock's mind as easily, as completely. He remembers too much and I'm sure he will come back a second time. Perhaps during the day when I am powerless to stop him.

School opens on Monday. I will allow Jane to go back to work. If there is gossip, then perhaps that will still it. And she will write coldly to Burke, telling him to stay away from her. If he comes, I cannot let him escape again.

After they had gone, I recalled the previous spark of lust I had felt, that Jane cannot arouse in me. Soon I must see Rebecca, therefore: the tiny flame of passion was for her. And perhaps I will also see the interfering priests.

Monday Night 24/25 September:

FIRST BLOOD

It has been a period of savage frustration. It is becoming impossible to follow any train of thought or action for any length of time because some tiny stimulus will always bring out the Dead lusting for blood and then I must go ravaging about the countryside on orgies of destruction.

Only two nights remain in my mind with any consciousness of my own will — two visits to the vicarage. The first was some ten nights ago. The church clock struck seven as I passed it like a shadow on that bright evening. I swung in an arc round the churchyard to where the trees around the old house almost reached the road, offering me shelter and easy access. Between the trees all was quiet. I slowed my steps and crept through the shadows like a panther, alert with dark purpose: Rebecca. The bright specks of animals and insects were few tonight — they had been thinning out for some time, learning to avoid the black figure which fed on them in the night. I spat and hissed at their fleeing forms. I would have howled but I fought for control, choking into silence as I crouched behind the vicarage garden wall.

I heard voices: "What was that?" Brother Warlock.

"What? I didn't hear anything." Old Mr Gore.

"It sounded like some sort of animal."

"Perhaps it was a cat. The woods are full of them, you know."

"Yes. That must be it," said the first voice. Brother Warlock's words were clear, his intonation revealing that he did not believe for a moment that the noise I had made was the cry of a cat.

"We are fortunate to have such an evening to sit out in this late in the summer," observed Mr. Gore tranquilly.

"Indeed," agreed Warlock. But his mind was elsewhere.

I pressed my cheek against the cold brick and sent my thoughts hunting his. At first his mind was tense, concentrating, alert to the slightest sound or movement.

Then he began to relax. He lowered his defences, and I crept into his memory and looked around. I saw surprisingly little at first: a childhood obscured, a restless youth, a young-manhood like many — like my own. And then the finger of belief touching him. And from that belief coming a tireless quest for knowledge never to be quite slaked in seminaries and universities. The paths and patterns of his knowledge twisting into distances beyond my ken. But then, suddenly, one path which riveted me, leading through the years of his experience: the memory of his first exorcism.

My hackles rose. More terrible memories, exorcism after exorcism. Here was a man who fought devils, witches, ghosts, all on their own terms. My panic made me clumsy, and suddenly he knew I was there, something was there, in his mind. I felt him jump into awareness and begin to identify the essence which had invaded him. My panic increased. Then abruptly, I saw two women stand in his thoughts. Rebecca, beloved daughter of his oldest friend — he was worried about her. He suspected that she was involved far more deeply than she realised in something which even he feared. But the other woman in his thoughts was Stana Etain, Countess Issyk-Koul. I froze, stunned.

And yet, I told myself, he did not, he could not, know her true, dark, evil power as the Dead. He only knew her as the priestess, the wanderer, the plague-carrier, the witch . . . an entity he must fight and finally control. Which would explain why he had remained in the village — he would not want to leave until he had laid her to rest.

But even as I considered this strange new situation, Brother Warlock's mind closed in upon me. As I was seeing into his own depths so he would see into mine in an instant. There was no time for coherent thought — the Dead, timelessly practise in deception and survival, took over and disguised me. I blundered forward, batlike, into the light of his awareness, fingers spread, body squat, broad, and dark-furred. I fell forward and flitted, screaming, towards freedom.

His mind started back in instinctive revulsion. I saw myself in the mirror of his thoughts, twisted by the instant of his fear, hardly recognisable. But as I broke free, the talons of his recognition raked along my back. My essence, and not my shape, stirred someting in him and word VAMPIRE filled his mind. There came a crash as he jumped up, overturning his chair, then reeled and nearly collapsed.

"John!" cried Hugh Gore. "What is it? Are you all right?

Footsteps stumbled on a path. Then Gore's approaching, firmer. "Here, John — lean on me."

"I'll be fine in a moment. A . . . a passing faintness, no more . . ."

I saw then in his mind another word: EXORCISM. He had applied for the bishop's permission, and so far it had been withheld, and now he feared that his strength was failing. I smiled,

"Come inside." Gore was solicitous.

"No . . ." Receding, too weak to enforce his wishes. "No,

really" — his friend leading him away towards the house.

The French windows screamed shut behind them. I was back in my body now, crouched against the garden wall. I rose and faded into the shadows, trembling yet from the narrowness of my escape. And then the Dead in me broke loose again.

Nights passed: the more it hunted, the leaner became the pickings. It was as though the cold of winter came each sunset to the countryside around Dunmow Cross. Small animals died, even a few dumb sheep. But there was no fulfilment, and the beast was never satisfied.

Last night, however, it seemed to remain asleep inside me when I stirred. Underhill's mind — *my* mind — drove me out into the night as soon as possible, seeking Rebecca still, and I prowled restlessly round the vicarage until all the lights were out. Then I crept up to the door and silently it yielded.

The hall was a bright cavern around me. I paused. Faintly from above came the sound of someone snoring peacefully: the old man. But other sounds were not as I had expected. As I crept up the stairway, my head moving from side to side, ears alert for the least noise, tiny gasps and murmurs of ecstacy came to me on the still air. The gallery stretched to either side like the arms of the letter 'T'. I turned left. The vicar's peaceful grunting came from behind, the sounds of lust from before me, on the right. And not from Rebecca's room but from Brother Warlock's!

His door was closed against me. I willed it to open and it swung inwards. But when I stepped forward my foot came to the threshold and would go no further. Yet the door was fully open. Confused, I put out my hand. It went as far as the edge of the door-frame and there, as if the door had been replaced by a sheet of glass, some invisible force prevented it from entering.

Brother Warlock might not know *whom* he fought against, but the power of his spell and the faint hated whiff of garlic showed me that he had all too clearly learnt *what* he confronted: he confronted the vampire . . .

Like a child outside a sweetshop window I pressed my hands against his defences and peered through. And the Dead, which I thought had left me to myself tonight, was there before me.

Within the room Brother Warlock writhed on his jumbled bed. And astride the sleeping man's loins crouched Stana Etain, Countess Issyk-Koul, ghost, pure spirit, *succubus* . . . His spells were powerless against her. As in a rodeo she rode his bucking body, her head lashing forward and back as he jerked. I hissed her name but she did not hear. She was in a kind of ecstacy, her face and senses closed to me, her long hands grasping his shoulders.

At last their movements reached a climax, and then quietened. "Now!" I thought, and stepped forward, but still my entry was prevented. Stana sat, slumped forward, her whole pale body jumping. There was no brightness about her, no life-flame. "Stana!" I cried, beyond control, but still she would not hear. She drew back the tumbled, red curtains of her hair with shaking hands and began to move again. Warlock groaned, and started to writhe in helpless response.

I whirled away from the doorway, hot with rage and passion. I stood erect, rigid in every fibre of my being. A great scream for Rebecca built in me. I fought to control it. Suddenly I sensed a movement, downstairs in the hall. I moved to the landing, but remained cloaked in shadows, staring down.

The door of the lounge opened and Andrew Royle came out. He turned and I heard this whisper, "Goodnight, darling." She, on the couch no doubt, make some noise in reply. He began to creep on tiptoe across the hall, slipping on his jacket as he did so. As he opened the front door I stood halfway down the stairs and watched him, the air about me suddenly cold as ice. The door closed behind him.

For a moment I hesitated, torn between my hate for him and my desire for Rebecca. Then I moved forward once more, passing across the parquet of the hall like the first north wind of winter. The door opened to me and I glided out. I was not aware of walking. I seemed to float over the ground, a column of darkness like smoke. My eyes burned. My wolf's tongue lay along my lower jaw, waiting. I was aware of every tooth in my long hot mouth.

He hurried down the side of the house and then along the path towards the graveyard. He vaulted easily over the low wooden gate and threaded his way amongst the tombstones.

I followed, drawing closer to his unsuspecting back with silent speed. Was Stana with me then? I do not know.

For some reason, in the very centre of that dead place he chose to pause. I saw my left arm reach out towards the shoulder of his jacket: a long hand, impossibly thin, absolutely bloodless. It closed on the cloth, sucking his warmth already through the bright strands. He did not jump. It was far too late for shock. As though deeply hypnotised he turned towards me. He had a young, open, innocent face, not unlike the little I remember of Underhill's face. His hair was tousled. He needed a shave. And behind his eyes a picture of Rebecca, naked and welcoming on the couch.

My left hand rested like thistledown on his left shoulder now. I pulled him towards me gently, like a lover. His chest brushed against mine. Our lips could have met. Gently, I took his soft-stubbled chin in my right hand, resting on my curled index finger, thumb closing on the girlish roundness beneath his lower lip, thumbnail brushing his white teeth, inches away. I turned his face into the crook of my arm lifting the lower jaw a little until his head tilted fully backwards and the column of his throat was mine for the taking . . .

There was an open grave close by the churchyard wall. I cut an extra niche in it two feet deep and laid what was left of him there. I smoothed the bottom of the grave flat over him. He will not rise. It was to have been like a lover's first kiss, hesitating, gentle. But the hunger overcame me and I lost all control. Now his body is completely destroyed and his spirit utterly vanquished . . .

Saturday Night 20 /21 October:

PLAGUE RETURNING

They are still looking for innocent young Andrew, but they will never find him unless they exhume Mr. Berry and look under the old man's box.

Now, today, Jane tells me that they are bringing in a crack medical team to be centred at the hospital. All the children at school have been inoculated. "Against what?" I ask.

"Some sort of flu epidemic, they think."

"Why is that?"

"Some of the children have been kept at home, complaining of sore throats and fever." Some fourth-years are ill, she tells me, many fifth-years, almost all the sixth-form girls. They complain of sore throats, restlessness at night, listlessness in the day, terrible nightmares, raging thirst, fever. Hospital tests reveal anaemia. There is talk of some strange infestation. Many parents want the school shut down entirely and fumigated from top to botton.

"What makes them suspect infestation?" I ask.

"Well, nothing concrete really. Just that in one or two cases pinpricks have been noticed on the children's skins as though some sort of insect had bitten them."

"Has any of these insects been found?" I enquire.

"On close inspection a flea or two. At least one case of nits and some ringworm. Pretty much what you would expect. Nothing unusual at all. It is so strange. Nobody can understand it."

I agreed. Oh, I agreed.

The sensation of lips pressed to hot hollowed flesh is among the most exquisite. Yet it is only the prelude to subtleties and complexities beyond belief. From the pulsing richness which bursts from the smallest incision in the throat to the cooler, lighter draughts coaxed gently from a vein below the ankle.

Ah, you will doubt me. This is a monster, you will say, without sense or sensibility, a night-walker capable only of the torn joys of the wolf. But, as is evidenced by what Jane says, my feeding since then might be confused not with the savaging of a hound, but with the sipping of a flea.

Like fine needles, my fangs break the skin. My tongue moves like a butterfly's wing to lap and savour. Is this then the feeding of a beast?

Take Margaret Allen, for instance, captain of the school. She is among the infected. She lives near the crossroads in Dunmow Cross. She is an only child. Her father, a farm labourer, caught mumps from her when she was three and is now impotent. He is a great simple giant of a man, quiet and gentle. He loves her more than life itself. He and his highly-strung little wife are distraught. They do not know what to do. There is nothing to be done, of course. She will not live for long.

Each night when they are all asleep I come tap-tap-tapping at her bedroom window. She rises like a ghost from her bed, lets me in and returns to her deep, troubled slumbers. I steal to the end of her bed.

Margaret sleeps, curled like a child, on her left side. I draw the blankets back gently. She may stir then, but she will not wake. She wears childs' pyjamas, decorated with pink kittens. I stand before her, lost in wonder at her simple beauty. Then I lean forward, dipping my face into the cool flame of her flawless silver life-force. My lips just brush the peach-down at her waist, then move of their own volition, exploring the curve of vital flesh cataloguing each miniscule change in temperature until a fat vein wanders like a hot wire from point to point across my tongue. The slightest pressure, the least movement of my head and the hot blood comes. And more, much more; the wonderful complexities of her life, her hopes and dreams, loves and hates — everything that makes the succession of the days worthwhile for her.

What animal could appreciate such things? What monster employ such artistry? More deeply than the most impassioned lover ever could, I have partaken of the essence of this girl. She is mine, but, in a strange and haunting way, I also am hers.

Thursday Night 1/2 November:

ALL HALLOWS

In Rome it was a saturnalian orgy in honour of Pomona, Goddess of Fruits. They call it Cake Night, Nutcrack Night,

Holy Eve, Hallowmass, Hallowe'en, All Hallows. To the ancient Celts, worshipping in their strange stone circles, it was Samhain, the first night of winter and of their New Year. Even in these enlightened times, the fires of the Druids, lit millenia ago to placate Arawn, lord of Annwn, the Abyss, have not moved away into folklore but just along a few days to Bonfire Night.

Whatever its name, for more than a week beforehand I felt All Hallows building in the atmosphere. In the corner of my eyes I glimpsed strange movements. There was the scent of the charnel-house on every breeze, and the taste of something rotten in the air. Such heart as I have was stirred at the promise of it. My restlessness dwelt in my long mouth; I fed often and widely. They expect to close the school soon for more children are ill, and one or two parents also. But no one will die as long as I can hold the Dead in check, for deaths such as this would breed my disease — Stana's Plague, the White Death — and reprisals. I cannot have that. My greatest strength, the most massive bastion protecting me, is the fact that so few people believe the Dead exists.

A year or two ago, in the Midlands, a man choked to death on a clove of garlic which he had placed on the back of his tongue to protect him from vampires as he slept. In his room were talismans. You smiled, I'm sure, if you read of it, more shocked than amused of course, but thinking : poor fellow, he must have been a *little* mad.

If you thought that, then you are mine. You could not even begin to protect yourself if we met one dark night, because you do not believe.

But if children began to die, then people might begin to wonder. If children began to rise again, hungry for blood, then even you would believe.

My nets, therefore, cast wide and shallow. I am the locust disguised as a butterfly — what I might devour, I sip instead.

On 28 October we returned from British Summer time to Greenwich Mean Time, and from that day, of course, my potential prey was multiplied and my hunting became less hit-and-miss. When the sun sets it is no longer nearly six o'clock, it is a little after half-past four, and there is still some bustle and vigour in the day. For a quarter of the year I have been chained to the night, but now it seems I have a toe-hold in the afternoon. Now I can follow the schoolchildren home, the office-workers, shopgirls and city secretaries returning from work. And when selection is make, addresses noted, company and possible protection sounded, then I simply wait until they are alone or asleep in bed.

But I was not the only one finding such easy satisfaction. Other things moved upon the air, thickening it like wood-smoke. What ever these ghostly essences were, their dark dancing grew wilder during those strange days until All Hallows Eve, and the evil of their power grew.

The sun set that night at five-and -twenty minutes to five. Even with the lid closed down upon my narrow bed I could feel the boiling of the air. I rose, caught by it, bubbling with excitement. Great things should be afoot tonight. Because it was a special occasion Jane exercised herself to the utmost, trimming my hair and shaving me, and by five I was abroad. The night wound around me, unnaturally warm and vital.

There was a wind and a thick toil of clouds overhead, as if the sky were an inverted cauldron full of sooty water at the boil. A new moon, thickening towards fullness, would slice the sky later like an ancient Druid's golden sickle, cropping mistletoe among the stars. The laughter of children, barely contained, whispered in the shadows. I thrust my taloned hands deep into my pockets. Had they been free, I think I would have leaped into the air as though I could take wing with sheer excitement. It was a night to ride the skittish winds like a leaf in autumn.

Already the graveyard was astir. Mist clotted among the gravestones, concealing the first thrusting fingers and arms as the smoke-thin essences of awakened spirits clawed into the air. I paused, looking over the black, dead, wrought-iron fence. The wind sending icy coils of mist to writhe around me. A quiet came as the ghosts strangely sensed my presence and paused in their unearthly movement, fearing me.

A lone hunched figure from the material world hurried down the side of the church — Hugh Gore, going about his futile business. The tall, pointed door creaked open, light flared within, the door screeched shut behind him. I turned restlessly away. Rooks rode the wind above the skeletal trees like untidy black kites, screaming. Rebecca . . . I turned into the long arm of the wood behind the vicarage. Only the plants glowed, already growing winter-dull. There were no animals out at all.

The tops of the high trees shook in the wind but I strode in still air as though I were just below the surface of some strange ocean. The garden wall loomed. I crouched behind it. Silence from the garden. I rose and looked across the long lawn. The back of the vicarage seemed to huddle in upon itself, the thickly-curtained windows glowing dimly. Smoke rose from a tall gaunt chimney only to be torn to rags by the wind, now sucked in a long thin column to the stars, now rolling in slow billows down the ancient tiles. I vaulted the wall and stole across the shaggy lawn. Splinters of quiet conversation were thrust into my straining ears. It was not until I stood right against the glass of the French windows that I realised the television was on. Round the edge of the heavy curtains I saw Rebecca. She was sprawled on the long sofa, tensely watching the screen. What she was watching I cannot tell, for the box to my eyes was a dazzling maze of electric circuitry, all so vividly ablaze that the lines which formed the picture were lost in the pervading fire.

I was content to wait there and observe her. Simply having her under my eye seemed to calm my restlessness. I ceased all movement and stood like a shadow hour after hour. She watched the screen intently, as if it were a shield against the night's unease. Her father returned. Warlock came and went. At last she rose reluctantly and snapped the bright machine off. As the church clock chimed out eleven o'clock, she went slowly upstairs. I did not enter yet. My ears sending threads like spiders' webs to catch the sounds of her movement, I listened as she climbed the stairs and went to her room.

Wanting to be sure the household was all asleep, I lingered another hour in the roaring dark. The church clock was tolling midnight as the front door yielded to me. There was silence as I crossed the hall, silence, and a potent whisper of evil. Something powerful in the house waited in ambush. My whole body prickled. My nerve-ends tingled. As I mounted the stairs I remembered my first blood, Andrew Royle. I smiled: Rebecca had not been too upset by his disappearance — there'd been no hysterics, no decline. I'd known she did not love him, but it amused me that not even the slightest gesture of remorse had been offered.

At the top of the stairs I became aware of a faint whisper of sound, the merest movement of lips. I paused. There was sanctity in the air: someone was at prayer. My interest roused, I moved forward.

Warlock's door was wide. I stood in the shadows outside the white-edged door-frame. My hand pushed round the wood and immediately met invisible resistance. Wise man — he was taking no chances. He sat at a darkwood desk, fully clothed, reading his prayers by the light of two votive candles. Around the yellow cones of light, the darkness danced like the waves of the sea. He sat on a hardwood chair, hunched forward, his elbows on the slope of the desk's lid, a book before him. His head was supported on his broad hands. His eyes followed the lines, his lips the words. I pushed the faintest trace of my awareness into his mind. It blazed with holy fervour. I staggered back from the doorway one arm up.

Such was the brightness of his prayers that the reason for them was almost hidden. But, narrowing my mind, I soon sniffed it out. It was the memory of his dreams that tormented him. With Stana, once sleep had stripped his defences away, he had plumbed the depths of sexual depravity. Underhill was bemused and sickened by what lurked there, but the Dead in me laughed savagely at the cesspit Stana had created within him. I choked on its laughter.

The shadows at his back were thicker now. He dozed, and his head slipped off his hands. He jerked awake. Too late. The moment his grip of prayer had faltered she was standing behind him, the candlelight glowing in the red pools of her eyes and on the terrible white blades of her teeth. I look like that, I thought.

She stood immediately behind him. She was naked. Her hands, long and almost transparent, reached forward to stroke his hair. The flight of prayer began again, faltered. Forgetting everything but the weariness she placed in him, he yawned. She leaned forward, her arms sliding around his neck. He shook his head, trying vaguely to clear it. She soothed his brow until his tired head was cradled on her breasts. Every shadow tempted, and Stana was already

121

behind him. Her hands moved on him, her breasts cushioned his neck. He breathed deeply, stretching his ribs with the fullness of his lungs as he arched his back, thrusting his head down into Stana's pale embrace.

He groaned in his passion and the sound broke into his sleep that was no sleep at all. He opened his eyes, saw her looking down at him. And into his mind there flooded the memory of the greatest of his strengths, his bishop, in full regalia, arms raised as he spoke the simple, dreadful prayer commanding a blessing on Brother Warlock in the Office of Exorcist . . .

He lurched to his feet and cast himself on to his knees by the bed. As I reeled from the renewed force of his prayers I saw Stana herself turn and take flight, all her shadows following in her wake. His prayer was like a cathedral towering in his mind, all its windows blazing with light. And its radiance tore at my senses as I staggered away, across the corridor and into the icy sanctuary of Rebecca's room.

I leaned by her bed. The power of Brother Warlock's prayers was left behind. I looked down, and was transfixed.

She lay in a cave of wonder, aglitter with life, resting on a double bed beneath a quilt ablaze with silk. She had slept so peacefully, the ghostly tensions of the night forgotten. Now she moaned in her sleep and the Dead awoke.

"No!" screamed poor, weak Underhill, "I must not . . ." But it was too late. One long hand, brindle-haired on the back and palm, yellow-clawed, knotted with tendons, had grasped at the edge of the quilt and thrown it back.

She lay on one side. The cold hand took her burning shoulder and laid her on her back. She unfolded like a rose, the long flame of her life-force lambent on the pale net of the sheet. How long we stood, the Dead and I, hypnotised by the rhythmic pulses of life beneath her silken skin, I do not know. The beast within me drew dark and savage strength from the sight. The lust she had once roused in my loins was nothing beside its power.

At last I moved. Left hand beside her right shoulder, right arm taking my weight, I lay on her gently, like a lover. She stirred voluptuously beneath me but did not wake. I rose on my elbows and turned her head on one side. The wind shrieked and beat upon the windows with invisible fists as though it would break in. Beneath her right ear the life pulsed, and my long mouth throbbed in answer. I lowered my lips until they brushed the warm curve of her throat. The wind screamed in the stone throat of a bricked-up fireplace deep behind the wall. The power of the beast hunched over me, its one love, destruction, its one joy, death.

I would have torn her throat out then. I was but the slightest gesture away from doing so. Then there was a noise behind me: tiny but significant enough to cut through my delirium. Like a lover caught *in flagrante*, I looked over my shoulder, and Stana stood in the doorway watching me. She held out one hand towards me. In it was a sheet of paper. I rolled off the bed, rose to my feet, and took the paper. As I did so she stretched her arms out like wings and crossed them over her breast. She was clothed now in a gown of the lightest of faery green. I unfolded the sheet of paper and read it.

Dear John,
I apologise for the unpardonable length of time for which the Synod has considered your urgent request. The last six months cannot have been easy for you under the circumstances. I am pleased to inform you, however, that agreement has now been reached and with all our blessings you may proceed with the full *Rituale* to exorcise those abodes of the noonday devil as you ask.
        Your brother in Christ
        Ralph
        Archbishop

When I looked up into the doorway she was gone, but I followed her out into the night, for I knew well enough that she expected us to stand together against the terrible threat of exorcism. And I think I hear her now as I write these words. *Together*, she whispers, *we will never be defeated.*

THE ROMAN RITUAL

Last Saturday afternoon Burke the psychiatrist returned. His footsteps on the gravel path roused me and I sprang awake in my narrow bed. There were hours yet to sunset and I was all but helpless where I lay. The doorbell rang. Jane was marking books from the school and did not immediately answer, but eventually the insistent ringing penetrated her apathy and she climbed wearily to her feet.

"Who is it?" she called from behind the closed door.

"It's Richard Burke, Jane. Hurry up and let me in — I'm freezing out here!"

"What is it that you want?"

"I want to talk, Jane. I must talk to you. Please open the door!" He banged upon it impatiently with his fist. She paused, uncertain what to do. "Jane!" he yelled, "open the bloody door."

At last, inevitably, the strength of his demands was answered by the obedience I had engendered in her. With arm at full stretch she unloosed the latch and jumped back like a startled rabbit as the door swung inwards.

Burke strode in, sweeping her into his arms at once and hugging her tightly as he kicked the door shut. Confused by his affection — for I had locked off that area of her experience amongst many others — she answered his embrace in the only way she now knew. Her body moved against his licentiously.

Shocked, he sprang back and his distaste washed through the place until I could smell it like smoke. "Jane!" he cried. "Jane, what has happened to you?"

Through his eyes I saw a thin pale characterless woman, washed-out and old. Her hair was lank. Her forehead was deeply hollowed at the temples. Her dull eyes were purple-ringed. Her cheeks were as hollow as her temples. Her neck was lined and scraggy. Her shoulders were hunched, her hands restless. Her clothes hung off her at breast and hip, and she was dressed in a slovenly, careless manner.

With a deep sense of shock I realised that I had seen none of these things. I, or perhaps the Dead, had seen her simply as Jane the body-slave, and noticed nothing else.

Burke led her, unresisting, into the lounge. He sat her in a chair and perched on the edge of another opposite her. "Jane, what is it? What is happening to you?"

"Tired?" It was a question. I had made her senses so dull. Yes. Yes, indeed she must be tired: working all day, being used each night by my unrelenting unfulfilled lust. She was not an individual to me, of course — no one was any more. Little by little over the weeks, the whole human race, with the possible exception of Rebecca, have been reduced to one function in my eyes, which is to be used for my sport.

"Look Jane, you must come with me! I'll take care of you, my darling. Dear goodness, why did I ever go away. I should never have left you." He ran his fingers distractedly through his hair. ". . . Look, I'll cancel my next few lectures. Take you to London. See you're all right."

A thin enough gesture, I thought, for the man who had left her in the first place to go on this lecture tour, content with the formal letters I made her write in reply to his own, happy to speak with her once in a while over the telephone, relying otherwise, on old man Gore and a strange priest to look after her.

And yet how well the Underhill in me remembered the bright dreams of fame poor Burke had had. How they had filled his life, given him a goal worth striving for in the dark days after his failure to cure Mrs. Gore. His love for Jane had been real enough, was still real. But first there had been Underhill between them, then Underhill's memory. How easy, therefore, to convince himself that the lecture tour, which would bring fame, position, enough clients for an exclusive private practice, was the surest way to win her in the end.

"You should have told me — you should have told me about all this in your letters!" he cried. "I would have come sooner. Made arrangements to stay." He sprang to his feet and began to pace. "What am I to do? I have to deliver a talk to the Royal Society on Monday. It is the one thing I cannot cancel. Jane! I must go back tonight. Come with me for pity's sake. I will take care of you. Come with me — *please*."

Jane can have understood none of this. She sat quietly in the armchair, twining her fingers in her lap. Finally he took her by the hands, sinking on one knee before her. "Jane, you must come with me . . ."

And at last I opened her dull mind and, as though she were a puppet taken up suddenly by the puppeteer, she sprang to her feet. "Now you look here, Richard," she said, "you have no right to come charging in here. There's nothing the matter — nothing at all. I may be a little tired but that's all. And it's not as if you *really* cared!" She tossed her head scornfully. "How many weeks is it now since you left me here alone? And sending the vicar down to see if I'm all right: hardly the act of an impassioned lover. You're a hypocrite! You profess undying love, but do you actually bother to come and see me? *No* . . .!" She collapsed in tears on to the armchair.

He was thunderstruck. "Jane! I . . ." he came towards her, arms reaching out to comfort her.

She jerked erect, eyes blazing, suddenly almost vital again. "Oh no you don't! You can just leave me alone, Richard! Get out of my house and leave me alone! Do you hear me? Just get out — and don't come back!"

Oh, how avidly did the Dead feed upon this delicious irony. That in striving so hard to win her he had finally, irredeemably lost her. And he was beginning to see that bitter truth for himself.

And so he went, sadly, back to London, and out of her life.

But there were other enemies to hold the centre of my interest at this time. Brother Warlock, having at last received permission from the Archbishop to perform his exorcism, was deep into his preparations. These were deceptively simple. He took communion morning, noon and night. The wafers and the wine were all that he consumed except water. Like a monk he rose every few hours through the night or paused in his labours during the day and said the service due to the hours. After the wild, dangerous, murderous strength of the Dead which so nearly consumed her, I did not dare to visit Rebecca again, but even had I desired to do so the way would have been barred against me by the priest's ceaseless rituals.

It was barred also against Stana Etain, Countess Issyk-

Koul. As if by mutual — though unexpressed — consent we sought each other out during at least part of those long restless nights and talked. She told me of herself, her lives. She told me of the night, of its wonders and beauties. She showed me places, holy and unholy, which might be important in our fight against Brother Warlock. For there was no doubt that we would stand together. In that we were of one mind. *We* were, after all, the Dead.

On Thursday evening as I swung open the lid of my coffin she was there, an emerald flame in the most shadowed corner of the cellar. "It will be tonight," she said. "His preparations are complete. It only remains for us to complete our own and then await him at the Round in the Broken Woods. He will come at midnight." She sneered: "With bell, book and candle no doubt!"

"What must we do?"

"To each his own. An evil deed, to give us strength."

"Is that all? An evil deed?" I was disappointed by the mean-mindedness of it. Where was the grandeur in a mere evil deed?

"To give us strength," she said again. "The more suffering it brings, the greater the power it leaves." Her blood eyes blazed, and I began to understand something of the enormity of the act required. And, as it chanced, I had a deed ripe for the doing.

Margaret Allen's protracted illness had caused devasting results in her family. Her mother had suffered a nervous breakdown and was on the edge of suicide. That quiet giant of a man, her father, had aged ten years and more, taken to drink and become dangerously violent. The destruction this simple sipping of the child's life was causing, gave the act an almost transcendental significance. There were moments when I felt like Macbeth, spreading wretchedness around me like a plague.

An evil deed.

They had removed her to a private room in the hospital for tests. The window yielded easily enough to me, and she lay fortunately sound asleep, on a white-painted, iron-framed bed. Careful not to touch this, I folded the bedcothes back. She did not stir. She rested on her side, one arm pushed under her pillow. She wore a pink-checked cotton hospital-

127

smock tied with three laces down the back. I turned her until she lay face-down. The smock rode up around her, revealing her upper left thigh and both of her calves. In the warm hollow behind her left knee I let my lips alight. She smelt like a puppy, and whimpered in her sleep. My fangs probed like a lover's fingers.

Where is the great evil in this? you will ask. Where is the grandeur in this painless leeching on the leg of a child? Tear her throat out if you would be wicked! Rip out her heart if you would lend strength to your damnation! Ah but wait, my hot-blooded friend. I look to the future. Her simple death will be the undoing of the mother. If I am gentle, my mark invisible, she will die apparently of pernicious anaemia. She will be buried in a week or so; but she will not *rest*. She will rise, return home to her father who must either destroy her or be destroyed. So they all will be undone — damned, perhaps eternally. All from a moment's sipping at the back of her leg . . .

Slivers of needle-sharp bone, too keen to waken her dull nerves with pain, probe her. Sliding past fine-stranded tendon, careful of swelling muscles above and below, avoiding the electric white worm of the nerve, nudging aside the slack-walled vein to stab down into the twitching tube of the artery. The long fine points opening the convulsing wall with more precision than any scalpel, and holding it wide while the blood gushes out, two tiny geysers fountaining on to my avid tongue. For moment after moment as the light thickens, there is only the sound of quiet sucking.

Then her breathing becomes hoarse and ragged. Her body writhes on the bed, shivers convulsively once, and lies still. The deed is done; the well is dry. And when the points of the fangs withdraw, why, you would need a magnifying glass to find the wounds. They are so fine at the tip, so razor-sharp and delicate, these fangs of mine. You will laugh, I know: but I must take care when licking the blood from my lips or I will lop off half my tongue.

I withdrew outside the window and towered in darkness, awaiting visiting time. Duly at half-past seven the door opened, the light went on, and, by the best of luck, both parents followed the nurse immediately into the room.

As soon as she saw her daughter's abandoned position,

Mrs. Allen knew. Even as the nurse reached Margaret's side and grabbed for her wrist, the thin, grey-faced little woman turned away and soundlessly collapsed. Her slovenly husband caught her under arms, and looked stupidly into the glazed surfaces of her suddenly doll-like eyes. Then he gave one great bellow of animal agony, cast his dead wife down beside his dead daughter and stumbled out into the busy corridor, weeping like a demented soul.

Evil enough? I laughed, believing so.

At midnight we waited, cloaked in black, among the trees of the Broken Wood beside the Dunmow Round. The church clock in the distance laboriously chimed the hour. The wind performed a devil's dance among the tree-tops, tearing away the last of the autumn leaves. Black clouds closed off the stars and moon. There was no light, except, to my eyes and to those of the phantom Countess, the lambency of life, dull green and winter-low, in the tree-trunks, branches, mosses, lichens, fat toadstools and stunted grasses all round. This was light enough for us to see by: the exorcists required a torch.

"It should have been done in daylight, surely, "quavered Hugh Gore as they came. At the first hint of doubt in this voice, Stana moved away from me, and when the two men entered the glade she walked beside the vicar, her serpent arms entwined around his neck.

"John, this is just plain stupid. We're playing the Devil at his own game here." At the mention of His name, she burned more brightly. Warlock silently erected a small portable altar. Sanctity dwelt on the air until a gust of wind tore through the trees at Stana's command to tip the table over.

"We should be home in bed," continued Gore. She pressed the icy length of her body against him. His mind filled with sensual thoughts and suddenly his defences began to stir — she had almost alerted him. Now she fell back and he quietened.

"No," John Warlock said. "It must be here. It must be here, and now"

They had to weight down their altar-cloth for fear the wind would claw it off and carry it away. It took them some time to fight their way into their flapping, recalcitrant robes. Stana's wind danced and howled more wildly around them.

Twigs began to fall like a rain of ice-green fire. Savagely the branches whipped each other. The whole glade began to tremble as though the earth would quake. Then Warlock, before his makeshift altar with its paraphernalia, religious junk, water, wafers and unlit candles, raised his arms and cried, "*Our Father . . .*" And the wind stopped.

The service got under way then, the young man saying the versicles, the old man the responses:

"*Save thy servant,*"

"*Oh my God, that putteth his trust in thee.*"

"*Be unto him, oh Lord, a strong tower,*"

"*From the face of his enemy.*"

And so forth.

And so on.

And there were prayers. An infinity of prayers, each word like fire in my ears: "Deliver this place from ruin and from the noonday devil send thy fear, oh Lord, upon the wild beast . . ." And worse: "I command thee, whosoever thou art, thou unclean spirit . . . that thou *tell me thy name*, the day and the hour of thy going out . . ."

While Warlock and Gore had been conducting their ritual, a wind had sprung up again, but this time it blew against us, Stana and me, where we stood shoulder to shoulder a little outside the circle, to the north, in the direction dedicated to the name of Uriel. Uriel, Raphael, Michael, Gabriel . . . As the prayers multiplied, so the wind seemed to grow, threatening to hurl us away, through Scotland and even over the end of the earth.

But as Warlock spoke these words, ". . . *tell me thy name* . . ." it seemed that a great bolt of lightning danced between the two of us. The darkness around us fell away so that our enemies could see us where we stood, bathed in vivid electricity. And it seemed that the lightning between us had, not only thunder, but a voice. From the deepest part of the sky it roared.

"I AM THE SHADOW IN DARKNESS, THE SILENCE WHICH SEEMS TO WHISPER. I AM NOT THE WALL BUT THE CRACKS IN THE WALL. NOT THE BONE BUT THE DUST OF THE BONE."

Warlock and Gore were blasted back by the force of it. Stana and I reeled alike and only the icy strength of it held us up.

Warlock held up his Book of Exorcisms. "I exorcise thee, most foul spirit, every coming in of the enemy, every apparition, every legion . . ." but his words were drowned by the thundering of the Dead.

"I AM NOT THE AIR BUT THE POISON IN THE AIR. NOT THE FIRE BUT THE ASH. I AM NOT THE EARTH BUT THE POISON IN THE EARTH. NOT THE WATER BUT THE DUST. I AM WHAT LIES BETWEEN THE STARS. NOT THE SPACE BUT THE ANGLE."

Gore was broken now, but still the man Warlock was granted strength. He crawled towards us awkwardly in his robes, on two knees and his left hand. Still with that black book held up before his face he cried, "I adjure thee, thou old serpent, by the Judge of the quick and the dead, by thy Maker and the Maker of the world. I adjure thee . . ."

"I AM THE VIRUS. I AM THE WORM. I AM THE FLEA. I AM THE SPIDER. I AM THE BAT. AND I AM THE WOLF."

The man was beaten now and he knew it. If he had other powers, they were not to be invoked this night. He caught up the fainting Gore and together they backed away. Still the black Book of Exorcisms was held up between us so that even we, victorious, were powerless against them. Staggering backwards down the path together they cried, "We pray thee oh Almighty God, that the spirit of wickedness have no more power over us but that he may flee away . . ."

But this last prayer also was drowned out by the thunder:

"I AM THE RELENTLESS HUNTER. I AM THE STEALER OF SOULS. I AM THE BRINGER OF TERROR IN THE NIGHT. YOU WILL KNOW ME WHEN I COME FOR YOU—

I AM THE DEAD AND I WILL ABIDE."

TO REST IN PEACE

Last night, more than a week after the Dead overcame Gore's and Warlock's canting, I found myself full of a burning restless energy. As soon as I was free of the shackles of the day I strode abroad. Only the greatest control kept me from finding my favourite victims and letting the Dead in me drink its fill and drain them until they died. But what I had done to Margaret Allen and her family seemed jest enough for the time-being; and I was still — though more faintly — concerned about the dangers to myself inherent in a return of Stana's Plague.

Soon, therefore, I found myself in the Broken Woods at the site of our victory. The air smelt strange. There was a heavy odour of burning and, indeed, the bushes around the point where the Countess and I had stood were badly scorched. But it was more than this. There was a distinct aroma of burned soil, a strange overlay of charred wood, leaf-mould, of the ash of dust and stone and this was mingled with the stench of long-dead air.

I started at north of the circle, where the smell was strongest, and began to explore the crisp black undergrowth in the mystic house of Uriel. All the bright life had been drained from the place and I searched almost blindly. I was used to seeing a green lambency about every plant around me, but here there were only shadows multiplying.

I believe now that Stana guided me. But at the time I thought I had found the pit by chance. A lifeless crater nearly six feet deep, I could not tell whether it was under the exact point where we had stood or if it was a little behind. In either case it took me utterly by surprise. The ground just tilted suddenly and fell away sharply, and I slid down into it until at its bottom my feet struck a strangely flat stone slab. I knelt down and let my fingertips investigate it. A little more than a square yard was laid bare — a granite slab cleft, as though by a thunderbolt, so that there was a crack in it just large enough for a man to squeeze through. From this cleft came the strange smell of stale air long entombed. Not unnaturally such an odour called to something deep inside me. Blinded still by the lack of life-flames, I crawled forward and sat on the edge of the hole so that my feet dangled below. Then, with the utmost care I eased myself over the edge and dropped into the black tunnel below. At first I did no more than stand there, then my eyes cleared a little. There was life down here: sparks of tiny animals, filaments of root, faint clouds of lichen — life enough to see by.

I was in a long tunnel, perhaps seven feet in height, which sloped steeply downwards on my right. After a moment more of exploration I faced downhill and began to follow the slope. After several yards I came to a flight of steps leading down to a high narrow door. Without thinking I ran down them and reached one hand out towards the handle. What made me hesitate I do not know — some ancient wisdom of the Dead. My fingers merely brushed the handle, yet even so a great flame seemed to erupt there, almost consuming my hand. I staggered back. For a second more, blue flames danced around my strange flesh. Then they died.

Cunningly wrapped around the iron handle I had touched there were wolf's-bane and garlic flowers, dead for so long that they contained no warning life-force — only their eternal magic, deadly to me. I went closer again. Carved on the door itself there was a feared and hated symbol. This place had been closed against such as I. Therefore I longed to see inside.

An hour later I once again stood beneath the cleft stone slab. I called up to the woman whom I had brought back with me and she lowered first the bag and then herself into my waiting arms. "It's dark," Jane said.

I remembered about the light she would need in order to see. "You have the torch?" I asked.

"In the bag."

"Get it out. You will need it."

Abruptly the beam sliced the shadows. "All right?" she asked.

A strange relationship, ours. To me she is a creature, totally bound by my will. To her, in the shadowy world I allow her to see, I am her mysterious lover, creator of and sharer in the adventures of the night. She does not talk of me:

our love is secret. My name in the daytime? Ah, a shifting thing like sunlight in water, glimpsed but not easily caught. My identity? A black cat amongst dark shadows. Sometimes far above her, sometimes at her side.

"All right," I said. She, bearing the light, went first down the slope. She moved slowly: careful but unafraid, lighting the place with her clear life's flame more vividly than did the torch. Over the fire-edged silhouette of her head, the bolts of thought flashed. Down her lithe back ran the electric river of her spinal cord.

It was the work of a thoughtless moment for her to break the spells on the old nail-studded blackwood door. She turned the iron ring of the handle and pushed her shoulder against the graven symbol. The door swung a little open, the hinge protesting bitterly, then stopped. There was a scent which in life I would have said to be the scent of roses. "What do you smell?" I asked her.

She took a deep breath and began to retch drily, leaning against the door-frame. Beyond the smell there was nothing to guide me. I felt a power in the place even more ancient than that around the door. I went in front of her and rested the fingers of my left hand on the edge of the door. Behind me, Jane straightened. The torch beam brightened the wood. There should have been the shadow of my head. Of course, there was no shadow. I pushed. The door swung away from me. The smell of roses intensified. She sank to her knees, choking.

I went forward but even to my eyes there was only the faintest light. A candle-power of old magic. Enough to make shadows loom. I called the woman. After a moment, still fighting for breath, she brought the torch to me.

It was not a large chamber — perhaps twelve feet across, made up of at least ten short-sided walls each mounting in a curve to a pointed vault. It was as though we stood inside a huge bullet looking upwards towards the point. On each of the walls there were painted scenes of sadism and sexual perversion. The torch light wavered, lighting more obscenities. I caught the woman and held her cradled in my right arm. The faintest of sensation as it brushed her clothing told me that feeling was returning to the blackened fist of my right hand. I willed it to move, but muscles beneath the blistered skin remained recalcitrant. I took the torch in my left hand and guided the beam myself. There was an altar in the centre of the room, its sides like the walls, lovingly decorated. A forest of stakes were painted there, each bearing strange fruit. White bodies, impaled, transfixed in a grim mixture of agony and ecstacy. Amid the laden stakes danced naked, blood-speckled children. So vivid was the artistry that the impaled ones seemed to writhe as you watched, and as you glanced away the children seemed to move. Lingering on the utter silence of the place there came the faintest echo of childish laughter.

There was about the room an air of brooding agony which I could not bear. If Stana had wanted me to find this place then it was here, no doubt, four centuries ago, that she herself had been discovered at her blasphemies and dragged away by the townsfolk to face the rope, the axe, the stake. Abruptly I wanted to get away, even from the leering, licentious gaze of the children dancing on the altar's side. "Come," I said to the woman. She led the way out of the tiny chapel, waited like a porter as I passed, and closed the door behind me.

I left Jane to walk home alone, content myself for the moment to dawdle. The restlessness which had filled me earlier was stilled. I wandered darkly through the deserted, silent village. Winter was well upon us now, and what had been a clear, starlit night adorned with a crescent moon was rapidly becoming palled over with a massive winding sheet of clouds. A wind blew from the north-east, bitter and still with a faint breath of the great black-pined steppes which had given it birth. That at least suited the new mood building up in me.

As I strode towards the crossroads, however, I detected a distant flicker of movement: someone, in the dark heart of the night, was creeping throught the back gardens of the little terraced houses away on my left. I suddenly caught the stirring of a familiar old excitement. I knew it but did not recognise it. Something deep within me was aroused. Hunched forward, cloaked in thicknesses of shadow, I crept down the tiny path between two houses.

There! Again! In the distance, a pale flicker. The air seemed to contain laughter — as had the air in the underground chapel — and the hair down my long back stirred. Eagerly I ran through the neat-clipped, winter-bedded gardens, vaulting easily over hedges, fences, walls, slowly drawing closer to the pale thing which scurried noiselessly down the length of the village. Every now and then it would pause, disappear into the shadows behind a house, and reappear a few minutes later. As I came closer I could hear, each time this happened, a gentle tap-tap-tapping on glass.

Down one side of the village we sped, then across the road and into the gardens to creep up the other side. This time the figure did not simply tap on the windows, but lingered longer as though expecting answers. At last an answer was received. A window opened. Another figure climbed out. I caught right up and watched them: two children in night-clothes whispering to each other and giggling in the shadows.

I realised then: it was the Fools' Game again, but strangely out of season. I drew closer still. And then I understood. The child who had just climbed through the window was bright and blazingly vital. The child I had been following was not: it was Margaret Allen, three days buried, now playing the Fools' Game in earnest.

And even as I thought this, the darker figure engulfed the bright one. The silver life-frame quivered and began to die.

I strode forward, but at my first movement Margaret, or the thing she had become, let go of the child she had been feeding upon and flitted away into the darkness. Her victim stood for a moment, dazed, then fell to the ground. I picked her up, put her in through the open window to the stifling warmth of her own lounge and left her there where she would come to no further harm. The longer the villagers remained unalerted to what was abroad, the better.

In the moments it took me to perform this act, Margaret had disappeared. I cast about in the gardens further down, but she was gone. But then, as I turned to go home, the wind carried a snatch of drunken song to my keen ears and, down past the shops from the direction of Braintree, came Margaret's father. Where he had been I have no idea, nor how he had contrived to arrive home at this time. But he was as drunk as any man can be who is still able to move.

I followed him as he wove down the dark, dead road. I

stood under the four-fingered signpost at the corner of the green as he fumbled at the front door of his house on the corner opposite. Eventually the door opened and he staggered in. I had no difficulty in slipping in after him a few moments later. He was crashing around downstairs. He had switched on the kitchen lights and was searching for something. Eventually he raised his voice and bellowed hoarsely to his dead wife, "Enid, where are my slippers? Enid . . .?" Then, even in his drunken stupor, he remembered.

He stumbled past me at the bottom of the stairs, blinded with hot, boozy tears. I followed him up, into his bedroom. He switched the light on at his third attempt. The room was tidy — strangely so, considering the mess in the rest of the house — and the bed was neatly made. Arthur stared around, as if trying to make some sense out of things. Then he dumped himself down on the edge of the bed and set about pulling off his boots. That done, he hurled them across the room, lurched upright, threw the bed-clothes back and froze.

She was lying where her mother used to lie, dressed in a long white nightgown. As the light struck her she opened her blood-red eyes and smiled, the needle-points of her fangs glinting. "Hello, Daddy," she whispered.

I cannot properly describe the sound he made. He staggered back. She rolled across the bed and rose before him, her arms wide in mute invitation.

"No!" he screamed and, turning, he blundered into me, where I stood on the landing. At the time I didn't think he even noticed the brief contact as he swept past on to the stairway. He took two steps and his knees gave out, precipitating him bodily down the stairs. The hunter in the child followed. With a snarl which rid her face of its last vestige of humanity, she bounded after him and threw herself bodily from the top of the stairs on to his back as he staggered erect. The weight of her pitched him forward again and she rolled over his shoulder. He was on his knees as she cast herself at him a third time, but now he was better prepared. A great ham-fist swung across her face, hurling her, snarling, into a corner as he rose finally to his feet.

I watched from the top of the stairs. Even the Dead was given pause, fascinated by the boundless, evil ferocity it had let into the girl's body. For the fourth time she charged, all white-bone fangs, red eyes and yellow claws. The man caught her by the throat as she leapt at him. They swayed together for a moment as her talons tore at his shoulders and chest before he hurled her away once more. As soon as he was free of her he turned and stumbled towards the back door. He left it swinging and ran into the yard. I thought he was making an escape, as did the thing his daughter had become, for she hurled herself across the room to pause in the open doorway, hands on the door-post level with her head.

For a second this tableau froze, the girl outlined against the dark rectangle as her eyes probed the shadows beyond. Then there was a great cry and a glittering arc of light swung past her head to crash into the upright of wood. The vampire staggered back and something fell to the ground. At first I did not realise that it was her right hand. Then, with a great scream, as mad and animal as her own, Arthur Allen erupted back in through the doorway, wielding a great woodman's axe. Like any creature wounded and cornered, she hurled herself into the attack but the man had her measure. The axe-head buried itself in her side, flinging her back against the wall. She attacked again, spitting blood, reaching out even with the stump of her right arm, only to be hurled back once more, gushing the blood of village children over the floor and walls.

I turned away long before it was over and vanished out of the front door into the shadows. My mind ablaze, I ran home to Jane. There was an hour or two before dawn yet and the sight of blood had aroused my lust.

Half an hour later he came. The great thundering of his fists upon the door jerked Jane out of my arms. She threw on her dressing-gown and went downstairs. I stood at the head of the stairs as she crept towards the bolted door. "Who is it?" she asked.

"Where is he?" cried the man outside.

"Who? Who do you want?"

"Underhill!"

"Oh, but Mr. Underhill is dead . . ."

The head of the axe burst between two planks of the door tearing the bolt cleanly from the wood. The door slammed back and Arthur Allen stood there, fired with a terrible lunacy, in one hand his logger's axe and in the other the head of his daughter, swinging by its hair.

"Where is he?" he screamed. Jane staggered back, her mind, thankfully, blank. After a step or two she fell, stuck her temple and lost consciousness.

Arthur swung his axe across his great chest, catching the haft just beneath the steel head, and strode in on stiff legs. I stood at the top of the stairs and watched him as he prowled, muttering, about the hall. Every now and then he would whirl and send the bloody blade of the axe howling through the thick shadows at his back. It was not until he reached the foot of the stairway that I heard what he was saying: "Here, boy; here, boy; come along, there's a good boy. Come here, boy: I won't hurt you." As though I were some kind of animal to be fooled by his kind words.

He would say this four or five times, then whirl around to hack at the shadows.

Satisfied that I was not lurking in the hall, he stumped off to explore the kitchen and the dining room. I flew silently down the stairs, scooped up Jane's inert body and carried her up to the landing, out of harm's way. Then I returned to the hall, and went to hunt the hunter.

He never really stood a chance. Even if his constant muttering had not given away his location, the bright flame of his life-force would have guided me. But finding him and finishing him were two different problems. Half a dozen blows from that axe had reduced the lithe, powerful body of his vampire daughter to something fit only for a butcher's shop. I did not want to share her fate. My right hand was still charred though beginning to heal. I crept into the kitchen which he had just vacated, looking for a weapon myself. There was a great crash from the dining room as he attacked the grandfather clock. His muted drone never varied. There was nothing in the kitchen which I could use as a weapon. My own talons would be more effective even than Jane's sharpest carving knife.

With stunning suddenness his mad blaze erupted through the door behind me. "HA!" he cried, swinging his axe up. I whirled and rushed forward in one movement, catching the kitchen table and pushing it before me. The narrow end of it crashed into his lower belly, hurling him backwards so that the axe blade cleft, not my head, but the table-top a foot before my face. The massive blow destroyed the table completely, and Arthur hurled himself forward once again through the mess of kindling he had made. I met him in the doorway.

For a moment we stood there, swaying, our arms raised and interlocked while blood from his daughter's ragged neck ran down them. Then, almost of their own volition, my lips spread wide and I struck at him like a snake. He staggered back. I turned and vanished once again into the darkness. This time there was a weapon in the kitchen — a heavy mahogany leg in the ruins of the table.

Arthur was on the prowl again, whispering, "Here, boy, here, boy," in his crazed undertone. Somewhere far beyond the edge of the world the first light of dawn was threatening. An early bird swooped across the black sky heralding the hated chorus. I crept into the hall. Repeating his lunatic phrase for the fifth time, Arthur swung round on the third step of the staircase and destroyed the banister behind. He paused, then hunched his shoulders and began to climb once more. He was on the fifth step when I rose up behind him and brought my makeshift club in a great blow on to his left ear. The power of it hurled him to his right, through the banisters, and flat on his face on to the parquet flooring below. The axe slid away across the hall. Not so his gory trophy, its hair wound tightly round his fingers. Incredibly, he heaved himself on to all fours and began to go after the axe.

I threw my club to one side, for it had splintered as I struck, and thrust myself after him. As luck would have it, I did not land well and sprawled half on to his heaving back. He shrugged me off with almost contemptuous ease, leaving his daughter's head now for me to catch up in my turn, and crawled on. His fingers closed upon the axe just as I skittered round in front of him. He reared up, trying to control the shining blade sufficiently to strike a final murderous blow.

I had no time for thought — only for action. I swung the weight now in my burned right hand, swung it back and downwards, then powered it up again in the most powerful blow I could muster. It took him under the chin, lifted him upright, drove his lower jaw up out of its socket, and hurled him back amid the wreckage of the stairs.

At that climactic moment there came a terrible, soul-destroyed scream from the landing. Jane stood up there. My concentration on the battle had been so total that I had not felt her stir and waken. Neither had I closed off her mind. Too late, I tried to do so now, only to find it already possessed with a thousand variations on one frozen, hideous image.

She had seen me clearly at last — she had seen what I had become, and she had seen what I was doing, and the vision of it filled her mind with revulsion. The creature at the foot of her stairs seemed more vile than any product of mankind's darkest fantasies. Yet she knew that it was real, that she had loved it . . . *and that she had made love to it.* And it stood now, astride the bleeding body of a man, frozen in the act of clubbing him to death with the severed head of a golden-haired girl.

This picture was the last thing that Jane saw. As I watched, the silver flame around her faded. The golden filigree of living thought about head and body disappeared. The pulse beneath her skin faltered and stilled.

"Jane!" I shrieked.

She toppled forward and pitched down the staircase. I flung the head away and went forward to where she was lying. If the shock of what she had seen had not killed her, then her fall had, for she was quite, quite dead. Gently I lifted her and, cradling her pale blind face to my breast, I carried her upstairs and put her to bed. The carrion down in the hall I buried. This house is isolated and its garden large: the chances, even if Arthur were traced here, of anyone finding him are remote.

The task completed, I returned to Jane and sat at her side and held her hand until dawn began to burn my eyes. Poor Jane: I would have cried for her once, but the Dead has no tears.

ALONE

I had not thought I could have felt grief, but for nights on end I have just wandered disconsolately through the old house like some mindless spectre condemned to repeat a pointless eternal round. Only her bedroom contains anything of her now: everywhere else is full of her absence. Her school-books unmarked, clothes to be washed, dishes piled on the draining-board. There are telephone calls in the light hours which interrupt my rest with their urgency, and letters piled each evening at the foot of the door. Letters from old pupils, people I have never heard of. Letters from Richard Burke begging forgiveness and understanding. Then there are letters from school demanding an explanation for her absence. People come knocking on the door, but of course I never open it. But I read the letters aloud to her each evening, in the lingering twilight.

One night I decided to return to the mysterious chapel we had discovered together beneath the witches's circle of stones in the heart of the Broken Woods. A sentimental journey or an answer to a summons? At the time I did not think to wonder. The wind was up, and gusting black clouds low across a moonless sky. The weight of the winter night pressed down on my shoulders like a coat of lead. I walked slowly along almost deserted streets, between seasonably festive shop windows. Nobody saw me. Never before had the sense of my otherness been so poignant within me, the totality of my loneliness so terrible.

Beyond the last street-lamp, the dark gathered round me like a congregation of old friends. All around, even in mid-winter, life was bright. Only the dead road and I were dark. The Broken Woods enfolded me like a shimmering cloud columned with green. I shivered with the intensity of my hatred for all this mindless burgeoning.

At the bottom of the black pit the cleft stone slab still gaped. I stood for a moment looking down at it, remembering how I had stood here once before with Jane at my

142

shoulder. The wind died. Silence crouched over me, and I swung round, fully expecting someone to be there. But only mocking shadows met my eyes. I slid alone into the hole, paused on the edge of the broken slab, then dropped into the dark, musty passage. I waited until the roots in the roof gave some of their light to my eyes, then I moved silently down the dust-carpeted slope. The door stood a little open, faintly aglimmer. This gave me pause, for I remembered that Jane had closed it behind me as we left. I crept up to the smooth lambent wood, therefore, and ran my fingers warily down its cool surface. Its magic against me was still strong. I braced myself, and pushed it further open.

Stana sat upon the altar as though upon a table-edge, one foot swinging in the air, her upper body leaning back on the rigid prop of her right arm. With her left hand she drew the red tresses of her hair across the bone-white dome of her brow. A delicately curved eyebrow was raised interrogatively above the expressionless blood-almond of her eye. "What is it that you search for?" she asked quietly. Did she mock me? I could not tell.

"Nothing," I told her. She looked down, smoothing the folds of her faery-green dress, her claws whispering.

"What is this place?" I asked.

"Surely that is obvious." She gestured to the painted walls, the point of the roof towards which the eyes were directed by the painter's artistry and which I now saw to be adorned with a picture of a beast, half-man/half-goat. "It is a place of worship."

"Your place of worship?"

"It is mine but I did not worship here. I came here. Others worshipped here."

"Because you know that what they worshipped was . . . is . . . a plaster painting only?"

"I know many things."

"But not that. What they worshipped, what you worshipped, you do not know its nature."

"Perhaps. Perhaps not."

"To know that," I said suddenly, "to know that for certain would almost be worth becoming this." I gestured towards my body. Immediately I knew I had enraged her, although there was no change in her expression.

"And what do you truly know of *that* or *this*?" she demanded. "You know nothing. Nothing at all. Come with me!" Abruptly she stood erect, her hand held out imperiously towards me. "Come — there is a thing I wish to show you."

Obediently I took her hand. The walls of her strange temple began to waver. Slowly she led me forward towards the door, but by the time we reached it, it had vanished. Like Dante led by Virgil down to the Pit I went, or seemed to go.

After some time we paused and she turned to me — we were at the very top of a precipitous cliff. She gestured down. It was black basalt rock and sheer as a wall. An ocean beat against the foot of this cliff, but it threw no spume or spindrift up into the whirling wind. It was an ocean of bodies stretching far beyond the shadowed horizon. How deep it was I had no way of knowing, but there were bodies enough to make it heave like a restless sea. Great waves swept in relentlessly. Greased by blood and sweat, those in the depths tried to claw their way to the surface. Those on the surface dared not rest or sleep, for fear that those below, made wakeful by agony, might supplant them.

Those on the surface who were strong enough crawled forward, hoping to reach the cliffs. If they could reach the cliff-foot, perhaps they might scale the massive basalt wall and escape altogether. And there were some that made it. The rock was glass-smooth and lined only with the tiniest cracks. Some who were thrown upwards by the heaving below caught hand-holds here. If they could avoid the clutching hands beneath which sought also to be pulled up, and could wedge fingers and toes into hair-thin seams, they could begin to climb. But the higher they climbed, the greater became the danger. If they fell more than a few feet, the human ocean below would open and they would sink to the bottom once more. And as they climbed higher, the cracks, blunted at first by the fingers of those unnumbered ones who had made it some way up, became sharper, glass-edged.

Even so, as we stood and watched at the outermost edge of the cliff, a pair of gaunt hands appeared. Bleeding fingers tipped with filthy, broken nails, pulled thin, torn arms into view. A bearded head rose with aching slowness over the black rock. The man saw our feet and looked up, eyes ablaze with hope of salvation.

Then his gaze fell on my companion. His motion froze. His face twisted in a mixture of terror and hatred. "You!" he cried.

She stepped forward towards him, hand stretched out to help, but he jerked away from her in an uncontrollable gesture of revulsion. "Do not touch me," he hissed. His hand-hold failed. His chin crashed on to the cliff edge. Screaming, he fell away.

She turned to me. "He loved me once," she said.

I went to the outermost edge of the cliff and looked down upon the ocean of writhing bodies which stretched as far as my eyes could see on all sides. How many millions were entrapped down there? Their cries gave life to a great rushing wind.

"But how strange it is," I said, "that, out of so many, the one who climbed the wall should know you . . ."

She looked at me then and I thought I detected sorrow in her still face and the surfaces of her crimson eyes.

"They all know me," she said. "These are those dead at my hand who died in sin. Some rose again, their corpses filled with vampire-spirits, some did not rise. No matter whether their bodies moved or remained at peace, this is where their souls abide."

Behind her, the hurricane of their cries almost drowned the surf of their agony as they lapped against the rock. "I knew them all, loved them all, destroyed them all. This is what _you_ have to look forward to. This is what being the Dead means. You tear, you sip, you infect and pollute others. We are the White Plague you and I. We are the tall figures in black robes who take the scythe to such as these. Behold! a pale horse, and he that sitteth upon him is the Dead."

I stood, stunned, scarcely understanding her bitter words. Then, abruptly she smiled and held out her hand again. "Come," she said, "enough of this. Let us return to reality: it is almost dawn."

I swung towards her, stung by that word 'reality', for I had thought myself to be in a circle of Hell, in a mansion of the Pit. And my mind had already raced towards that glowing conclusion: if Hell exists, then so does its opposite. So

145

that all the evil and good in all places and times had fallen into a beautiful pattern.

And now she had destroyed the symmetry with that one sharp word. I swung towards her, therefore. "Reality?" I said. "Returned to reality? Is this place then not *real*?"

She laughed, a joyless sound. "Real?" she whispered. "*This is a dream!* You did not think any of this really exists, did you?" She threw her head back and howled with triumphant laughter. And before the echoes had died we were back in the underground chapel.

I have not visited that cavern again. In time I will find out for myself what is real and what is not. Certainly I cannot rely upon Stana for guidance. But why should I do so, in any case? I do not begin to understand her. I think my most fundamental error has been the assumption that because she takes the outward shape of a human she is in fact touched by some humanity. She is not. And on those rare occasions when I can see myself clearly nowadays, I am appalled by the extent to which even my own humanity has withered quite away. And yet I crave sensation. I am sexually insatiable, which is no more than a metaphor for the most delicate sensations of the soul. I am sexually insatiable because my organs, although functioning perfectly, are without feeling. And because consummation is forbidden, it is the more avidly sought.

Only the grossest excesses seem able to move me now: rage, lust, agony, terror. Because I cannot feel the gentle delicacy of love, I crave it. I crave conscience also, but that too has gone. Ah, how early that began! With the fear of water, with the failure of mirrors, I cloaked a growing ruthlessness under the urgency of my pretended mission to save Rebecca, not seeing for a moment where this would lead. How could I have been so self-deluding? Only self-pity remains, and is exquisite. Let me wallow a little longer. After all, no matter how wise I might have been what could I have *done*? Once Stana's stake had pierced my palm, my path was fixed. And now . . . and now I feel, ah, *I feel*, so sad . . .

Burke came back last night. There were letters at the door's foot when I rose and I collected them together to read in the evening to my quiet Jane. A little after seven o'clock the doorbell rang below. We sat in silence, Jane and I. The ringing was repeated at length and with great urgency. The door-handle rattled and fists beat upon the still scarred wood. I have buried Allen's body, but I cannot make the door perfect again.

"Jane!" Richard cried.

I put the letters down and rose to my feet. The bell began to ring once more. I moved along the landing and down the stairs. The hall was full of his noise. His finger on the bell, his fist on the locked door, his voice on the evening air like the howl of a hunting-dog. "Jane! I know you're in there! Answer the door. Jane! It's Richard! I've come to take you away."

I stood beside the door scant inches from him. My left hand reached out until its fingernails stroked the black wood where his face must be. Feeling came: hatred, ice-cold and welcome. I stood with my mouth stretched in a smile and felt wonderful, beautiful hatred for this importunate man.

Then the sound stopped. He stood silently, lost in thought, then turned away. His footsteps receded down the path. I knew very well what would happen next. There was no need for haste. I went along beside the stairs and down into my cellar to await events.

They began with the smashing of a pane of glass upstairs in the study. A window slid up coming into position with a bang! There was a scuffling sound as he climbed carefully across the sill. Feet placed individually and almost silently on the carpet. Would he open the curtains or creep forward in the dark? A footstep, a stumble, a crash!: he had become entangled in the curtains and upset the small table beside the window. He had chosen the dark, and it was not his element. Silence. He stood frozen. He had been in communication no doubt with Warlock and Gore, so he knew that something was terribly wrong. Yet he had come here alone, to face he knew not what. What brought him? Mere professional curiosity? The need to challenge his disbelief? Even love? I could not tell.

Footsteps moved across the room. I smiled to myself. Childe Roland to the Dark Tower had come, in search of a fair damsel to rescue. He would find her soon enough. Hinges squealed as he opened the lounge door. His leather soles clicked on parquet flooring. I seemed to grow: I had the momentary impression that if I moved at all my head would strike the ceiling. I towered there in the cellar's blackness. He came past the locked door at the top of the cellar steps, his heavy footfall growing louder and them softer again. He went into the kitchen. My eyes burned. My teeth throbbed as though a tuning fork had been struck against them. My hands, the right one fully healed now, were hooked at my sides.

"Jane?" he called.

My whole body shook with tension. His footsteps drew near once more. As they receded towards the front door again I sped up the cellar steps and into the thickest shadows of the hall. He stood looking at the wreckage of the banister. He wore jeans, a black shirt open at the neck and a ski jacket. As I arrived, he glanced up as though startled, but he could not distinguish me from the sea of blackness all around. He had a flashlight which he turned once more upon the stairs and crossed towards them. He paused, swung round suddenly. The torch beam cut through me where I stood in shadow behind him. His breathing filled the hall like a gale of wind. His cheeks were white, his hair and beard were wild. He had the face of a man who has been terribly torn on the rack between duty and desire. Abandoning Jane, albeit at her angry command, had cost his conscience dear. How I envied him. And how I hated him — that such a creature should have feelings so much more subtle than my own.

He turned back to the shadowed staircase and began to climb. I crossed the hall in three long strides and crept up close behind him. I could hear his heart thundering in his chest. A web of light flickered all along his back and down his legs as the muscles jumped with tension. A stairboard creaked. He cried out in sudden terror, his scalp a vivid crown of gold as all the tiny muscles jumped to raise his hair erect. Then he moved on, his breath clouding above his head as he panted on the freezing air. He reached the landing, hesitated.

Once more he called, softly, "Jane?" Then he crept away from her bedroom as if he already suspected what he might find there.

Together we checked the rooms in which Underhill had once lived. He searched the bathroom — I preferred to stay outside its maze of iron water pipes. But at last there was nowhere else for him to go. He crept up to her bedroom door and stopped. Terror flickered over his skin like sparks. It was as if he knew there was something terrible in there. Did he have second sight? Or . . . I sniffed the air: ah yes — he could smell her. And yet he still went in.

The door squealed open for him. The torch beam wandered around the room and found her as I had kept her, in a warm nightdress, propped up in bed. The yellow light made her face livid. The look of horror with which she had died was faded now, for the flesh had bloated and sagged. The eyes were dry and filmed with grey. A small track of something green wound over her slack, purple lip, down her chin and on to the neck of her nightgown. The smell of her was overpowering. He choked, staggered, and yet moved on forward.

I moved backwards then, sweeping towards the head of the stairs. "Jane!" he cried again, this time in the unbelievable certainty of what he had discovered. I heard his fingertips against the cloth of her nightgown. Then he gave a sobbing scream and came back through the door at a stumbling run, his mind a whirl of images overlaid most strongly by the idea of the police — to whom someone should have gone long ago. He tripped on something. The torch fell from his hands to land on the floor, pointing uselessly at the wall. He did not see me at first. He was still looking back over his shoulder as he staggered to regain his balance. Then he stooped, groped for the torch, and there I was, towering above him. As I could see him amid his silver life-flame, so he saw me, darkness of darkness, shadow of shadows, red-eyed, white-fanged. He cowered away, his face convulsing in horror. "No!" he choked. "Oh God, no!"

"Yes," I whispered, moving slowly forward.

Disbelief, like a cloud, around him. But it could not save him. Gently I leaned down and gathered his face in my left hand, thumb down the left side of his jaw, the spider-scar crouching on my white skin. His eyes bulged over the edge of my hand. His breath and the beginnings of a scream trembled against the sensitive fur on my palm. I tightened my fingers until I felt his cheekbones begin to crack. Agony cleared his mind. And in it I saw, in this his dying moment, his reason for having returned to the house. Love. Love for Jane. In his own way, no matter how imperfectly, he had loved her.

I closed my hand to a fist. His face crushed like a sheet of paper. I twisted his jerking head back until the neck snapped, and sank my fangs into the offered column of his throat. I hurled him away and down the stairs. As he crashed from step to step the bright flame of him began to fade. Finally it guttered and died on the dim parquet. I descended, kicked his remains away from the foot of the stairs, depression suddenly weighing me down.

As midnight stirred, my mind cleared and I seemed to be sickened by what I had done. By what the Dead had done. A confusion of feelings lingered briefly: sadness for the dead man rapidly became sadness for myself. Sadness and bitter loneliness.

Even Jane, my creature through many months; Jane, consigned by chance to oblivion and silence; even Jane had had someone to love her, to search for her and try to save her.

Who could ever love me now?

Sunday Night 9/10 December:

STANA'S PLAN (i)

As soon as I shrugged off Underhill's vapid melancholia I began to look for the Countess Stana, and pursued my search to the exclusion of all other things except feeding in the night. She was not in the strange chapel beneath the buried circle of stones in the Broken Woods. She was not in the graveyard or the crypt or the tombs of the church, though I waited for several nights hoping she would come. She had no lair in the village that I could find. She did not rest beneath the finger-post at the crossroads on the green in the grave where once she had lain.

I did not see her as I followed the shopgirls and the secretaries to their snug homes in the evenings. I did not feel her near me as I sipped willing bodies. How full this winter will be of laryngitis, pharyngitis, bronchitis and the mild blood diseases — iron deficiency, anaemia: if only the local doctors knew. Stana was not there in the night as I moved about silent streets, sated and searching for her. Nor in the cold grey dawns like this when Edwin brings me home to keep my journal, no, my *nocturnal*: my journal of the night, in the house with Jane in her yellow-stained bed, and the remains of the psychiatrist at the foot of the stairs. Sooner or later someone, the police no doubt, will come and find them and take them away. But until that happens they are at least company for me, of a sort. Tiring of the search and growing impatient with my helplessness, I decided to console myself with a sight of Rebecca. I had not visited her for some time, fearing my weak control over the Dead, and what the beast might do to her. At midnight, therefore, I went to the vicarage and stood before its blackwood door. There was no wind or movement in the earth during those moments, and as the chimes struck the door swung slowly inwards at my command. The house was quiet. The old man and his daughter were in bed. I mounted the stairs. The landing lay open and dark on either hand. The door to the spare room where Brother Warlock had slept was open. Idly I entered. Much of the man remained — clothes, shoes, cases — but of the exorcist himself no sign.

I was lingering there, trying to ascertain the reason for his absence and the date of his return, when I heard the faintest breath of laughter. At first I did not see her for she was lying cloaked by shade, but then, as I stood bemused, Stana rose in a parody of Venus from the sheets. She was clothed from throat to ankle in her gown of faery green. As she swung free of the bed she smiled at me, teeth agleam, eyes lighting the room like the embers of a fire. "He is not here," she said. "But he is not so far away that I cannot reach him when he sleeps."

We talked then. It was her time, sated as she was with her torture of Brother Warlock's sleeping mind, for confidences. She told me of her suffering after the staking and dismemberment, when she had existed, blind, deaf, dumb, bound to the grave by the crossroads. This was as near to Hell as she could imagine, fighting through countless days and nights to remain as an entity, to hold together a character, a mind, an identity as all her strength was sapped away by the nothingness around her. She told me how memory faltered and faded. Madness beckoned. What lay beyond the final plunge when all knowledge of self would be gone she did not know, but it was the only thing which truly terrified her. So she had used it, for four hundred years, used her terror and her hatred to remain individual, to remain strong, to remain the Countess. Until by chance I had at last released her into personality and the spectral semblance of a body, so that she could wander freely.

It was a sombre night, this night, and we talked of sombre things. One subject of discourse especially held my interest. In all the centuries of her existence as the Dead, before she came to Dunmow Cross that one last time, she said, her sole abiding grief had been that she was always alone. In all that time there had been no single companion immortal like herself. Solitude was a state of being I should try to avoid above all others, she said. Even the burden of immortality grew light if shared. And here she was willing to help me. She would have offered herself, of course, but she had form only, and no flesh, while I was young and great in power. Now was the time, therefore, for me to choose one and fit her to be my eternal companion.

How would I do this? I asked.

There were rituals, she said: if I would allow her, she would aid me in their performance. My part, after choosing my companion, would be to ensure that her spirit was educated swiftly in the ways of the Dead — swiftly but gently, for some spirits were weak and might break beneath the strain. Further, the carrion flesh must be stripped away skilfully and in a certain manner. And I must not only take the essence of my chosen mate, but give to her also of my own essence, in so far as I am able. I must wrap her gently in toils so thick and strong she could never escape, even should her wishes be contrary to my own. Had not even I tried to escape my fate? — my victim might also try to seek oblivion rather than eternity.

"Choose your partner carefully," she told me, "and then we will begin."

But she knew as well as I did that the choice was already made.

(ii)

When all the vicarage lights were out on Monday night I commanded the front door to yield to me. Impatience barely held in check, I crossed the glimmering hall and mounted the stairway to the landing. The old man was deep in sleep, his dreams stinking of purity. Stana was not in Brother Warlock's room but I knew well enough what to do, even without her.

Rebecca's gown was of white cotton buttoned demurely to her throat. I sat upon the edge of her bed and slipped quietly into her dreams. We dreamed together through the long dark night.

At the first most distant stirring of dawn in the restless air I unfastened the buttons of her nightdress and pulled the bodice wide. The column of her throat beckoned me from its shadowed hollow to the full curve of her chin. Yet fearing the ravening of that monster, the Dead, even though it grows sluggish within me at the ending of the night, I pressed her wrist, only, to my mouth, content to ease my needle teeth amongst the tendons there. In a moment I had searched out the strong beat of her pulse and filled my mouth at its perfect fountain.

Tuesday night passed in the same way — as did each night for the rest of the week. Remembering Stana's instructions, I interfered more in her dreams, until she came to regard my intrusion there as something natural and desirable. Our dreams were always chaste. It was not until later that I wished to feature as lover and master — for the moment I was content to be her friend.

And I talked. I talked about everything under the sky, promising her such experiences, such wild visions. Her body jumped with anticipation; her heart pulsed with excitement — and yet I was careful to sip at her wrist only.

Tonight, however, I felt it was time to move one step further. As her dreams stilled in the dullest hours of the night I decided to awaken her.

How many times I actually placed my hand upon her shoulder only to pull it back again before she stirred, I cannot tell; but eventually something in me was sickened by this timorous hesitation, causing my long fingers to close on her burning flesh and shake her with unnecessary force. She sprang awake immediately and I felt ripples on the air as her senses expanded around her. "Father?" she whispered — why she whispered I do not know. "Father, is that you?"

Already my will was closing around her, not absolutely, as it had closed around Jane, but strongly enough to hold her. She smelt me first, and that alerted her. Visions of graveyards came into her mind because of the stench of my body. Then she saw some dull light on my face from the uncurtained window. Curve of eye-socket, thrust of cheek-bone, resolute line of jaw. A wing of brindled hair above an ear. I turned a little towards the light — it was as though I could see my reflection red-eyed in her mind. At last recognition came. "Edwin," she breathed.

An avalanche of conflicting emotions came. Love, respect, trust engendered in her dreams. Terror, revulsion, disbelief born of her waking mind. I raised my left hand and rested it on her broad brow, gathering her throbbing temples into finger-roots and thumb-joint. Her mind lost force and power. "Edwin," she said again. Then, "How can it be you?"

But before I could answer she had thrown herself forward, arms about my neck. With my chin pillowed on the muscle at the back of her shoulder I strove to hold back the beast within me while the flame of her body pressed against mine. Such breath as I chose to take fanned her hair as her sighs stirred mine. Warmth drained out of her full flesh and into my chill bones. I felt only that, only that and the burning needles of lust, the joys of coming destruction, a heady sense of victory over a formless good. The first step was taken and there had been no stumbling. She loved me. I took her to the window and let her gaze upon the night. "All this is mine alone," I told her, as though the darkness were some precious jewel, "but I have awoken you so that you may share it with me. I am King here. I want you as my Queen."

For the rest of the night I told her, while awake, what I had promised her in dreams. This time her face shone, her dark eyes glowed with the thought of it. Then I led her back to her tumbled bed. "Tomorrow night," I told her as I raised her wrist for the last time to my mouth, "we will begin a little Odyssey upon the ocean of the night."

My lips moved upon her burning flesh. A moan whimpered almost silently far in the back of her throat. At that passionate sound my gums burst aflame. I fought the monster down. Shaking as though with fever I placed her arm beside her body on the bed. She slept immediately. I was crouched over her when the door burst open. In the twinkling of an eye the Dead had whirled me away into the safety of the shadows.

Mr. Gore's head came round the door. "Rebecca?" he whispered. "Rebecca, are you all right? I thought I heard . . ."

His voice trailed away as he saw by the light from the open door that she was asleep. He stood in silence for some moments, his eyes probing the darkness beyond her. Perhaps he sensed my presence. Certainly the stench of his fear was strong about him. His hand brushed the light-switch, faltered, and dropped to his side. He turned and walked away down the bright corridor as if all the weight of the world was resting on his shoulders.

(iii)

On Monday night the vicarage door was bolted and barred. Faintly but potently on the blackwood was marked a cross in holy water. The old man thought he could keep me away . . . My laughter was lost amid the chimes of midnight as I went round to the side of the house where the ivy glowed, winter-dull, but strong against the brick. In a moment I was outside Rebecca's bedroom window. She paced restlessly in the room, not yet undressed for bed. She wore a black polo-necked pullover against which the silver crucifix upon her breast caught the light mockingly. There was a stench of sanctity, as though prayers had been said in the room. The window also was barred against me with more holy water. "Rebecca!" I called to her with my mind.

Her pacing stopped. She looked fearfully at the window but saw only the night. I called her again. Her will rose. Something in her forbade her to listen to me, but when I called her the third time it died.

Without further thought, she crossed her arms upon her stomach, fingers to the waistband of the pullover, and with one sensuous movement she lifted it over her head. The silver cross and chain became entangled in the woollen folds and were cast aside. Then, bare-breasted, she crossed to the window. She used a hand-towel to mop up the water from the sill and threw the window wide. Immediately I was in, forming out of a tall column of darkness behind her.

She turned back towards me, shivering suddenly in the icy night air. The church clock intoned the half-hour. I held out my hand and the last of her resistance crumbled as she accepted it. I said, "Dress quickly. We have much to see."

Our path took us past the churchyard. We stood outside the wrought-iron fence and I passed my hand before her eyes so that she would see as Stana and I saw. The mist billowed up above the frosted ground. The graves lay in neat rows, trim, well-tended, full. A rat crept from the splintered corner of a tomb. A breath of wind set the mist to rolling like a strange sea. From the grave nearest to us there suddenly thrust a dead white hand, clawed and clawing. Another. Arms like sticks. A face like a skull half covered with grey clotted clay and ill-tanned leather. Rebecca turned away, revolted. Another and another rose, mindless horrors capable only of echoing the wind and stumbling a few yards from their resting-places. Neither cursed nor damned, I told her, too insignificant to warrant anyone's attention. Pity warred with her revulsion, a lingering vein of humanity. I recognised it, but it was a stranger to me. What sort of a sickly power would care for these? I thought. "This is what you may expect from life after death, my dear, in spite of all *their* cant!" I gestured up at the quiet church. "They are things of no account. Come," I said, and led her onwards.

I took her then to my house. I showed her this place, my lair, the chair and desk I have moved down here so that I can keep my journal of the night. I showed her this book itself and read her some passages from its crowded pages. I showed her my narrow bed, saying, "It does not look much, I know. And yet what else is there to look forward to?"

I took her through the hall, past the stinking wreck of Burke at the stair's foot, and up to see my Jane, bloated now almost beyond recognition. "That is the best you can hope for," I told her, leading her out into the night.

Tuesday night found me picking my way easily through Gore's ineffective maze of charms. I took her to the Broken Woods, to the circle made of stones. There was an oddly confused reaction to these things in her mind. Writing it down now, it strikes me more forcefully than it did then. She knew the place well enough and the half-buried, mossy stones of the Dunmow Round, scarcely more than ankle-high but all aglow with occult power. Folk memories danced vividly and erotically as she recalled rituals once held here. Behind these memories, strongly associated with them, was her fear of madness and the curse of the Dead which she had for so long sought to escape. But underlying all, so deep and devious as to be almost invisible, there lurked another drive, the strongest by far. A drive not wholly Rebecca's own. At the time, when the Dead was strong in me, I hardly paid it any attention. Now in the dawn when the Dead is weak I am more disturbed.

But it was not the stones alone which were my object. I took her to the pit which had been hollowed by the power of the Dead as it fought the Roman Ritual through Stana and myself. I lowered her through the cleft stone down into the passage, slipped down behind her and we walked to the chapel. A sort of revelation overcame her when she opened the door and saw inside. Breathless with wonder and growing passion she studied the walls, craning her head back to follow the paintings to the pointed roof. Abruptly, she took me by the hand and led me to the altar. She climbed upon it and lay back, extending her neck and throat. Then, like the couples on the walls, she writhed as I drank at the bright thrusting fountain of her life.

The next night, Wednesday, presented even more spells to forbid my entrance to her room, but still, for all Gore's senile cunning, they proved ineffective. His defences were half-hearted and without pattern or force. He had meant to await my arrival himself armed with some paltry protection, but he had gone to sleep kneeling at his bedside.

Rebecca wore a nightgown woven of pure white silk completely apt to my purpose, for I had come to baptise her. She lay still as death but when my fingers brushed her forehead her eyes sprang wide and her lips parted in invitation. Deep rhythmic breathing surged in her throat and she writhed slowly in an excess of desire.

"Sit up," I ordered. She obeyed immediately, thrusting herself erect, her back straight, hands folded and pressed into her lap. I sat half turned towards her on the edge of the bed. In some distant part her mind suddenly exploded into absolute terror. As I controlled it, my fingers brushing the hair away from her face, her cheek rubbing sensuously against my hand, I was moved for a minute to self-recrimination. The power of the Dead hid it well from whatever vestiges of humanity still remained in us, but the woman and I both knew, somewhere deep in our hearts, the true horror of what I was doing to her. I was taking a creature of light and life, of joy and mortality, and making from it a monster like myself. And, for all the deluding passions of power, a monster is what I knew myself to be. A thing that rational creatures, whether of no account like Gore, or capable of wielding power like Warlock, must loathe and condemn. I was the leper infecting his most dearly beloved so that I might not be lonely in my obscene damnation.

And this was the moment for such thoughts, while there was still time. The blame was not mine that I was what I was: and from that a whole dreadful sequence of events must follow. Yet now, now the step I was taking was new, and newly vile . . . But the power of the Dead, like a thunder-cloud over the moon, effortlessly rode down my stunted conscience. I smiled, feeling my lips stretch over my fangs. Her chin rose fractionally, her eyes opened, heavy-lidded, and her throat was offered. "Not yet," I told her, "later. First it is your turn."

Slowly I pulled my tie off and began to unbutton my shirt. A second or two was sufficient time to open it fully, revealing my lean chest, ridged with ribs and forested with rough black hair. Only down the very centre of my breastbone did the flesh gleam dully. Rebecca's eyes rested here, entranced. I rested the long curved yellow claw of my left index finger at the hollow of my throat. For a moment it remained there, then it began to move downwards, the edge of the talon parting the dead skin and flesh as efficiently as any razor. Cold blood came, pale and thin. I took her by the back of the neck and pressed her mouth to it. As she sipped like a kitten from a bowl of milk, my fingers unloosed buttons at the back of her nightgown. By the time I had them all undone her mouth was at my throat. The wound was healed beneath her lips. Her eyes glowed with a new light. Her breathing was raucous — she had become a thing compounded entirely of lust, and this was the time to answer her desire with my own.

The final stages of Stana's ritual were simple. I must show her the beauties of my state so, for the next two nights, as the old man snored obediently in his room, I led her out again. She no longer needed to change out of her long nightgown. She no longer felt the cold. My power over her was so strong that she might already have been dead. Looking through her eyes I saw it all anew, and the dizzy joy of it washed over me once more. It was all too beautiful — how I longed to destroy it.

Street-lamps soared around us, elegant curves of bright blue power exploding into their dazzling brightnesses like sky-rockets frozen. All around us, fine indigo nets of cables sparkled. People and animals made her catch her breath with the beauty of their living as they hurried past.

When the village was quiet I led her up the still, dead ribbon of the road to the Broken Woods. The faint phosphorescence of winter-dead fields called to her with soothing beauty. The tall trees clothed in green fire made her laugh with joy. Even in this season there was some life here. I caught her a dull-burning rabbit. Together we tore its flesh and drained it.

Now there is only the final part of the ritual to be performed. The time is not quite right. I will kill her on a night of power; when, I do not yet know. She lies there now upon her distant bed. If I wish it she will open her eyes and I will see through them. She is mine now utterly. I sit here, sated — for I have drunk her blood and used her to the full — keeping my dark nocturnal at my desk in Jane's cellar while the sky begins to lighten. My body does not need to be with hers any more. Even should oceans part us I can touch her with my mind. Wherever she is, or will be, ever, I can feel her, hold her, see what she sees, know what she knows. She will do what I tell her instantly and without question. While still she is a creature of flesh, until I grant her the final power, I am the puppet-master and she the puppet. We are utterly and completely one.

Saturday Night 22/23 December:

FINAN'S EVE

Finan's Eve is the Winter Solstice, Lucy's Day, Midwinter. The day has seven hours and the night seventeen. No sooner had the sun set behind flat, slate clouds than I was up and about. Long before the street-lamps could surge into life, when even the old man Gore would still be awake, I stood before the blackwood vicarage door. It was bolted, blessed, and would not yield to me. I tried to form with my mind the cavernous hall so that I might enter there as I had exited my grave so long ago. All I saw was a bowl of holy water and a prayer. Laughing at this dogged repetition of his aged folly I proceeded to look in at the windows. All were sealed against me. There were more prayers. White wafers. Water. In Rebecca's room there were strings of garlic and a terrible excess of worship.

She lay still and sleeping on the bed, her night has become the day, and her day the night. But she was bound down and protected. A new hand here: someone who knew the Dead for what it is. Even before I saw him I had guessed who it would be. Rebecca's bedroom door opened. Brother War-lock came in and sat on the edge of her bed. Gore entered also, dark-eyed and bowed with fatigue. Warlock said, "Sunset." They both looked fearfully at the window.

I could not see Rebecca clearly for the rituals forbade the entry of even my mind into the room, but I knew well enough now she would look — pale and languorous upon the sheets. To the men's eyes sick unto death; to my eyes more beautiful than ever.

"Thank God you're back, John," whispered Gore. "This thing has grown terribly since the Roman Ritual. I had given up all hope for her."

"No," commanded Warlock. "You must never give up hope, Hugh. With God's help she will come through."

"But you have not seen the new power of this Hellish obscenity, John. I warn you, have a care. Each night for the last week I have laid out the charms exactly as you suggested and waited up myself, but each night it has come regardless and taken her. My flesh is too weak, John. My flesh and my faith . . ."

"No, Hugh. Do not doubt your faith. I have been trained to this for many years and practised the rituals all over the world, but even I have never come across an evil such as this. How such a power has been allowed to escape from the Pit, I can hardly imagine, but we can only pray faithfully for sufficient strength to chain the beast again."

"I am frightened, John. Not only for my daughter. I am terrified for my very soul."

161

"So am I, Hugh. I am fearful for all of us. God send us grace. And power."

"Amen."

Rage came, that they should stand in my way. Thunder rumbled in the clouds. *Rebecca!* I called silently, battering with all the power of my mind against all the walls of prayer and magic. Faintly and at a great distance I felt her stir.

"John! I think she is waking up."

"Yes. The night is upon us." There was the sweetest sound of terror in his voice.

Rebecca! I called again, summoning all my monstrous strength. She sat up, but her eyes remained fast closed. "Dear God," whispered Gore. "It is summoning her. Even through your prayers and spells, John. It can reach out its foulness and she will answer it!"

Come to me! I ordered, and she began to move, swinging her legs off the bed, placing her feet on the floor. "*John!*" choked the old man, such agony in him that I nearly howled with joy. But then Warlock took her, whispering some foul prayer. I felt my grasp upon her slipping. "Here," whispered the white wizard, "drink this". Something was pressed to her lips. I heard her teeth chime against silver and I lost her.

"God!" she screamed, her shrill voice filling the room like the most sickening stench, "God help me! Father! Brother John! Give me strength! I don't want to die! Daddy, Daddy, I don't want to die."

"Hush, my child!" The old man enfolded her in her arms and half carried her back to bed. "With the Lord's help we will come through. Hush now, go to sleep."

"Oh Daddy, it is so horrible. Oh dear God!"

"Hush now, Rebecca. Save your strength."

"Let us pray," said Brother Warlock. He came towards the window, his suspicion like a hot wind upon my face, but he did not see me there. He turned his back, broad shoulders blocking the room from my sight, and the three of them filled the night-time with the terrifying volume of their worship.

Anger bitter in my throat, I climbed down and began my search again. No door would open to me. At first it seemed that all the windows also had been sealed with spells, but then I found that the window of a cellar, its sill at ground level behind a rosebush, had been forgotten. At my insistence it began to open, my will upon the rusty hinges like oil. In a moment or two I slid through it and dropped like a shadow to the floor.

Sensing nothing untoward, guided by hate and thwarted desire, I crossed the little basement room and mounted the steps. Silently, again at my will, the door swung open and with the merest whisper of sound I walked into the hall. Facing the stairs, I closed the door by leaning back against it with my shoulders. The place was heavy with holy magic. I felt as though I had suddenly walked into a stifling tropical storm. Bowls of water gave off their steamy power. Wafers filled the air with clammy warmth. Everywhere the fetid, overpowering stench of garlic. Crosses everywhere fashioned of wood, silver and iron, filled the place with a thunder of their potency. There was even a sort of fence made of black briars at the foot of the stairs. As soon as I moved the powerful lightning of the spells cracked about me. My hair stirred with fear and yet I *would* go on. Some way or other I would reach Rebecca now. Therefore I strode forward across the hall in spite of everything they had placed there to protect themselves against me. Therefore I fell into their trap.

Suddenly the old man came out of the bedroom along the passage at the head of the stairs. Before I could do anything, his eyes met mine. "Sweet Christ!" he whispered.

I pounced towards him, but my steps faltered even before I reached their briar wall because light caught the great silver cross he was wearing round his scrawny neck. "It is here!" he cried. "Warlock, the thing is here!"

His right hand took the silver and thrust it out before him as he stumbled down the stairs. I staggered back a step or two as it flamed in his hand with dreadful power. Then Warlock too was at the head of the stairs above the old man. He held in his hand a bottle of water and as soon as he saw me he hurled it. I threw myself sideways instinctively, but I was not the target — it shattered against the cellar door, painting across my only escape-route a pattern of brightness whose strength I would not easily overcome.

"I was right," he called to Gore. "It *is* Underhill."

Prayers stumbled into Gore's reeling mind. He nearly choked himself with the silver chain, thrusting his cross at me. But I had no time to consider him too deeply. Warlock had come striding past him, similarly armed. My whole being was trembling with massive rage at their temerity. My eyes burned as never before and on the surfaces of everything facing me, a blood-red light began to glow.

"His eyes," cried Warlock, kicking aside the briars, "do not look at his eyes!"

He caught up a silver bowl and hurled it at me. He was being so careful to avoid looking in my eyes that he missed me entirely. His mind signalled that he wanted help. "Hugh," he cried impatiently. The old man began to approach me slowly. I fell back. Walls gathered behind me. Warlock caught up a cross of wood. Its foot had been sharpened. There was a mallet there also. Gore began to mumble prayers aloud. They closed towards me. My mind reached out in all directions, commanding the children of the night to help, but I feared I was too late.

Then abruptly there came a terrible scream. Rebecca stood at the head of the stairs. The two men turned towards her. I launched myself forward in one desperate dive, my fingers clawing the air as though I might take flight. Even as my scream echoed hers I was standing beside her at the head of the stairs.

"Quick," cried Warlock, but he was already too late. I swept her up into my arms and ran down the corridor. The window at the end was sealed with prayers, and although the sharp glass did not touch me, the prayers cut at me till I screamed as I dived through it into the welcoming night, keeping tight hold upon her as we fell safely to the ground.

In a few seconds of flight we were in my only refuge — Jane's home, and safe for the moment in the hall. But now they knew who I had been in life, it would take them only minutes — as it had taken mad Arthur Allen only minutes — to work out where my lair would lie in death. I began to cast about immediately for some sort of weapon which might stand against them. But they gave me no more time. The front door slammed open. Brightness washed over us, dazzling me. I staggered back, stunned. Warlock's voice bellowed the words of a prayer. He and Rebecca's father each brandishing a length of wood topped by a blazing bundle of oil-soaked rags, advanced into the hall. The men were both festooned with charms and talismans against the power of the Dead. Their words chained me. Warlock had a leather satchel slung across his shoulders. The point of a stake and a mallet protruded from it. Gore's hand moved. Drops of holy water like molten lead rained on my arm, leaving holes in my flesh which smoked.

I turned away and would have raced towards the shadows, but one of them threw a tangle of blackthorn briars which bound my feet and held me. I fell forward, dragging myself across the littered floor to the foot of the dusty stairs. My taloned hands gripped banisters and steps. I began to pull myself up. But Warlock was on me too quickly. He grasped my shoulders and hurled me on to my back.

"Look after Rebecca," he called to the old man. His foot slammed into my belly. "Where is Jane Martin?" he shrieked at me. But I was too far gone in rage even to form words. Screams and hisses and roars bellowed from my throat as though I were some sort of cornered animal.

"Where is she?" he demanded once more. But even had I wished to fling the answer in his face, I could not find the words. For the briefest instant there was black bitterness in me as I wondered, *What sort of creature have I become if I cannot even speak?*

Warlock threw down his torch upon the tiles and lurched forward, his knees crashing into my arms, pinning them. His hands went to the satchel, to the stake and the wooden mallet. He began to pray again as he removed the engines of my final destruction. On the other side of the hall the old man was only just able to restrain his daughter as I summoned her to my aid with all the power I could muster. I was not strong enough to overcome the rituals and spells, or the force of a loving father's arm, but the Dead in me overcame something else.

In the blackest moment of my rage, I heard something moving in the shadows. A shambling step behind Warlock: he did not hear it. A floorboard creaked upstairs. He did not care. He had the stake out now. The head of the mallet was caught in the lining of his bag. Another step behind him in the shadows. Another. The mallet came free. He reared erect, his mouth drowning me in a wild torrent of prayer. Our eyes met, his aflame with fervour and victory. He did not fear my gaze now. The point of the stake rested on my chest. The mallet swung up and back to the full stretch of his arm. His whole body tensed to drive it down . . .

. . . and the right hand of Richard Burke closed upon it, while his left arm, too bloated to bend properly, swung ungainly round the Brother's neck. Dead for weeks, he had yet been summoned to my aid. The faceless horror of his head caught the light for a moment, as his back straightened. It was a haphazard mess of putrid flesh. Then Warlock was lifted from me. Burke's dead muscles began to crush the life out of him. He struck back wildly with the stake. I tried to free my legs but the black thorns sliced my fingers, threatening to entangle them also. I looked around. Rebecca hung fainting in the arms of her father. Both were on their knees, the old man white as candlewax, watching Warlock's grim battle. Rebecca could not help me. And still I could not free myself.

I writhed, screaming in agony and frustration. Then, softly, a hand fell on my shoulder. White bloated fingers comforted me. Jane. She came down another step, her body massively swollen, her gait uneasy, for she could hardly bend her dropsical legs. She moved completely into the light of the torch on the ground. Gore gave a choking sound, dropped his flaming torch, and slumped forward unconscious. And at last Warlock had gained some inkling of what he might be fighting.

His eyes bulged. I could see his mind begin to crumble. He drove his stake in one more time and Burke's dead grip broke. Warlock sprang to his feet and swung to face his adversary. Burke, the stake through his chest, took one last convulsive step and crashed to his knees. As he finally toppled forward, the whole foul semi-liquid ooze which had been contained in the cavern of his skull burst forth and cascaded down upon the priest.

Warlock's reason snapped then. He staggered back, turned and fled, trailing a wild scream behind him. Burke's corpse rested on all-fours for a moment, shaking its empty head as though slightly puzzled, then it slumped slowly to the ground and lay still.

My feet came free. Jane looked up at me out of the blind, crusted sockets of her eyes, then subsided on to her right side. I rose, kicked her unresisting hulk aside, and ran across towards Rebecca. As I approached she began to stir and the movement roused her father. He saw me towering above him, my tall silhouette black as the night. He whimpered and began to crawl backwards, flushed with the red glow of my eyes.

He was beneath my interest. I turned away and raised Rebecca to her feet. This simple gesture was enough to halt the old man's flight. "In God's name," he yelled, imbued with new strength, "in God's name I bid you . . ." He grasped my shoulder, swung me round and waved his silver cross in my face.

But the full power of the Dead was upon me now, as it had been in the moment it overcame the Roman Ritual. My left hand closed even upon that most powerful of talismans and wrenched it from the old man's grasp. "Dear God!" he choked.

His feverish hands found a bottle of holy water. I carelessly knocked it aside. Overcome, he fell to his knees then, and held up before his face the white disc of a communion wafer blessed, no doubt, by the Archbishop himself. "Our Father," mumbled his terror-slackened lips, "which art in Heaven . . ."

Delicately, as any child prophesying love with a flower, I plucked the wafer from his fingers and crushed it into dust.

When I took him by the shoulders, he was actually crying. "No," he pleaded, the depth of his terror making him say it gently, as though to the child of a friend. I lifted him to his feet. There were no more prayers, no more crosses, wafers, garlic, silver or holy water. Only his flesh stood between me and his blood, and that was old, and tired, and very thin.

His daughter stood and watched me while I emptied his body. As his life-force died I turned to her and pressed my lips to hers so that her mouth was filled from my mouth with the last of her father's blood. Then we collected everything in the house that would burn readily, and piled it in the hall. We moved my narrow bed and this journal out into the garden. Finally I hurled her father's still smouldering torch into the pile we had made.

Long before we had reached the vicarage, where I had decided now to make my home, the flames from Jane's house were staining the sky with crimson.

STANA'S CHILDREN

Of course, Saturday's local newspapers were full of the fire and the tragic deaths of Miss Jane Martin, Dr. Richard Burke and the Reverend Hugh Gore, together with the mysterious disappearance of Brother John Warlock.

Rebecca had been disturbed early on that morning. She was, naturally enough, distraught at the news, but, no, thank you, she really did not wish a policewoman or any kind neighbour to keep her company. There would be much to do, yes: she would contact her family's legal advisers after Christmas. In the meantime, having given a statement to the police, she would prefer to be alone.

She spent much of the rest of the day fighting off well-wishers and one to two reporters. Late in the afternoon, just as I was rising from my narrow bed in one of the vicarage cellars, I heard her sudden laughter. I found her up in her mother's library, reading the doggerel which was the folk-memory of the words used by Stana to curse the Gore family:

> Women of blood, look to blood,
> Make of blood your bread.
> Feed on blood until your blood
> Feeds the Dead.

There was real joy in her laughter. The curse was worked out at last — but with none of her mother's madness. No horrors touched her now: only the weird joy of eternity. As she stood before me I searched through her mind for traces of sadness but there were none. She had been sufficiently educated in our dark ways for there to be no loss — least of all the death of her father — that could touch her.

The weekend passed in a distant bustle of activity. The whole village seemed to visit her at one time or another, their petty minds brushing the feather-ends of my sleeping consciousness. How was it that none of them suspected anything? The whole community should have been restlessly alert. Deep within me, I found their childlike innocence disturbing. Surely some race-memory, some collective unconscious should have warned them what was in their midst? The unsettling coincidences of the accident at Rebecca's New Year's party, the change in Underhill, the arrival of Warlock, the murder of Theresa Potter and her lover, Underhill's suicide, the change in Jane Martin, the disappearance of Andrew Royle, the deaths of Margaret Allen and her mother, the disappearance of Allen himself, strange doings in the Broken Woods, and now three more deaths. And Brother Warlock still to be accounted for . . . Surely someone must have suspected something?

But no. People today are far too sensible. How much more wise had been their forebears of four centuries ago. They had realised what was happening in their midst. But even Gore, who should have known so much better, had looked upon their ruthless self-defence as ignorance and blasphemy. How willing had been even Underhill, caught in the very middle of it all, to discredit the last strong barriers which superstition might have built. Oh, brave new world that has such sensible people in it.

On Sunday the vicar of Great Dunmow came over to hold services in Gore's church. He told Rebecca how well she looked, considering. In his mind, however, there was the deepest trepidation. She looked so thin and wan, and pale as death.

Ah, but at night, the sickly listless day creature was replaced by my vibrant, joyful companion. Stana's plan continued to work itself out surely and perfectly. We fed on each other's coldness. We used each other, passionlessly but to excess, as her senses died like mine and fulfilment became more and more elusive. The night was a dark shell around us during those haunted hours, as we extended the strength of our flesh and consumed each other, wildly, intemperately, madly. How our desire would have ended I cannot guess, had not tonight brought what it has.

After a day made oppressive even in my deep lair by Christmas and by the endless troupe of sympathisers and well-wishers about the house, I rose exactly on the point of sunset. The last old lady had been ushered away without an offer of tea, and Rebecca sat, dark-eyed, bone white and on the edge of collapse in the quiet, dusty lounge. Her hair was in untidy rat's-tails, her cheeks had collapsed. The skin strained on cheekbones and stretched like tissue over jaw-line. Even her lips were thin and colourless. Then I touched her.

At once she sprang to life. Her eyes were deep and sparkling. A delicate colour suffused her flesh. Her hair became glorious, alive with red highlights. She rose and stretched like a cat. She yawned and suddenly her lips were full, her teeth, pale and sharp as the teeth of a cat, glistened in her coral mouth. The points of her breasts thrust passionately against the black wool of her dress. "Was I asleep?" she asked, her voice deep and vibrant.

"Almost."

"All those old women." She shuddered with the simple luxury of one observing a fate which can never befall her. "And they all say the same thing: so boring. 'How will we exist without the dear vicar?' 'What will we do for comfort.' 'Where will we go now for understanding?' All selfish, concerned only with how his absence upsets them or their little plans!"

Her mouth twisted in contempt. As she spoke of them, so for a moment I could feel them, the whole village, bustling around, each one self-importantly centred on his own little actions. The families of them, mothers, fathers, children, centred on the getting of gifts, on feeding, on drinking. Napier and his family above his butcher's shop, Grant the greengrocer sharing the evening with widowed Mrs. Browne above the papershop, he the more nervous. Pride the haberdasher with his unruly brood. Morris and his family above the farm-supply shop. Seven more in the dining room of the sexton's cottage, and all within a few hundred yards. Nearly a hundred more within the mile south across the village. Potter, recovered from the death of his daughter, is doing extra business at the George because of the notoriety. He has opened specially for the men in from the farms. All of it battered at the edge of my consciousness, stunning me for a moment with the sheer contemptible industry they put into being alive. Like ants teeming about a nest.

Then Rebecca said, "Look at me! I must get out this! Black is all very well for you, but I must have colour. Green! I will never wear anything but green."

"Green is bad luck," I said, uneasily. "The faery colour."

"Nonsense," she chided lovingly. "What have we to do with luck?"

After six we ventured out. The streets were quiet. The darkness had long since ceased to be clear crystal blue, and was at the moment thick under a heavy overcast sky. We walked through the village. I watched them hungrily behind bright windows beyond the flames of their Christmas trees. Never had the village seemed so close and vital around me. Any of the hastening little candles of life still abroad on the streets who chanced to brush close to our cold hunters' senses paused, surprised that the darkness should so disturb them on Christmas night, and then hurried on, not looking back. We walked south while I savoured Dunmow Cross like a hundred grains of salt on the back of my long tongue, then, opposite the black shell of Jane's house, we turned and retraced our steps.

It was after seven when we reached the skeletal trees of the Broken Woods. A movement in the shimmering undergrowth caught Rebecca's eye. Her hands closed on my hand and I turned. Something was indeed there for a second, and then it was gone. Not a rustle, not a footfall, not a breath.

The woods remained silent about us as we prowled. At last our aimless steps led us to the Dunmow Round. Here too there was stillness, but a stillness tense with expectancy, as though every shadow were a panther set to spring. The pit beckoned to us so we scrambled down its side, the woman leading me. She dropped first into the tunnel and stood silently as I followed. I thought we would go to the chapel but Rebecca turned the other way. "Where does it lead?" she demanded.

When I shrugged she was off at once up a slight slope, past a crest and down again along the narrow twisting passage. I followed her along the dusty flags, brushing away the cobwebs and roots which hung in profusion from the roof. After a few yards the stale air became heavy with a strange smell which I did not recognise until too late, for it was an odour foreign to me now for many, many months. The aroma of cooked meat.

At the end of the tunnel was a huge stone wall, blackened but solid. We paused. I would have turned back, but my companion suddenly threw all of her weight against one side of it, and it slowly began to grate open. "It's a door!" she exclaimed, her voice made guttural with the effort she was making to move it. "Help me. We'll open it!"

The smell of smoke lay on the still air and all at once I knew where the doorway would lead to. "No," I said, and would have turned away, but I was too late.

Rebecca gave a final convulsive heave and the stone swung fully open. Beyond it, was only darkness. Even my eyes could not probe the shadows, and so I paused. Rebecca did not. Her body followed the motion of the great stone door and she was gone into the cellar of Coul Hall, where the Dead had slept her days away in her great stone coffin, and where her children had been staked and piled around the walls.

No sooner had Rebecca and I entered the ash-filled chamber than there was light. I do not know where it came from, for I was too intent upon what it illuminated. More like bundles of wood than ever, the children were still piled round the walls. The heat of their burning had destroyed many, but others, more tightly packed perhaps, had survived — black, shrivelled, ill-formed. In the middle of this chamber Stana stood.

"My Lord, my Lady," she said, almost mockingly, "I bid you welcome. You must not mind my children." She flickered like a tall green star, the glow of her mounting power almost equal now even to the flame of Rebecca's fading life. "My children fear and envy such as you," she continued, gesturing to the roasted horrors piled against the walls. "So do we all. Fear your power and envy your *flesh*."

I thought I saw hatred in her as she said it. Her words flowed on like water. She directed our attention again to the burned corpses of the long-dead children. They looked like bundles of black rags loosely wrapped around twisted sticks of varying length. Some were surmounted by pocked black melon heads. "These of course are of no account now," she persisted. "They are like all good children, to be seen but not heard." I thought there was great sadness, in her voice, but she rounded upon us then so that her voice, had it actually moved on the the air like a human voice born of a muscled and gristled larynx, might have filled the room and echoed.

She gestured at our bodies with her unsubstantial, ghostly hand. "But you — " she cried, "you both have homes, castles, a safe refuge. How much more power can you exercise when you do not have to use so much spectral energy simply to *exist*!"

Rebecca had already grown impatient: I had put the blood of the beast into her veins and now it burned to be assuaged. She caught at my arm, turned her back on Stana, and without another word we left the burned-flesh stench of the place and followed the passage back down towards the chapel. Behind us Stana could be heard singing, for her children perhaps, a lullaby of hate.

I took Rebecca's hand in mine and led her in to the underground chapel. Everything in that strange place was as we had left it. We threw our clothing on the altar and there we made our bed.

She fed at my breast blood again, long and languorously, as a prelude to our copulation. When she fell back at last, she had drawn an excess of strength and passion from the night and from such cold blood as she had sucked from me. She was a fury to be ridden, controlled, mastered, in a battle which neither could lose or win, the waging of which was its own object. Tooth and claw we used, shouting our agonies and barren ecstasies. At one time I was master, then she — rising above me like a wild succubus.

But finally, at our last and cruellest coupling, when the most perfect ecstasy was frenziedly, futilely demanded, there had to be a further passage of blood. She lay beneath me, her hair afire with lust, her face — to my strange eyes which could not see water, pocked with perspiration, hollow eyes wild and red. The edge of the altar came across the back of her neck and she threw her head back, laying open to my burning lips the pale column of her throat. What more natural then for me that, as I thrust for the last time, I should lean down to slide my razor fangs into the waiting flesh? And what more natural also, since I had weaned her to it with such infinite care, that she should throw her ecstatic arms about my head to hold it there?

The blackness swirled in my mind as deadened nerves almost brought me to climax. Her cries fled from my ears. The only sensation my body held was the brushing of my

173

needle teeth against the pulsing pipe of her artery. This was enough for me. Then her body allowed her one last shudder of fleshly ecstasy, and the arms behind my neck spasmed as her thighs rose beneath me. Thus, as she cried aloud again, the walls of the artery in her neck were split apart and her life sprang boiling into my mouth.

The ground shook around us. At the moment of her death the earth quaked. Nerves ran from my arched spine to every corner of the land. In that instant when her life throbbed under my lips and was gone I felt the land of Britain spasm and shake with her. *We* have done this, I thought. Our power is such that when she dies the earth quakes.

After a while I raised my head. Realisation of what I had done slowly came to me. Her head rolled to one side, a dead weight now, no longer at her command. How can I describe my feelings? Horror at first. Bitterness. Black rage. And yet what *had* I done? I had completed the final stage of Stana's plan. It was inevitable, after all. In order to join me as my eternal consort, Rebecca had to die. Wearily I climbed down from the altar and began to dress myself.

Then, with equal care I dressed my quiet lady. I gathered her up gently and carried the feather's weight of her out into the passage. A moment later we were back in the Broken Woods. In the centre of the Dunmow Round, my lips on her throat once more healed the wounds my fangs had made. Not even the most thorough autopsy would reveal how she had died now. The darkness cloaked me as I took her home. No one saw the tall black figure with the girl's corpse like a twisted rag across his arms, flitting from shadow to shadow. The church clock struck the half-hour of some small hour as I carried her across the green. I laid her cold corpse down beside her front gate, on the ground where it would be found in the dawn, then I returned to my narrow bed where it lies, here in its small cellar room which no one ever enters. I sat myself down beside it at a massively long oaken table, stored here for numberless years, and took up my pen, and this my journal of the night.

THE PIT

In the dawn when the monster within me is weakest sometimes I say to myself, Edwin Underhill did not die of gas. Jane returned and found him unconscious, his mind utterly destroyed. He is now committed to an institution for the criminally insane. He sits in a corner, semi-comatose, unaware of the passage of days. In his mind, in his mind *only*, his body is a vampire, host to the Dead. He has not risen from the grave and haunted the night. He has never sucked blood. There has been no death for Jane, Burke, Gore, Rebecca, the rest. There was no earthquake in England on Christmas night.

These things are all impossible.

Today as I lay sleeping I saw, as vividly as if I had been standing at the graveside, Rebecca's funeral. There was an air of desolation amongst the little congregation. They were poignantly aware of the tragedy: first mother, then father and daughter, dead like the Allen family. Afterwards, as they trailed away from the silent graveyard, I heard them agreeing sanctimoniously amongst themselves that it had been a terrible year for Dunmow Cross, almost as if some obscure curse were working itself out. Miss Simcox, bulked out against the cold by her best black funeral coat, shook her head as she lingered beside the raw earth mound, thinking of the coroner's courtroom where she had first heard the doggerel curse:

> Women of blood, look to blood,
> Make of blood your bread.
> Feed on blood until your blood
> Feeds the Dead.

Who — what — are the Dead? she wondered, and she looked around at the grey gravestones, as if expecting to see us waiting there to feed on her blood. Then she shivered, thrust her hands deep into her overcoat pockets and walked off laughing. But there was no humour in the laughter.

As the sun finally set, I sprang out of my narrow bed and moved out into the evening. In Jane's garden, undamaged by the fire or the firemen, the black-boughed bush that grew out of the stake stood stark against the scorched wall, its blossoms like great splashes of blood against the brick. I reached out carefully, selecting the stoutest of the branches. It felt cold and firm under my hands. There was power in it, but no bright surge of life, even though it was in full bloom for the second time this year. When I tore the limb away, the sap in the tear-shaped wound on the stem was red and thin.

I took my offering up to the graveyard. All the mourners were gone. Wreaths and bunches of flowers were piled on the bare brown earth. I kicked them away and laid my branch — three feet of it, straight, strong and laden with flowers — along the length of ground under which Rebecca's body lay. I stayed for a moment, eyes closed, head bowed, listening to her as she writhed beneath me and screamed in the coffin, experiencing the first panic moments of her re-birth. Eventually, I knew, she would appear out of a column of mist at the grave's head to be dazzled by the explosive glories of the night. I lingered only a few seconds, then walked away into the busy bustle of the village.

My head was a dizzy swirl of hopes and fears. The greater my emotion, the greater was my fight to hold the Dead still. Have patience, I told it. In a little while we will have a consort, a partner, a mate, and we will go hunting together like grey wolves in the night. We would take the country by the throat, find ourselves slaves to serve us, like Jane, mindlessly in all things. Such passion rose in me that I almost howled out loud. The Dead was like a force too great for my body to contain. I felt that I would explode.

When Rebecca would come to me I did not know, but I knew where she would look for me and I knew I should be there when she did come. I wandered on, slowly retracing my steps. Although she must acclimatise to the night on her own, she would come to me after that. She would come to me as her creator, consort, lover and master. The church reared over me again, the bright clock-face showing some unremembered hour. She would not rise until the streets were empty. I passed the black wrought-iron graveyard fence, looking across the misty ground. Her screams had quietened. I turned away and went towards the Broken Woods. I walked amongst the tall green flames of the trees. Many hours passed. The night drew in, thickening the air. Clouds rolled down from the icy north. A wind moaned. Distantly it bore the sounds of merriment as the creatures of Dunmow Cross wound up towards the celebrations of the New Year. I strolled back towards the vicarage, remembering this last week when I have wandered aimlessly abroad, waiting for the funeral, waiting for Rebecca.

The sky seems never to have varied during these nights — it has been overcast, always threatening rain. If the streets of the towns where I wandered were individually dazzling or dark, the clouds remained always bright. To my sensitive eyes, the dust in each invisible droplet that made up the great misty masses, caught and reflected the light from below, multiplying it until the whole sky always seemed to contain lightning. There was a wind from the north-east, wet and cold as steel, carrying something of the sea over the flat marshes and low banks of East Anglia. This wind, doubly wet with evaporation and the threat of rain, actually attained form, as though it carried a black mist within it beneath the strangely blazing clouds.

This vision remained with me, the sinister dead black fog sweeping towards me. No matter where I was, abroad or in my narrow bed, it came towards me and covered me.

It was with me tonight, as I paced restlessly in the bright hall of the vicarage. My mind strayed outside the walls of the old house, impatient for knowledge of my creature, questing, alone, defenceless. Suddenly a great spear of ice seemed to pierce my head. My hands came like white spiders clutching across my temples. A wall struck me on the back. I fell to my knees, and in my agony, the Dead took over, dragging me upright and unleashing such a fire of rage in me that the spear melted away and the agony in my mind faded. With the beast still in control, I raged through the house looking for the source of this unexpected attack, but there was nothing. Every nerve agonisingly alert, I finally fell back into an armchair downstairs. The wind began to whimper. The villagers' revelry continued in the distance. And in the graveyard something stirred.

As vividly as the spear of ice, a vision of the cemetery rose before me. The mist writhed tidally amongst the grave-stones. A column of darkness rose erect in the centre of the place and stood there, trembling with power. I stood up immediately and crossed to the window, looking down towards the church. The mist was there, black to my eyes, enveloping the tombs and gravestones. The clouds broke open and there was a little moonlight to make the marble monuments glisten coldly. It seemed to me that there were figures moving amongst them. I was suddenly struck with the feeling that I was in fact among the audience when I had thought I was on stage.

I glanced around, my hackles rising. Something was happening down there to which I was not party. Something of great power and moment, about which I knew nothing.

At the centre of this strange shadowy movement rose the column of darkness and even as I watched, it fell away to reveal a pale figure standing in the moonlight. It turned towards me as though aware of my scrutiny, then it stooped, picked something up, and began to come towards the house. It was Rebecca and she walked like a queen. I moved back, unwilling to be seen waiting like an inferior. Emotion swelled in me and the beast stirred. I quietened it with a promise. Soon now, I told it, soon. I passed through the rooms alone for the last time, as I thought. My hearing stretched beyond the closed door, seeking her footsteps, but there was only the wind bearing excited chatter and laughter from the village. I settled at the foot of the stairs, drawing myself up to full height. If she was coming to me as a queen, I would receive her as a king. The waiting was not long.

The latch on the door moved, the tongue grating out of its socket. The hinges groaned. The door swung inwards and she was there, a flame of power before a wall of darkness. I stood silent. She moved forward, the brightness of her magic suddenly flooding the hall.

"Do you not bid me welcome?" she asked, her voice sweet and heavy on my ears.

"You are welcome . . ." I said. It had been in my mind to greet her by name: Rebecca; but something stopped me. The first icy awareness of the truth.

That this was Rebecca's body I had no doubt — the full

red waves of the hair; the pale vibrancy of the flesh; each curve, hollow and length of her described my lover. But the thrust of her teeth distorted her full, soft mouth. The cheeks were collapsed into dark hollows beneath the cheekbones. Something too fundamental had changed in the blood-red pits of her eyes.

"Am I welcome?" she taunted me. "Am I truly welcome, my little man?" She swept towards me, electric with power, burning with cold evil. I staggered back, stunned. She threw up her head and laughed.

"Stana!" I cried. "What have you done?"

She paused before answering, bringing her right hand forward to show me the bough I had laid on Rebecca's grave. As she answered me, she began to tear the flowers from it and scatter them at her feet until she seemed to stand ankle-deep in blood. "I have returned," she said.

The laughter died in her. Even that poor obscene relative of humour, stilled. She became like fire frozen in ice: utterly calm, utterly still, utterly evil. "I have returned that my will may be done."

I still did not comprehend the full madness of her plans, the evil of them. "But what is your will, Stana?"

"Freedom. Freedom and revenge."

"Freedom from what? Revenge upon whom?"

"Freedom! Can you be so stupid, so ignorant of our ways that you *still* do not understand? With this body . . ." Her hand moved, bringing the black stake she carried down against her thigh with a vicious *crack!* "I now have identity. I now have *power*."

"But how can it be?" I cried. "You are mine. I made you. I took you. I moulded you . . ." I stopped, realising that I was talking, not to Stana, but to Rebecca, who was dead. I had not moulded Stana who stood there, clothed in Rebecca's body. She had moulded me.

My mind began to work then, coldly. If I could not have Rebecca, why, then Stana might do to replace her. "Shall we sit down?" I asked her.

She nodded but I thought I saw the slightest of sneers at my lingering human ways. She followed me into the sitting room. She sat at one end of the settee and drew her legs up until she was curled like a cat, leaning against the arm. Her crimson eyes were on mine. She waited for me to start talking. She was like an animal: absolutely still while you were watching her, moving only when you looked away. Power sat on her pale shoulders as easily as the cold silk of her faery-green dress.

"I came to you for help originally, because I am alone," I said. "I needed . . . *need* . . . a partner. A consort."

"Yes?" Without emotion.

"Will you be that partner?"

There had been little emotion in her from the second she came through the door, but now it exploded with terrible force. "You?" she spat. "Consort to you? If you are sufficiently humble, I might allow you to become my body-slave. You are fit for nothing else. Let me tell you something about yourself: I have controlled you, overseen your every thought and action from the moment a few ounces of your blood gave me a measure of release. You have felt your little surge of power and you think yourself a king. You are *nothing*. I am the Dead and you have never been anything but my *creature*."

I sat, stunned, the meaning of her words terribly at odds with everything I had come to believe about myself, about the Dead.

"What is it that you want then, Countess?" I asked at last.

"What I have wanted for centuries, little Edwin. Things you cannot begin to imagine."

But I could imagine. She had told me once herself. The one thing which had kept her in existence through the four hundred eternal years of total nothingness to which this village had condemned her: revenge. The desire for revenge beyond the bounds of reason, beyond the bounds of human imagination.

I sprang erect, my ears listening for the latest sound from the houses near and far around me. It was not yet midnight, yet strangely their revelry had ceased. The wind brought only the sound of its own wailing. In the houses there was utter silence.

She stood up. Her eyes dwelt on me for a moment, mocking and contemptuous, then she turned and crossed the room to the window. She threw it wide before I could move, and was gone into the greedy throat of the night. In a second

180

I was at the window, my eyes searching for her, but seeing nothing. A sense of terrible danger swept over me then. What monsters could she summon? What madness was she about?

In a matter of moments I had raced through the village down as far as the empty shell of Jane Martin's house, more than a mile from the vicarage. All the houses crowding the sides of the road were ablaze with electric light, but over the whole place hung brooding silence which stirred terror deep within me.

The nearest house on my left belonged to the Fullers. Father, mother, two boys and a girl. They always had a large noisy party on New Year's night. All the windows were bright. The door stood wide. Not a whisper, not a movement stirred. I ran through the dull garden and into the Fuller's cramped hall. There had been people here — I could smell them on the air. The lounge was cluttered with decorations. Glasses, tankards, pint-pots stood on the floor and tables, some still half full of liquor. More than one cigarette still burned in the overflowing ashtrays. A half-eaten sandwich lay on a plate. Upstairs and downstairs, the place was deserted.

Across the road at the Harveys' house the television played quietly to an empty room. The settee before it still glowed with the warmth of bodies recently removed. There was a smell of blood like iron on the air, and of something else which made my hackles rise.

Only in the George was there noise. I crept towards it carefully and looked through the windows before I entered. The bar was completely empty: only the juke-box played raucously, giving the illusion that the place was tenanted.

As I moved on through the empty village, my body grew so tense with its strangeness that I jumped at even the mindless whimpering of the wind and hunched forward, ready to spring into the attack at the slightest stirring of the shadows.

In the gutter outside the dark hulk of the Allens' house I saw the faintest point of brightness. My interest engaged, I crouched like a nervous predator on the prowl. It was the silvery brightness I associated with life. Something there was alive or held the memory of life, some tiny animal lying vivid

181

at the dark curb's foot. As I crept towards it I scented once
again the iron odour of blood and paused. Silence. Stillness.
In the most shadowed part of the street it lay where the
circles of brightness from two street-lamps did not quite
overlap. The tension in me made my flesh crawl. I rushed
out of the darkness to snatch up the bright thing and scuttle
away to safety once more. It was a hand.

Curled in my palm, the fingers perfect and closed, the
nails gleaming, the knuckles dimpled, still glowing with
silvery life was the hand of a small child severed neatly at the
wrist. I threw it away with an exclamation of impatience and
the sinister shadows gobbled it up.

They closed around me then, those shadows, seeming to
teem with evil movement, while I continued to search the
deserted streets. As I reached the top of the village and the
crossroads themselves, I experienced the deep conviction
that if I swung round suddenly, I would find those shadows
creeping up behind me in an unstoppable tide of dark evil.

I cannot adequately describe the horrific tension which
gripped the whole of my body as I moved up above the green
towards the vicarage and the Broken Woods. If the shadows
in the village had seemed sinister, here they bred monsters
beyond imagining. Nor were they silent any longer. They
whispered wickedness and destruction, yet they were utterly
impenetrable — there was nothing *living* in them. They
pressed about me as I went up past the last houses opposite
the green to the church hall, dilapidated and boiling with
darkness. I found that I was walking in the middle of the
road, far from the whispering hedges. Where was Stana?
What was she doing? It required every ounce of the Dead's
dark strength within to force my footsteps farther. The
strangeness of the night closed around me like bars, and
there, beyond the pool of the last street-lamp's shadow
ringed light I froze, caged by terror and the dark.

Then, suddenly, away on my right, came a roar of sound. I
swung round. Beyond the first thin trees, beyond church,
graveyard and garden, the vicarage was ablaze. For an
instant I stood, watching the flames licking up out of the
windows, the smoke already rising from the roof. Then I took
a step towards it.

And a figure burst out of the hedgerow before me, bellow-

182

ing with terror, running in a strange crippled manner. I saw the frog-face of Miss Simcox, strangely scarred with claw-marks. I saw the life-brightness of her made more vivid by her fear. I saw the wicked gleam of the carving knife in her right hand as it rose and fell, slashing at the darkness surrounding her.

I leaped backwards. She blindly staggered past me. At first in my fear I thought it was the shadows themselves which were attacking her, but then my mind cleared and I saw — I saw and shrieked aloud that what I saw might not be so.

Hanging all about her were Stana's children. Given a sort of monstrous life by their mistress, the blackened, crippled, all but limbless creatures, which had lately been piled like wood around the cellar walls, had come crawling out through the door Rebecca opened, along the corridor, out of the pit itself, through the shadows to begin the Dead's revenge.

One of these things — a black torso with stick arms but no legs — was fastened in her neck. Another hung like a bat on her stomach. The carving knife came down, cut through its crumbling, cindered flesh, buried itself deeply in the coroner's own belly, and was jerked up again. At her heels, like lizards, two more scuttled. They had arms to the elbow, legs to the knee, yet they kept pace with her on all-fours, their teeth snapping audibly on the air as she stumbled away into the dark woods, screaming and stabbing, screaming and stabbing.

The sight filled me with a great rage, and freed me from the bars of terror that had been caged around me in the dark. I broke away, and ran into the Broken Woods also. Here I crushed much underfoot — whether it was winter-brittle branches or fire-crisped flesh and bone I do not know. Such was the fury in me that I did not care. The village was *mine* — that she should bring her foul lunacy into *my* lair. The blind strength of the Dead within me rose with irresistible passion. By the time I burst into the circular clearing of the Dunmow Round, rage sat on my shoulders like storm clouds and I could feel the lightning of my power crackle away from my dead flesh to present the whole of my head and torso in a bright avenging aura.

The ground was a seething mat of the children, heaving like the sea. Here a twisted arm, flesh in black rags on stick-bone, would be thrown up, there a head, bald, earless, gaping pits for eyes and nose, hunter's teeth snapping, white against the cindered face. The stench was sweet, overblown, utterly sickening, and the sight so horrible that it was not until a warm rain touched my face that I looked up and saw what the children had done.

Like the picture on the side of the strange altar in the chapel buried below, there were bodies in the trees. The leafless branches of the trees had been torn back to make strong, sharp points, and on to these had been driven every living soul in Dunmow Cross that night. Through breast, belly, groin, head; through back, through front, from side to side; from shoulder to thigh, from fundament to gaping mouth, every one of them reared up there, impaled, and their blood rained down in misty clouds upon the soft night air.

She stood there, drenched from head to foot, the red blood clotting already and crusting about her. She swung to face me as I kicked aside the twisting offal on the ground. "A pretty harvest," she cried, throwing up her arms in a wide gesture at the trees. "Fruit in midwinter!"

She tilted back her head and laughed. Her hair swung, matted solid with blood. It cracked and flaked away from the ghastly flesh of her throat. It broke in a million wrinkles across the thick red mask on her face. Her beautiful face which was Rebecca's.

"And this is your revenge?" I demanded. "This is why you returned?"

"No!" suddenly her laughter died. "This is only the beginning. I will be revenged upon them all. ALL OF THEM."

So simple. So monstrous. All of them. Not all in Dunmow, or all in Essex, or even all in England. Just *all*: simply that. All who had a body while she did not. All who had a soul while she did not. All who had blood while she had none. All who had tears. All who had dreams. All who were alive, when she was not.

And she would do it, if I should let her. I kicked my way through the last of the circle around her. I held up my left hand. The spider-scar upon it blazed. Stana's hands fell to her sides. Her fingers brushed the top of the black stake from Rebecca's grave, driven into the ground by her legs.

"I cannot allow you to do this," I said.

"You're too late to stop me, Edwin. Far too late!"

She launched herself towards me as she spoke. I whirled aside. Her hooked nails whispered past my throat. She landed in a crouch, snarling. I threw myself towards her as she sprang erect and we met claw to claw, fangs bared, shrieking the purity of our hatred. Her head twisted and she went for my throat. My hands closed around her neck, pushing her back to arm's length, out through the circle to the very edge of the trees. She had expected to overcome me by the inhuman viciousness of her attack, but she had forgotten how well one of her own kind would know her. My fingers closed, sinking into her cold flesh. I could never choke her, of course. Even to break her neck would be insufficient. I would have to tear her head off. And this I was set to do. I felt the bones of her neck beginning to part when the man came stumbling out of the woods beside us, chanting in a voice like thunder.

At first I saw only the febrile brightness of his life-force in the corner of my eye and the blaze of his torch as it flared in the wind. Then his black-clad figure appeared, his eyes blazing with madness. In his right hand he held a great golden cross. "Lighten our darkness we beseech thee, O Lord," he was chanting. "And by Thy great mercy defend us from all perils and dangers of the night."

The sight of what he held so close, and the power of his words, caused me to sicken and turn aside. Stana twisted from my grip. I staggered back. The wild man came towards me, his hair flying. I recognised him then: it was Brother Warlock.

"Run, child, run," he shouted to Stana. In his desperation, blind to everything else around him, he saw only Rebecca's body wrestling with me. And I was the vampire.

He thrust the great gold cross closer, until I felt the flesh around my eyes begin to wither. "I have destroyed you," he screamed at me. "I have found out your lair, found out your coffin, your vile resting place, and burned it! Yes, and burned the whole vicarage around it!"

There was foam on his lips as he returned to his prayers.

"Thou shalt not be afraid for any terror of the night . . ." He was mad now himself, raving, but his words like blows to my head, the cross like fire before my eyes. I fell to my knees and then on to my back, wriggling and hissing. He arched over me, his prayers destroying all my strength, ". . . for the pestilence that walkest in the darkness, for the sickness that destroyeth in the noonday."

A hand brightly jewelled with claws came out of the darkness and fastened in his hair. His head jerked round, and he saw her properly at last: her red eyes, her teeth, the blood coagulated on her dead white flesh. And, beyond her, he saw the villagers arrayed upon the trees and her children creeping below them in the sodden grass. His face froze, eyes staring. One thin blue vein throbbed on his forehead. Of course he had yet another prayer — his last which was no longer his armour, but his epitaph.

"My soul is among lions," he cried, wrenching away. He swung around to face the clearing properly. All the children were still. "I lie among the children of men that are set on fire" he raved, and charged amongst them. I pulled myself to my feet. Stana watched him run amongst the little silent bodies. "Whose teeth are spears and arrows and their tongue a sharp sword . . ."

The Dead in the woman finally tired of the sport. She turned to her children and spoke a single, soundless command. The demented man in the midst of the clearing staggered now as small black hands closed on his leg. "They have laid a net for my feet," he howled, his voice breaking.

One of the children reared up, its little face level with his belt-buckle, its little fingers tearing at his breast. The mass of them heaved around him as more of them slithered up through the tunnel and out of the pit in the ground. More hands caught him, more lipless mouths, more little fingers. His movements slowed.

"They have pressed down my soul." He half turned and threw the cross, his last and only defence, at the woman he had come to save. She caught the thing and laughed. In her laughter there stirred such an excess of evil power that all the woods shook. "They have digged a pit before me," whispered John Warlock, defeated at last, falling to his knees, "and I am fallen in."

186

I was on my feet, stealing back, in among the trees. The children fastened on to the man and carried him silently, like ants, across the clearing. As the trees closed around me, I turned, obsessed with the need to go and check whether he had spoken the truth about my resting place, my narrow bed. But Brother Warlock's shrill scream drew me back, appalled, to the edge of the clearing. He was spread across a tree, higher than all the rest. The children hugged at his limbs, weighting them down as he convulsed in his death throes. Stana stood beneath him, her hands raised. He brayed his agony one last time, beyond prayers, and the point of the branch erupted from his black silk shirt-front. A great fountain of blood pulsed out into the air. And Stana stood beneath this scarlet cascade, and her laughter rang against the sky. The dead man convulsed, heels drumming against the tree, hands flapping, head rolling. I turned and left the Hellish place.

The vicarage was indeed ablaze. I stood before it, deafened by the roar of the flames, all but blinded by their massive light. Great billows of smoke carried sparks like shooting stars, whirling up into the sky, Overcome with frustrated rage, I raised my hands, and immediately wind came from behind me, a great gust of it pushing the hated fire back. What was left of the front door gaped. The hall was burned out, a hollow shell where there were no longer any flames. The wind fell. Smoke poured down again. I raised my hand once more, and once more the wind stirred, more forcefully this time, lifting the flames to the upper floors and blowing the smoke away. If I could trust the wind to remain steady, I might risk a moment or two in the hall, perhaps even in the cellar, to see if Brother Warlock had spoken the truth. My shoulders writhed uneasily at the thought of what would happen to me if I had nowhere to hide from the daylight.

The wind blew constantly from the south. Its strength began to increase slowly. As long as the roof-beams held I might risk a quick rush into the vicarage. I paused for only one moment longer as my friend, the south wind, carried the sparks and flames from the blazing house into the woods at the end of the garden and up into the Broken Woods, setting them instantly afire.

Then I was running forward, up the stone path, under the heavy lintel, into the house itself. Above me, the gallery was gone, and the second storey was a great dazzling cave. I looked for a moment at the roots of the flames which roared like a continuous thunder-roll. Sparks and glowing splinters of wood fell around me, my hands constantly busy brushing them away, the beautiful wooden parquet of the flooring had gone, leaving bare black boards that reached out to a ragged edge, torn away, I guessed when the landing and the stairs collapsed. Below, to one side, beyond the rubble, the cellar was relatively undamaged. Without further thought I ran lightly forward and leaped down. The terrible roaring of the flames was quieter here, the constant deadly rain of sparks less heavy, even the air was clearer. I began to search through the rubble. There were shrivelled planks of wood covered with blackened, blistered varnish — so Brother Warlock had not lied: these, then, were the remains of my coffin . . .

Only the old oak table remained and, beneath it on the stone floor, this book, pen still wedged between its pages as a book mark. I bent to pick it up.

Suddenly a great weight crashed into my back. Talons sank into my flesh, fangs stabbed down through my shoulder, grating on bone. The weight of Stana's body and the power of her leap threw us both forward on to the ground. Something clattered away under the table. Her grip broke as she scrambled vainly after it. I rolled wildly on to my back, caught at her hair. Through the gap in the cellar roof I could see that the wind was faltering. The flames were creeping back down the walls, smoke gushing out through the holes where floor joists had rested.

Then Stana's arm rose across the flames, weighted with a jagged brick. I wrenched my head away as it swung down, but I was not quick enough. The brutal piece of masonry crashed into the side of my face. I felt my cheekbone crack. There was no real pain, as there had been no pain from her fangs or her talons, but I was vividly aware of how such injuries would weaken me. My arms closed around her chest and gripped till her ribs began to crack.

The brick came down again, destroying more of my skull. Ribs split in her breast. We swayed like lovers in an embrace.

Claws flashed towards my eyes. I released her and she sprang away. I leaped to my feet. A great peal of thunder sounded over even the rumble of the flames. A blizzard of sparks whirled in the air. The beams were cracking. The roof was settling. In moments it would crash down upon our heads.

She caught up a smouldering lath of wood from my coffin and charged. I stepped back. My foot caught against a fallen beam on the floor and I fell. She leaped upon me, and the lath of wood plunged through my left shoulder, pinning me to the ground. I writhed wildly. There was pain at last, like boiling lead in my veins. She crouched astride me, twisting her makeshift stake. My collar-bone snapped. My upper ribs began to shatter one by one.

"You brought the wind," she hissed. "You caused the flames to carry to the Broken Woods. *You!* My revenge, my children: for the second time you have put the torch to them!"

Her knees crashed on to my belly. She hunched forward, her weight still fully on the stake which held me all but helpless. I could see that she was crying. Tears of blood wound slowly down her face.

Then her head reared up and her mouth spread wide. Her tears clotted on her icy cheeks and her eyes burned with triumph.

My right hand searched in the smouldering debris beneath the oak table for something to stop her fangs. My fingers brushed a hard edge as she struck. My hand closed, whipped it up in a blur of speed, and thrust it across her mouth. Her teeth snapped shut like a mantrap, fangs sinking into it. It was the stake. The stake that Stana had taken to the Broken Woods. The stake that she had then brought here and with which she had intended to destroy me. It had been lying where it had fallen when she leapt upon my back.

She reared up, the black wood wedged tightly across her mouth, for the moment helpless. Both hands flew to grasp it, and I rolled free of her, the stub of lath still sticking from my shoulder. She tumbled forwards, fighting to get the stake out of her mouth. I knelt on one knee beside her, caught at it and dragged it from her grasp.

"No!" she screamed, "Edwin . . ."

I pointed the sharp end downwards, and brought it down upon her breast with all of my remaining strength. The faery-green silk of the dress ripped open. The white skin puckered and tore. The flesh parted. The ribs caught the point of it for a moment, then reluctantly spread apart, snapping away from the breastbone. Like the finest-pointed stiletto under the massive force of my strength, the long blunt piece of wood slid down into the red cave of her chest, seeking her heart. The blood which filled her body burst out then, and her wild convulsions sent the cold liquid in fountains on to my face. Her throat, rattled. Her fingernails, clawing the concrete floor, split away and peeled back. The point of the wood slid past the inside of her shoulderblade beside the twisting column of her spine, and split like her nails on the cement beneath. Her mouth gaped wide, the rag of her tongue escaped her gleaming fangs and flopped obscenely on her cheek. The light in her crimson eyes dulled.

Abruptly by my side stood the twisted shape from Underhill's first nightmare. It had almost no boundaries, almost no will. I was briefly aware of its agony, and then it was gone.

The corpse staked there no longer held anything of Stana Etain, Countess Issyk-Koul. I looked down at her: she was my lady. She was Rebecca Gore, and she might have been lightly sleeping, were it not for the black stump protruding from her breast. Her right hand lay upon the scorched cover of my journal, and I picked the book up.

How long I would have stood I do not know, but suddenly the roof beams sagged a little further and the blazing wreck of the building settled, showering bright death all around us. A spark or two flamed in Rebecca's perfect hair and Edwin, now strong in me, was revolted at the sight. I used the oaken table as an aid to climbing up out of the cellar with my quiet lady and my book, and then I drew it up after us and carried it all out on to the village green.

But the Dead had not died in me. As soon as I had laid Rebecca on the table, a new thought struck me, and the Dead threw back its head and laughed. "In my beginning is my end," quoted the faint working remnant of my schoolmaster's soul. I caught up a burning branch and carried it to the southernmost end of the village. In a moment that too was aflame. Laughing wildly, and cursing, I lit the outskirts of the whole village. By the time the church clock told three o'clock, entry to the village on all fronts was forbidden. Each road was closed by fire, each pathway and garden was ablaze.

I staggered back to the village green where it all had begun, exactly twelve months ago. Rebecca lay on the table, decorous in her death. The journal lay at her head. Wedged in it still, its bookmark pen. Now, more than ever before, we, the Dead and I, have light enough to write by. Idly I flicked my journal open, and began . . .

Now, when the first ray of sunlight hits this body of mine, it will turn to dust. But slowly. First the flesh will begin to boil. Bubbles will rise to burst in gaping craters. I will swell up, seething, thick with putrid gases. My bones will become brittle, and long before oblivion comes they will splinter and collapse. A thing without precise form, I too, like Stana, will cry then my few burning tears of blood, before the lances of sunlight shrivel up my eyes within my head. The bones of my skull will fail. The great round of my brain will tear apart the thin sac of my face to pour in a stinking mass on to the spongy remnants of my shoulders.

And I, that part of me which is eternal and will abide, will be aware of all of this, will watch it taking place, will *feel* it taking place. And, after that, what horrors will remain?

For the Dead, for the damned, damned Dead, there will be eternal nothingness. The failure of eyes, of smell, of taste, touch and hearing. Only thought will remain, to madden, as Stana was maddened. Thought, and identity.

Identity. I.

Edwin Underhill.

I fear, oh dear God, I fear that I too, like her, will abide. I am this thing's identity. I will remain that part of the Dead which knows *who*, if not always what, I am. I will exist beside it, inside it, as blind and deaf and dumb and damned as it is. Always.

I am the relentless hunter.

I am the stealer of souls.

I am the bringer of terror in the night.

You will know me when I come for you —

I am the Dead and I will abide.

Yes. I fear that is true, now. I am the Dead and I will

abide.

Even as I write these words I can hear it whisper to me.

The fire is dying and there is the first paleness in the sky. Not long. Dawn will come in its own time and catch me mid-thought, mid-sentence.

I can hear the monster whisper to me: Remain king of the night: the spider, the bat, the wolf, the stealer of souls . . .

That way I would become like Stana: utter and absolute evil. And I, Edwin Underhill, would be a part of it. And the choice, even now, dear God, is mine. Such conscience as I, Edwin, have in the dawn, is all the feeling there is left in me. What power will I wield if I hide from the ancient sunlight? The power, ultimately, to spend my eternity observing all feeling's degradation and final death in me.

Or, in anguish, I can cease.

It is so nearly dawn. A few moments more and it is done.

There will be little more remaining of my lady and me than of the place we have destroyed — dust, ashes, a few crumbling bones. Hardly enough to warrant even a modest monument.

How bright the sky is becoming. Through the pall of smoke below it drains the life out of the last low flames in the black house-shells around us. I had forgotten how lovely the sky can be, now at sunrise.

On such a monument as there may be, write this epitaph — I saw it once, in a prayer-book in Rowena Gore's library, and it is fit for such as we:

What profit is there in my blood,
When I

— light, Rebecca. I see day —

must go

— listen! Rebecca, a lark! I believe I hear a lark in song, there, high in the eastern —

OH DEAR GOD IN HEAVEN, GIVE ME STRENGTH.

Down
Go down